D0974520

"Brown does a remarkable job introducing, developing, and sustaining the reader's interest by keeping it real. . . . *Sittin' in the Front Pew* will keep you laughing, crying, hoping, praying, and reaching into the deepest emotional part of yourself."
—Winston-Salem *Chronicle*

"Perceptive. Engaging. *Sittin' in the Front Pew* . . . shoos away the blues."
—*Bay State Banner*

"Reading [it] is a great escape. . . . *Sittin' in the Front Pew* will make you laugh and cry. The characters are people you know or are related to."
—*The Detroit News/Detroit Free Press*

"A touching and humorous story about family, grief, and honoring loved ones . . . [It] will move you, make you smile, and help you understand what it really means to be a family."
—*Detroit Urban Spectrum*

The Shirt off His Back
#1 *Essence* Bestseller

Fannin' the Flames

ALSO BY PARRY "EBONYSATIN" BROWN

Books published by The Random House Publishing Group
are available at quantity discounts on bulk purchases for
premium, educational, fund-raising, and special sales use.
For details, please call 1-800-733-3000.

Sittin' in the Front Pew

A Novel

Parry "EbonySatin" Brown

BALLANTINE BOOKS • NEW YORK

2006 One World Books Mass Market Edition

Published in the United States by One World Books, an imprint of The Random House Publishing Group, a division of Random House, Inc., New York.

ONE WORLD is a registered trademark and the One World colophon is a trademark of Random House, Inc.

This book contains an excerpt from the forthcoming book *What Goes Around* by Parry "EbonySatin" Brown. This excerpt has been set for this edition only and may not reflect the final content of the forthcoming edition.

Originally published in trade paperback in the United States by Strivers Row, an imprint of Villard Books, a member of The Random House Publishing Group, a division of Random House, Inc., in 2002.

ISBN 978-0-345-49490-0

Cover photograph © Robert Lewis

Printed in the United States of America

www.oneworldbooks.net

OPM 9 8 7 6 5 4 3 2 1

TO ALL MY GIRLS:
Nicolle, Michelle, Shanelle, Krystal, Krysten, Symoni, and Nierah

IN LOVING MEMORY OF MY:
wonderful mother, Colethia Naylor (1932–1992)
loving brother Donnell Naylor (1956–1996)
devoted sister Renee Johnson-Morgan (1960–1999)
precious granddaughter Kendra Dawn Kirby (5:15 A.M.–10:15 A.M.)

From the Heart...

To my Lord and Savior Jesus Christ, to God, the Father, be all the glory. I very humbly thank You for how I have been blessed with the gift of the written and spoken word. Lord, I thank You for loving me when I wasn't smart enough to love myself.

I must begin with a very special thanks to Michelle Brown-Kirby for suggesting the concept for this novel. As always, Nicolle Brown, you used your keen eye to critique the story and, of course, you were right on point. A mother couldn't be more blessed than I am to have you as my daughters.

I cannot begin to show the appreciation I feel for my sisters, Mary McClain-Sims, Lorraine Sims, Jackie Naylor, and Beatrice Johnson, for their unwavering love and support. You always tell me how proud you are of what I've accomplished, but it is I who am proud to be one of Miss Co's seven.

As an oasis in the middle of the desert brings overwhelming joy to the weary traveler, Neville Abraham, so have you brought love and joy into my life. I've woven many of your one-liners throughout this story just as our souls have intertwined. My heart sings a new song because of you.

To Glynda Ard, my best friend and confidante, I extend my heartfelt gratitude for the years of encouragement and understanding. Your love has been a constant, no matter the circumstance. You are truly as rare as a black diamond.

When we allow God to direct our path, people like Portia Ophelia Cannon find their way into our lives. You have been a consistent source of love, strength, and support from day one. You have worked tirelessly to make my dream a reality. You always give the shirt off your back, making you someone very, very special.

Twania Hayes, as my oldest and dearest friend you saw the butterfly struggling to make her way out of that cocoon. You nurtured and encouraged me until I saw what you saw. How can words adequately thank you for what you've done to make a difference in my life?

When Wanda Wilson came to sell me insurance almost ten years ago, who would have ever known the love, laughter, and tears we'd come to share? I can't imagine what my life would be like without our friendship. You and Don sell books almost as hard as I do just because you love me. When is that next bid whist party, gurl?

There have been so many who have been instrumental in my rise in the literary world. When I decided to just dip my pinky toe in the pool filled with words, I never realized what a package deal this happened to be. First Melody Guy, who brings new meaning to the word "patience." Thank you for doing all you can to make us both a success.

Everyone needs a *shero,* and I must bow down to mine, Victoria Christopher Murray. You have been not only a mentor, but a true, true friend and sister. Your blatant honesty has kept me on the straight and narrow. Everyone needs a friend just like you!

Jamaica Carter, you have been a friend for several years who has encouraged, praised, and held a sistah's emotional hand since the day we met. Thank you for making me laugh when tears would have been so much easier.

African-American booksellers play an enormous role in the success of our work. They have been responsible for so many new authors receiving their much-deserved recognition. There is one bookseller who stands head and shoulders above the rest, and I must give honor to her yesterday, today, and forever more ... the grand diva of booksellers, Ms. Emma Rodgers.

I would like to add a very special thanks to my advance readers who reviewed the manuscript along with my editor. I know you will be pleased as you read the pages that follow to see your recommendations come to life. I humbly express my thanks for selflessly giving of your talents: Stacey Turnage, Nicolle Brown, Glynda Ard, Vanessa Woodward, Cynthia L. Thompson, Lisa Bobbitt, and Michelle Brown-Kirby.

Last and most assuredly not least, to my friends who took care of a sistah in her self-published days on the road: Dan Navarro, Philip Wood, Lloyd Nelson, Tyrone Campbell, the Tocruray family, and my brothers and sisters with the International Association of Black Professional Fire Fighters.

Prologue

Turning to wave good-bye as I slowly walked the endless steps toward the gate where the Boeing 767 awaited, I tearfully begged my sisters not to let the miles that would separate us cause our hearts to break the synchronized rhythm we had known all our lives. Daddy never let a holiday or special occasion go by without demanding phone calls be made assuring us that distance was not a reason for separation of the heart.

I knew they loved me, but I never seemed to be a part of their everyday thoughts. They were always having family gatherings for one reason or another—mainly because they wanted to be together. They were always eating, drinking, and playing cards until the wee hours of the morning. There was always one sister missing. Me, Glynda.

Minute pieces of my heart seemed to be left behind with each step. I psychologically dropped heart crumbs in hopes that my sisters could find their way to me. I felt juvenile and just plain silly. I wanted nothing more than to go back to a time before my daddy had left me; a time when life was so much simpler; a time before secrets had been revealed. I don't remember walking the quarter mile to Gate B7 or giving my boarding pass to the agent. The pain in my chest had suffocated my conscious mind.

"Hello, may I help you find your seat?" I was greeted

by a very warm and friendly aging flight attendant whose name badge read FLORENCE. She immediately noticed the tears falling from my eyes, which could not express the emptiness I felt inside.

"Are you alright, miss?" she said, lightly touching my arm.

Her compassion only opened the floodgates as I started to sob.

"Please, may I show you to your seat?" asked the woman who was certain to be someone's grandmother as she glanced at my boarding pass. The days of flight attendants being runner-up contestants in the local beauty contest were long gone.

Although I knew I wasn't the first passenger to have absolutely no authority over her emotional state, I was so ashamed, nonetheless, of my lack of control. "I'm so sorry, I can find it. But thank you. I just buried my daddy last week. I'll be fine in just a few minutes."

"I'm so sorry. My name is Flo," she said tugging on my arm just enough to pull me in her direction.

Totally unaware that I was preventing the other passengers from boarding, I gladly moved closer to the kind woman of Norwegian descent. Today was no different than any of the other days since I had received the call that would forever change not just my life, but the lives of all the people I loved as well as people I hardly knew. I was in a total haze. Repeatedly the air filled with my words, my voice, but who was saying them? Surely it wasn't me.

"May I get you something to drink?" Flo whispered.

"No, I'll just find my seat. But you're so kind for asking."

"If there's anything you need to make your ride more comfortable, just let me know. We're not full today. I'll

make sure you're seated alone once everyone boards."
Flo was happy to be able to offer me special attention.

"Thank you. I would really appreciate being alone.
Again, you've been so kind." I turned, wiping at my
tear-streaked cheeks.

As I settled into my seat, I had never felt so alone.
What was I going to do without my daddy? The man
who had been my rock since the day I'd burst forth into
this world more than thirty-seven years ago.

Edward Zachary Naylor had been a strong black man
since he was a teenager. He had been raised in the poor-
est section of Baltimore's east side. He'd shined shoes
and delivered groceries for small-denomination coins to
buy clothes and shoes to attend school. His mother, who
worked in the kitchens of rich white folks, had told him
that as long as he paid his own way, he could stay in
school. She could do no more than provide shelter and
food for her two sons, Edward and Thomas. Their father, Edward senior, had been killed in a poker game
when the boys were five and six years old. Edward was
determined to join the army as soon as he turned sixteen
and make enough money so his mama wouldn't have to
scrub other people's floors to eat.

He joined the army the day after he graduated from
high school in the summer of his eighteenth year. His
mother died of a stroke before he finished boot camp.
On the bus ride from Fort Leonardwood, Missouri, back
to Baltimore for his mother's funeral, Edward met Lorraine McLean. Lorraine was the most beautiful woman
he'd ever seen. She was tall and sat up very straight. Her
long black hair was pulled back so tightly into a bun
that her eyebrows seemed raised by the tension. When
she spoke, she reminded him of the white women in the
fancy department stores downtown. She was dressed like
them, as well. Her clothes were meticulously pressed,

and her white gloves surely must be covering the most perfectly manicured nails. Not at all like the girls he'd known back on Baltimore's east side. She was on her way to Coppin State Teachers College. She was going to shape young minds. Right there on the Trailways bus on his way to bury his mama, Edward decided that this woman was to be the mother of his children.

Lorraine had no inkling what the polite young man had in his head, but she was sure she'd never see him again once they debarked at the Baltimore bus station. The forty-eight hours they'd shared had been very special. Her heart had gone out to him. He seemed so deeply saddened by the death of his mother. She remembered what she'd always heard her mother and aunts say about a man who loves his mother. *Girl, when a man loves his mama and treats her right, he's a good man.* Edward Naylor fit the bill perfectly. His grief, of course, was the primary source of his heavy heart. His greatest disappointment, however, was that he would never be able to take care of his mother the way she had provided for him all his life. He would make some lucky young woman a wonderful husband. She wrote her name and mailing address at the college on a piece of paper and told Eddie to drop her a line if he felt alone, was missing his mama, and just needed to talk.

My daddy had that piece of paper the day he died.

I remembered my mother telling me that story a million times as a little girl. She reminisced about how her Eddie had written to her every week. Their letters were the talk of the college dormitory and the barracks in the Thirty-second Infantry. All of Lorraine's friends had teased her that Private Naylor was in love with her. She protested that they were only pen pals and that he was grieving the loss of his mother. He found comfort in her letters and they were just friends.

On the other hand, the men of the Thirty-second Infantry wanted to know when Ed was going to propose!

On his last furlough before he was to be discharged from Uncle Sam's Army, Edward Zachary Naylor went to attend the graduation of his beloved Lorraine from Coppin State Teachers College. That night while they walked hand in hand through Druid Hill Park, Edward asked Lorraine to marry him. Though completely surprised, she graciously accepted the ring and promised her everlasting love to the man she had come to love more than life itself through his letters. They were married the Saturday after his discharge from the army at a small church in St. Louis, Missouri. Lorraine's entire family was in attendance. Edward's only family had been his younger brother and best man, Thomas.

I was remembering that familiar story when Flo interrupted my thoughts. "Ms. Naylor, we have another seat for you where you can have a little privacy."

As I buckled my seat belt, I heard the doors being closed and the flight attendants announcing the various door cross-checks. Was this how an inmate felt when he heard the prison doors close behind him for the first time? Separated from everything and everyone he loved as his life changed forever.

1

The Call

"Why is the phone still ringing while I'm saying hello?" Saying it aloud must have startled me awake. Only then did I realize I had been answering the phone in my dream.

"Hello?" I groggily answered.

"Sissy, is that you?" There was only one person who still consistently called me Sissy as an adult, but this did not sound at all like my oldest sister.

"Renee, what is wrong with you? And why are you calling me at two-thirty in the morning? You know I get up to go running at four-thirty." I held the clock radio in my left hand and the phone in my right.

It never dawned on me that Renee would not call me in the middle of the night unless something was wrong, terribly wrong.

"Are you alone, Sissy?"

"Yeah, Anthony is on his two-week reserve assignment. What's wrong, Renee?" I bolted awake and pulled myself up in bed. Renee had never cared if I was alone before.

Her voice cracked as she spoke. "Oh Sissy!" Renee was crying.

"You are scaring me, Renee. What the hell is going on? Is there something wrong with Derrick or one of the kids?"

"Sissy, it's Daddy! Sissy, Daddy is dead!" she screamed into the phone.

The room started spinning as I laid my head back on the solid oak headboard. She hadn't said my daddy was dead. She was screaming, so I knew I'd misunderstood. "What did you say, Renee?"

"Daddy is dead! We're at University Hospital Emergency Room. You gotta come home, Sissy. You gotta get on a plane now!" She was no longer screaming, but sobbing so hard it was still very difficult to understand exactly what she was saying.

"Give me the phone, Renee!" I heard Collette snap at her. "Why you just gonna blurt some shit like that out at her in the middle of the night. I told you to let me call, but nooooooo!"

"Hey, Sis, you okay? Did you understand what Renee was saying?" Collette's demeanor had drastically changed as she took the phone.

"Collette, it sounded like she said that Daddy is dead!" He can't be dead. I talked to him last night.

"It's true, Sis." Now Collette's voice was cracking.

"What are you saying, Collette?" This time I was screaming. There was no way my daddy was dead. I'd spoken to him just before he went to bed. He'd told me he loved me and how proud he was of me for passing the bar! My daddy was *not* dead.

"Where's Anthony? You need to calm down!" Collette immediately regretted the statement.

"Calm down, you calm down. He ain't here. What happened to my daddy?" As usual, Collette was trying my patience.

"He was my daddy, too!"

"What do you mean was?"

"Daddy is gone, Sissy!" Collette, using my pet name, started sobbing into the phone.

"What happened, Lette? Please tell me what happened to my daddy!"

"He called Dawn to tell her he loved her and while he was on the phone he stopped talking. She was screaming for him, but he wouldn't answer. She hung up and called 911 and then went over there. She called us from her car, and Renee and I met her there. When we arrived, Dawn was waiting on the porch to tell us he was dead when the paramedics arrived. But they were trying to bring him back. They tried everything, Sissy. They did, they really did." Her voice trailed off.

"Oh my God! Oh my God! Oh my God! Not my daddy. Not my daddy!" I screamed to the universe, not to my second youngest sister.

"Glynda, you need to call somebody!" This time it was Dawn on the phone. "We have each other, but you're out there all alone. Can Anthony come home? Can you get in touch with him?"

"Dawn, tell me my daddy is not dead! Tell me it's not true!"

"Sissy, it *is* true. He called all of us last night to tell us he loved us. I guess somehow he knew it was his time. He looks so peaceful. He's with Mama now." Dawn's many years as a pediatric nurse had imparted such a soothing way of talking. She dealt with the worst kind of death of all every day—the death of children.

"Dawn . . ." I had wanted to tell her I didn't want him to be with Mama. I wanted him here with me. I wanted to scream, in thirty years Mama could have him for all eternity, I needed him now! The words held up in my chest. My mouth moved, but no words formed. My daddy was dead.

"Glynda, you there? You okay?" Dawn was barely audible.

"I'm here, but I'm far from okay! How can I be, Dawn?"

"I know, Sissy. It was a stupid question. Can you call someone? You don't need to be alone."

"I'll call Rico. She's on call tonight. Dawn?"

"Yes, Glynda?"

"He called us all to say good-bye?"

"Yes, Sissy, he did."

"Hello." I knew it was Rico, but I didn't want to just blurt out the horrible news.

"Hey gurlfriend! What're you doing up in the middle of the night. I thought this privilege was reserved for us medical professionals. You lawyers got those banker's hours." Rico sounded more like it was three in the afternoon than three in the morning.

Rico Martin had been my friend since the day we met at the library more than seventeen years ago. Rico was in her senior year at the University of Southern California, and I, a junior at California State University at Dominguez Hills. We were both trying to escape the madness at our respective apartments. USC had won a spot in the coveted Rose Bowl, and the parties abounded. My roommate was in college to get her swerve on with whoever was willing to swerve at the moment. I just wasn't in the mood to listen to her proclaim love for a stranger, *again*.

Rico and I had so many books spread out across the massive table that no one dared to try to join us. We worked in silence for two hours before we engaged in conversation.

"Hey, want a cup of coffee? My treat," Rico said as if we had been friends for years.

"I'd love some, but I'll buy my own," I said, digging for change in my jacket pocket.

"You can buy the next round." Rico winked at me.

"Sounds like you're in for the long haul, too."

"Yeah, I'm pre-med, and tests don't stop because we got into the Rose Bowl. I'm Arico Perez. But my friends call me Rico." She extended her hand.

"Hi, Rico. My name is Glynda Naylor. My friends call me Glynda." We both laughed.

"Nice to meet you, Glynda. What's your major?" Rico's deep Hershey's bittersweet-chocolate complexion, with the distinctive features of a true African descendant, accented by hazel eyes and unruly curly jet black hair made me think her last name was Johnson or Williams, not Perez.

"Double major, English literature and business. The English is for me; the business is for my daddy. He said I have to be sensible, unless I want to teach for the rest of my life." I immediately felt comfortable with Rico.

"Ahhhh, I understand about family pressures. I'm the first in my family to go to college, and everyone wants the golden child to be a doctor. I really want it, too. But sometimes I feel like I have no choice in the matter." Rico was putting on her jacket.

"Well, my sisters and I had no choice on the college thing, but I was the only one brave enough to go away to school. All the others are in school back in Maryland."

"How many others?" Rico stared at me curiously.

"Three."

"And you're all in college at the same time?"

"Actually, the baby is still in high school. My oldest sister got married at nineteen and then went to college two years ago. Daddy doesn't have to help her, but he says if she's trying to make a better life, he's going to help her any way he can. But that's just how Daddy is."

"He sounds like a wonderful man. What about your mother?"

"Mama died ten years ago in a car accident—drunk driver. He's been raising us on his own ever since."

"Wow, I'm sorry to hear about your mother. My mother raised three of us by herself, because my daddy, whoever the hell he is, had other plans." Rico had a distant look in her eyes as she spoke.

"Sorry." I didn't know what else to say.

"What do you want in your coffee?" Rico smoothly changed the subject.

"I like it the way I like my man—black with just enough sugar and cream to take the bite out of it."

"I heard that!" We slapped five.

A month after that cold rainy night we spent in the library, Rico and I became roommates. We had moved up from one apartment to a better one, then another, until we bought a house in the prestigious View Park neighborhood for African-American professionals who had arrived. We'd shared the house until Rico married Jonathan Martin two years before.

Everyone, except me, had been amazed when the renowned pediatric trauma surgeon married the UPS man. Jonathan made Rico's heart, not to mention other vital parts of her anatomy, sing!

"That's what you think!" My poor attempt at humor didn't fool my best friend for a minute. "Thank you for returning my page so quickly, Rico," I said, trying to keep the tone in my voice even.

"What's wrong, Glynda? You and Anthony have another fight?"

"No, Rico. It's Daddy. He . . ."

"What, Glynda? What's wrong with Papa Eddie?"

Rico had adopted my daddy as her own on our first visit to Baltimore together.

"Rico, Daddy died tonight." I spoke just above a whisper.

"What? CVA, MI, what?" Rico had slipped into her medical jargon without thinking I'd have no clue what she meant.

"We don't know yet, but we think it was a massive heart attack."

"Oh my God, Glynda! Let me get someone to cover for me. I'll be there within the hour. Have you called Anthony?"

"No, he's in the desert on reserve duty. Besides, I called you first. I'll call his company and leave a message. Rico, please hurry."

I never seemed to need anyone for anything. Rico had always been the one who was so dependent in our relationship. When she heard the desperation in my voice, she knew tonight I needed her, and I knew she would move heaven and earth to get to me.

"I'll be there, I promise you! Just hang on." The authority in Rico's voice made me know she would handle everything when she arrived.

The phone rang almost the instant I touched the OFF button on the cordless phone. "Gurl, just get over here and stop calling me."

"Who're you talking to?" It was Collette's voice on the other end of the connection.

"Oh, Lette, I thought this was Rico calling back."

"Is she coming over? God knows you have been there for her."

"Lette, don't start. You know she's on her way. She just has to get someone to cover the ER for her. Anyway, how y'all doing? Are you still at the hospital?"

"Yeah, they have us in this nice quiet room. So we can

make the arrangements and call family. We need to pick a funeral home. I'm going to put you on speaker so we can all talk. We can't agree."

With the touch of a button I could hear my sisters' voices. "Are you guys doing okay?"

"I think we should call Morton and Dyett." Collette spoke first, ignoring my inquiry.

"Why Dyett? I don't like the way the funeral home looks on the outside, plus his cars are not as new as Brown's on North Avenue," Dawnelle interjected.

"Well, March is the premier funeral home in the city. They have the most locations." This time it was Renee.

"I think we should use the other March funeral home. You know, he's the cousin of the one with all the locations. They're really nice people. I met them when Delores's mother died." I couldn't believe we each had a different preference.

"Well, the March chain is definitely out. They're so expensive. You're only paying for their name. That's why I suggested Dyett. They're reasonable," Collette said.

"Daddy has all kinds of insurance. Money isn't of any concern." I was livid. I couldn't believe Collette's tight ass was going to try to penny-pinch with *my* daddy's funeral.

"But that does *not* mean we're going to spend an obscene amount of money just because it's there. He took out those policies so *we* would have the money, not some slick funeral home," Collette yelled.

"Why are you screaming, Lette? I bet you've already called your broker, haven't you?" Dawn did little to hide her annoyance.

"We're not scrimping on this funeral. Do I make myself clear? Daddy sacrificed everything for us, and we will *not* cut any corners." Now I was the one yelling.

"We'll set a budget and anything over that will come out of your share, Dawn." Collette was relentless.

"What the hell do you mean her share? Who do you think you are? Whatever we decide will be paid by all of us. I don't think we should spend more than we have to, but I do know my daddy was a classy, hardworking, strong black man, who gave only his best in life and will receive no less in his death." Renee began to cry.

"What about Estelle?" I asked softly.

"What about her?" Collette's words dripped with disdain.

"We should ask for her input; after all, they were engaged. How's she taking the news?" I knew this was a very touchy area with Renee and Collette.

Estelle Taylor and Daddy had been friends for more than twenty years. Estelle was a nice enough lady who loved her some Edward. They had worked together on the midnight shift at the plant for all of those years. Their friendship turned to love after Estelle divorced her husband of twenty-eight years when she found out his taste in a mate had changed to someone younger and of the same gender. Daddy had been such a comfort to her. She literally threw herself into his arms, but he told her she needed time to heal. If genuine love for him was what she felt and not rejection from her husband, then he would be patiently waiting.

Being the wonderful man who we knew him to be, Daddy was there through all of her ups and downs. Estelle just always seemed to be around doting over Daddy. Dawn and I thought it was wonderful since he'd lived alone since our mother's death. Renee and Collette hated her. On Father's Day the year before while we were all at brunch, Daddy announced he was in love with Estelle and he wanted our permission to ask her to be his wife. I ran around the table and kissed him on the left cheek, Dawn leaned over and kissed him on the right one. Collette and Renee stared at him as though he had just confessed he was Timothy McVeigh's coconspirator.

"She doesn't have a damn thing to say about this funeral. He was our father, not her husband. She was just using him anyway." Renee was adamant.

"How can you say that, Renee? You know she loves Daddy as much as we do. You have never given her a chance. And Daddy sure made it clear on Father's Day that he loved her, too." I was trying to hold back tears.

"Renee and Lette want to call her to give her the news, but I think we should go over there. This is horrible news to have to deliver over the phone." Dawn pleaded her case, silently asking me for reinforcement.

"Well, I'm not going," Collette stated flatly.

"We told Sissy on the phone, and she is no better than his daughter," Renee volunteered.

"Well, I can't make y'all do anything, but if you aren't going to do it in person, you need to call her immediately. She does deserve that. Maybe she can help decide what funeral home." I knew it was hopeless to try to change their minds.

"She doesn't have a damn thing to say about this! How many ways do I have to say it?" Collette said.

I could sense Collette's hostility even though I wasn't present in the small room. "Lette, you're not running this, we all are, and I say we ask for Estelle's input. She was going to be our stepmother in six weeks." I was *not* backing down on the issue. It gave my anger a great outlet. I needed to be mad at something or someone. It didn't seem right to be angry with Daddy.

"I agree with Glynda." Dawn spoke up quietly.

"Oh, isn't this just wonderful. We're split down the middle." I could almost see Renee shaking her head as she spoke.

"I have a suggestion." Dawn waited for someone to ask her to continue.

"Well?" Collette asked.

"They have to do an autopsy anyway. That'll happen later today. By the time the body is released, Glynda should be here. We can make the decision then. That way, we'll have had some time to calm down, think it through, and get some input from Estelle. She can have the deciding vote." Dawn felt pleased at her rationale.

"Autopsy? They're not cutting on my daddy! And I done told you, that woman has no say-so, let alone a deciding vote!" Collette was fuming.

"Lette, we have no say in the autopsy. The state has to determine the cause of death; that's the law. And stop talking about Estelle like she was some kind of stranger. She is a nice woman who I happen to like a lot. She's meant a lot to Daddy." Dawn tried fruitlessly to win Collette over to her way of thinking.

"This is getting us nowhere. I agree with Dawn. Let's leave the funeral home decision until I get there this afternoon. Y'all go on home and start calling the family. Has anyone called Uncle Thomas?" I changed the subject, trying to defuse the impending war.

"We called, but you know he turns his ringer off at night. We left him a message. We'll drive by there when we leave here. I guess you're right, we can decide on the funeral home when you get here. We need to stop disagreeing. Daddy would be so mad at us." Renee's tears started up again.

"You know, Renee is so right. He wouldn't have it! We're acting like those sisters on *Ricki Lake*." Collette was finally starting to make sense.

"I'll call you back as soon as I get my reservation. I'm going on the Net to get the first available flight out. I love you all so much. Please let's not fight anymore. Promise?"

"We love you, too, Sissy," Renee's crying started a round-robin of tears from all of us.

You'd never have believed the four of us had been at one another's throats less than five minutes prior. Everyone fell silent for what seemed like an eternity. I spoke up first.

"I'm going to put on some coffee. Where can I reach you all?"

"We're going over to Daddy's. The paramedics broke down the door to get in. We need to secure the place until we can call someone out to fix it. Sister Greene is staying there until we get back. We'll make the calls from there. We'll stop by Uncle Thomas's first though." Renee's voice was weak.

"I'm going over to tell Estelle. She shouldn't have to hear the news over the phone, and she's right here in the same city with us." Dawn wouldn't accept any flack from Renee and Collette. Her mind was made up.

"That's a great idea, Dawn. She'll really appreciate you for it." The battle lines were clearly drawn.

"Well, I'm through with the matter. Let Miss Fast Ass do what she pleases. I'm just not going with you." I could feel Collette rolling her eyes.

"Nor did I ask you to go, now did I?"

"Sisters, please!" I longed to be in the same room with them instead of on the phone twenty-seven hundred miles away.

"Okay, Sissy, we'll behave. Just hurry and get here. We'll call you from Uncle Thomas's house. This is going to almost kill him. You know how tight he and Daddy were." Renee took charge.

"I love y'all so much. Promise me we'll stay strong for

one another. We're all we have." My voice cracked as if I was on a cellular phone in a valley.

"I love you, too, Sissy," all three sisters said in unison.

"Call me after you tell Uncle Thomas. And Dawn, you call me again after you tell Estelle. Dawn and I will deal with Estelle if you two have a problem with it. But she will be involved, and there will be no further discussion on the matter." This time you would have thought I was the oldest and in charge.

"Okay, okay, truce," Renee said.

With that, we sisters said good-bye, and the connection was broken.

True to her word, Rico was slipping her key into my front door an hour and five minutes after she had hung up the phone. She had defied all the traffic laws set forth by the state of California. She'd made the drive from Orange County to the Antelope Valley in forty-eight minutes.

When I moved from the spacious home we'd shared in View Park, I ended up in Palmdale. Living in the high desert was the only way I could afford to continue law school and pay a mortgage at the same time.

Rico smelled coffee brewing and knew where to find me. As she entered the ultramodern, spacious, black and white kitchen, I dropped the creamer onto the granite countertop and ran to her. We spent several minutes crying and holding each other before Rico finally spoke.

"Come sit down, Glynda. You're trembling all over."

"Oh Rico, what am I going to do without my daddy?"

"I don't know, Glynda. I don't have a clue." Rico sat, speechlessly pondering the possibility of life without Papa Eddie and his *always* optimistic attitude.

"But at this moment we need to focus on what it is we need to do to get you to Baltimore. I'll help you pack and stay with you until I put you on an airplane." Rico finally spoke, running her hand over my braids.

"You're not going to the funeral?" Anger replaced my tears.

"Of course I'm going to the funeral. But you need to get to Baltimore today, and even if you take an early flight, it will be afternoon before you get there. I'll be there in a day or so. I have some loose ends to tie up. But you know I would never let you go through this without me. You think his commanders will let Anthony come to the funeral?" Rico was still stroking my hair.

"Probably not. Since we aren't married. This'll be all the ammunition he needs to use against me for that marriage thang. Damn!" I tried to laugh.

"Let me get us some coffee. Have you called the airline yet?" Rico was opening and closing cabinets like it was her own kitchen.

"Not yet. I have only made the coffee since we spoke. My sisters called again after I talked to you to ask what funeral home we should use. We spent most of the time arguing. We all had a different opinion. But I think we really argued because if we didn't agree, no one would have to make the call to the funeral home."

Rico only stared at me as she wiped up the spilled cream.

"How can I call a funeral home and tell them to go pick up the remains of Edward Zachary Naylor? Tell me that, Rico!" I was raising my voice without meaning to yell at my friend.

"Did you call Anthony's company yet?" Rico didn't have an answer to my question.

"Not yet. Will you call for me?"

"Of course I will. I'll get online and find you a flight, too." Rico was doing what she did best—handle situations in a crisis.

Rico had known on her first emergency-department rotation that she worked best under extreme pressure. It was her surgery rotation that made her know that God had given her an extraordinary gift in her hands.

I'm not sure what happened after Rico picked up the telephone. I only heard her muffled voice in the distance as I stared into the empty coffee cup. I didn't even understand what I needed to do to fill the cup with the dark liquid I love so much. I'd wait for Rico because she'd know what to do.

In what seemed like only a few seconds, Rico was sitting across from me holding my hands in her own. These were the same hands that had healed so many broken bodies. Could she heal my broken heart?

"You're all set. Your flight leaves at eight fifty-seven from Los Angeles. So we'll have to leave around six to get you there in time. We only have an hour and a half to get you ready. We need to pack. I left a message with the company clerk, and he promised to get it to Anthony's company commander. Jonathan is going to meet us at the airport. He wants me to tell you how very sorry he is."

Rico had handled it all. Within minutes she would have me packed and in the shower. She'd even dress me if I seemed incapable. Rico took me by the hand to lead me toward the master bedroom. With each step my movement became more difficult. My feet dug into the plush peach carpeting, causing Rico to pull my arm slightly. Each tick of the grandfather clock in the alcove under the winding staircase announced the beat of a heart broken into a million pieces.

My sanctuary awaited me at the top of the sixteen stairs. With each grueling step my resolve was weakened. I couldn't make this climb. I needed to rest.

Rico felt my hesitation. "Come on, gurl. You can make it. Just a few more steps."

As I finally reached the top of the stairs and stepped through the double doors into my bedroom, I caught a glimpse of my reflection in the oak-trimmed mirror. I looked defeated. I gathered my strength to speak. "Renee and Collette don't want Estelle to have any say in the arrangements. I think that is so wrong. What do you think?"

"Why do you think they feel that way?" Rico seemed to always answer my question with a question. She should have been a lawyer, or better yet a psychiatrist.

"They've never liked her. Dawn said she'd go over to tell Estelle on her own because she didn't want to break the news over the phone. They refused to go with her."

Rico held me by the elbow as she guided me to the king-size bed, sitting beside me as she touched my face gently with her delicate fingers. Tears once again filled my eyes.

"Why did this have to happen, Rico? Daddy was so happy and appeared so healthy. He was going to retire in two years and start to travel the way he always wanted to do." I was in her arms again, sobbing.

"We can never know or understand how destiny can appear to rob us of so much. Papa Eddie lived a wonderful life though, Glynda. You know how pleased he was with the way you all turned out, and when I graduated from medical school, there was no one in attendance who didn't think he was my dad. Including Mama!" She was brushing tears from my cheeks and my braids from my face.

"I know, but it was just way too short. He should've lived until we were his age!" Now I was angry.

"We can't say when one has fulfilled their earthly purpose." Rico's voice was so soothing.

"I guess you're right."

"Are you going to be okay sitting here? I need to start packing."

"Yeah, I think so."

I watched Rico in silent awe as she moved from my walk-in closet to my dresser drawers, picking and choosing just the right clothes. I stood to go into the massive bathroom that adjoined my bedroom, but my legs abandoned me. I couldn't move forward or return to the sitting position. I tried to ask Rico to help me, but my vocal cords were paralyzed. What was happening to me? Was I having a heart attack?

I stood in this position for several minutes before Rico realized I was in trouble. As she approached me, the room started to spin and I felt as if I was falling through a deep dark hole. Everything went black.

2

A Friend in Need

"Glynda?" It was Rico's voice. But she sounded so far away.

"Rico?"

"Come on back, gurlfriend."

"Man, my head hurts. What happened?" My eyes were slowly starting to focus.

"Well, Miss I've-got-this-all-under-control, you fainted." Rico's voice was sounding normal again.

"I fainted? I've never fainted before in my life!"

"You're fine. Your vitals are returning to normal. You were only out for a short time. I'm just so glad I was here. You did hit your head on the floor before I could get to you. That's why your head hurts. The extra thick padding that you just had to have paid off. It buffered your point of contact, so I'm not too concerned about it." My friend had such a kind way about her. I do love this woman as much as my sisters.

"My sisters! What time is it?" I realized I had a plane to catch.

"It's almost four forty-five. I'll have you packed in a few minutes. If there is anything else you need once you get there, call me and I'll come by and get it before I leave. Or I'll just buy it for you when I get there. Are you okay to take a shower?"

"Yeah, my head is clearing now. I feel a little disoriented, though."

"That's to be expected. Your body shut down rather than deal with the trauma. Let me help you up." Rico stood over me as I still lay on the floor.

"I sure do feel heavy."

"You are heavy!" Rico was straining to get me to a standing position.

"See how you are. I'm laying here in a traumatized state, and you gonna crack on my weight." I was feeling better with every passing second.

"Now you know if you give me an opening, I'm going to step boldly through it."

"Silly me, I definitely should've known better. I'm going to get showered. If the phone rings, just answer it. My sisters are supposed to call when they get to Uncle Thomas's place. This is going to be so hard on him. Daddy and he were inseparable."

"Glynda, gurl, this is going to be hard. Period! I've been so lucky. I've never had to bury anyone I truly love."

"Even though I was young when my mother died, I still remember how bad it hurt. But it was nothing like what I'm feeling now. I have pain in my chest. I feel like I have a hole in my soul. I knew Daddy would die some day, but I expected him to be almost eighty or ninety. He was so healthy, Rico!" Tears once again began to fall.

"We'll know more when we get the autopsy report," Rico whispered in my ear as she embraced me.

No more words exchanged between us as we went about our duties getting me ready to take the worst flight of my life. I stood in the shower and tried to let the water wash away my sorrows. I couldn't seem to get the water hot enough, nor would it pound my body with the force I craved. I needed something, anything, to cause me enough external pain to dull the anguish that was tearing me up inside.

"Glynda, you okay in there? Uncle Thomas is on the phone." Rico was yelling through the opaque white mist that filled the plush room that before had soothed my sorrows away no matter how grave, until today. Today was different. No black marble Jacuzzi tub made for two, no scented aromatherapy candles, no wine chilling in the crystal ice bucket, no trashy romance novel, not even Anthony's tall, handsome, Adonis-like body could have soothed my pain today.

"Okay, tell him I'll be right there. How is he?" I knew the answer before she even spoke.

"He's crying. He said for you to come to the phone or for me to bring it to you."

Uncle Thomas and I were almost as close as Daddy and me. Uncle Thomas had two sons, whom he hadn't seen for years. My sisters and I became the center of his universe as he tried to fill the void left by his sons' absence. Uncle Thomas had dropped out of high school to join the army, planning to serve Uncle Sam until he was forced to retire. But a sniper's bullet in the jungles of Vietnam had changed all of that. He returned to Baltimore and, after much rehabilitation at the VA hospital, went to work helping other soldiers to grasp the ring of hope that meant a normal life.

Through it all Daddy had been an anchor for Uncle Thomas. Daddy had tried desperately, but in vain, to reunite Uncle Thomas with Thomas junior and Michael. Their mother was an unhappy woman who did all she could to keep Thomas away from his sons, including moving them from Baltimore to Anchorage, Alaska. She was one of the few women who worked on the pipeline. Even after Thomas junior and Michael graduated from college, they settled in the Pacific Northwest. I wondered if they would come to their only uncle's funeral.

"Hi, Uncle Thomas," I said quietly. "How ya doing?"

"Glynda, why mah buddy go and leave me like dis?" Uncle Thomas sobbed.

"I don't know, Uncle Thomas. I don't know." My tears started anew.

"When ya comin' home, baby gurl?"

"I'm getting dressed now. My flight leaves at about nine. I'll be there at five-fifteen. Will you come to the airport to meet me, Uncle Thomas?"

"Course I will, Glynda. Ya know yo' daddy would want me ta come git chu. He worried 'bout chu bein' way out dere. Did you evah know dat?"

"He would never tell me, but I knew he did. He was really sad when I told him I wanted to stay out here after graduation."

"Yeah, dat sho' 'nuff broke his heart. But he undastood. Yes sah, he did. He was right proud of all y'all girls. Right proud."

"Uncle Thomas, I have to leave for the airport real soon. I need to get dressed. Where're my sisters?" I asked as I saw Rico pointing to the Swiss watch I'd given her several Christmases before.

"Dey right here. Dawn's cryin' pretty hard. Collette's takin' care of her. Aiight, baby, I'll see ya tonight, 'bout five fifteen."

"I love you, Uncle Thomas."

"Ya knows I loves ya, too, Glynda."

I fell onto the bed, the heaviness of my body returning. I feared that I would faint again if I didn't sit at least momentarily. Rico brought me my underwear and I stared at them, not exactly sure what it was I needed to do. I was so happy my friend was taking care of me.

"You need some help with that, gurlfriend?" Rico broke my trance.

"I was just sitting here wondering exactly what it is I'm supposed to do with these clothes. Is that wild or what?" I had to laugh at my own ineptitude.

"Not as strange as you may think. I deal with families in trauma all the time. It does very unusual things to us psychologically."

Once I got started it all became natural, and I don't remember getting dressed. The next thing I remembered was Rico putting my matching American Tourister carry-on and hang-up bag in the trunk of her emerald green BMW M5. When the automatic door locks released the button on the passenger side, I only stood staring. What was I supposed to do next? Rico leaned over to open my door. I slid in feeling like a four-year-old.

"I feel like a little kid, gurl. I don't know what I'm supposed to be doing," I said as I fumbled with the seat belt.

"That's why I'm here." Rico patted my hand.

The familiar voice of Carl Nelson, host of the early morning talk show *The Front Page,* filled the car. So much had happened in such a short time. Between the time I'd gone to bed and now, my world had crashed down around my feet and the sun hadn't yet come up.

"When will you get to Baltimore?" I needed my friend by my side. I wanted her to leave with me now.

"I should be able to get out on the red-eye flight tomorrow night, which will put me in Baltimore Thursday morning at five. I'll rent a car. Don't worry about anyone picking me up."

"Gurl, you can drive Daddy's car!" For the first time since I'd gotten the call, I felt as if I had a solution to something.

"I don't want to cause any confusion. You love me, but I'm not so sure about the rest of your sisters. They may think I'm trying to take over. Besides, I'm really hoping Uncle Thomas's boys will come, and then they can use it. We'll need a lot of people to drive to do all the running around. Don't worry about me, okay?"

"As much as I hate to admit you're right, you *are* right. Collette would be the main one."

Rico only laughed and nodded her head in agreement.

"Dang, I wonder if Dawn went by Estelle's yet? I forgot to ask if she was still going when I talked to Uncle Thomas. You know I really like her. She was so good for Daddy. He had been so happy since he asked her to marry him. I think she has been in love with Daddy a long time. Even back in the day when she was married. But you know Daddy wasn't even going there. Then even after she found out that her husband's tree branches swung however the wind blew and she left his ass, Daddy still held back."

"I know. He was a good man, Glynda."

"When he thought she'd had enough time to heal from all the hurt, he asked us if it was okay for him to marry her. Can you imagine a grown man with grown daughters asking for their permission? He told us he'd been in love with her for many, many years, even when she was still married, but that he respected her, her husband, and himself too much to make a move. My daddy was one of a kind. They broke the mold. Anthony says all the time that he can never measure up to Daddy, and that's why I won't marry him. Do you think that's true?"

"All I do know is that Anthony is a wonderful man and that I'm going to do what you did for me with Jonathan. I'm going to give you a reality check. That man loves your week-old dirty drahs. And he isn't going to keep begging yo' ass to marry him. He would walk on broken glass spread over hot coals for you, and *you* betta recognize."

I turned and stared at Rico. She rarely spoke to me in this sistahgurl tone.

"This is the same advice you gave me when I was too caught up on what Jonathan did for a living to realize that it was the size of his heart I should have been noticing. This kind of happiness doesn't come twice in a lifetime, and I owe it all to you. What kind of friend would I be if I didn't return the favor?"

"This isn't the time to talk about this, Rico." I tried to be angry.

"You may be right. And you know I'm here for you every second of the day and every step of the way, but the one you need is Anthony, and because you have denied the man the one wish that would complete his life, he probably can't be here. I love you so much, Glynda. I just want you to have it all. And despite what anyone says, you *can* have it all."

Tears began to fall once again. "I know you're right, gurl. I do love him so much. You're a true friend. Most people wouldn't tell me the truth the way you do. What am I going to do without Daddy?"

"I wish I knew the answer to that one. But you do have me. And you have Anthony. We could never replace Papa Eddie, but we can help you heal slowly. We will just love you." Rico reached over and pressed her soft hand on top of mine.

A sense of peace washed over me, and I reclined the seat and closed my eyes. The remainder of the trip was spent in silence. I tried to think, but grief just crowded my mind to the point that nothing else would fit.

"Just drop me off. I don't need help to the counter." I could tell my request startled Rico.

"Oh *paleeze*! My best friend's father just died and I'm just going to leave her on the curb. I don't think so!"

"You never walk me inside. You slow the car down and throw me out the door."

"I'm not that bad!" Rico had to laugh at herself.

"You know you are! But I can't take a long teary good-bye right now, plus I'll see you on Thursday."

"You know Jonathan is meeting us here."

"Oh, that's right. I'll just hug his neck and send him on his way. He's a really good man, too. You know this is going to make him late on his route today." Just the thought of Jonathan's six-foot-four-inch mega-muscular body waiting to hug me warmed my heart.

Jonathan and I had become friends immediately after his first date with Rico. She'd told him that I was the one responsible for her acceptance of his request to have dinner with him. He said that he had to meet the woman who'd changed his life forever. The first time we played pool I skunked him. He never even got to take his first shot. He'd called me Minnesota Slim. To this day he still calls me Slim.

As we sat and debated about the pros and cons of drop-off versus walk-in, I was startled when the passenger door opened. There stood Jonathan with his dimpled smile.

"Hey, Slim. How ya doing?" Jonathan's deep voice was a natural manifestation of his massive body.

Just seeing him with his warm, brown, puppylike eyes opened the floodgate of tears once again. "Oh Jonathan, what am I going to do without my daddy?"

"Oh Slim, don't cry!" His voice cracked.

"Honey, get her bags out of the trunk. She doesn't want me to walk her inside. Will you do it? No matter what she says, stay with her until she gets to security.

She'll pick up her ticket at the counter." Rico was leaning over me to talk to Jonathan.

"Of course I will, baby. Do you know when the funeral will be yet? I really want to be there for both of you. I need to represent for my man Anthony. I know from my military days they aren't going to let him off to come. I want to put in for an emergency vacation this morning."

I stared up into Jonathan's face. "Funeral?" It was the first time I had actually thought that we'd have a service with flowers, music, people speaking softly, shaking our hands and telling us how sorry they were.

Jonathan looked at Rico as if to say, What do I need to say here? "Will the funeral be in three or four days?"

"I don't know." I couldn't breathe.

"I'll let you know, honey." I heard Rico say, though it seemed she was somewhere far away.

Jonathan retrieved the bags from the trunk and sat them by the rear passenger door as he extended his enormous hand to help me out of the car. He wanted desperately to say something, but nothing seemed right. "Come on, Slim, let's get you on this plane."

The touch of Jonathan's strong arms made me long for Anthony. Rico was right. There was no reason I wasn't Mrs. Sanders, except my own stupid issues. I blindly followed him inside the terminal, where thankfully there were no lines. As we stepped to the ticket counter, Jonathan placed my bags on the scale and took charge.

"Where's your license, Slim?" he asked, awkwardly looking for my wallet in the abyss known as my purse.

Silently, I passed him my license.

"Ms. Naylor. You're checking two bags through to Baltimore?" Debbie, according to her name tag, asked.

"Yes." Jonathan answered.

"Did you pack yourself?

Did I pack the bags? I couldn't remember.

"She packed them herself and they have been in her control the entire time." Jonathan answered with such authority Debbie dared not question him.

Debbie continued to key what I presumed to be pertinent data into the computer. In a matter of seconds she returned my license and a boarding pass. With a well-rehearsed smile she said, "Enjoy your flight, Ms. Naylor."

Jonathan walked me to the escalator leading to the security area. Looking down at me with his warm puppy-like eyes, he smiled. He hugged me tight and whispered, "I'm so sorry, Glynda. I just wish I could fix this thing. Rico and I will be there for you just as soon as we can. I promise."

As I stared up into his handsome, weathered face, I knew they would do just that. Friends are the part of heaven that God puts right here on earth.

The flight attendant offered the passengers a choice of water or orange juice before takeoff. I chose a glass of orange juice and took the little yellow pill Rico had given me. She'd simply said, "This should help you relax and sleep on the plane." Of course, I had forgotten about it until the moment I sat down next to the middle-aged businessman of European descent who spoke with far more cheer than I was ready to receive. The seating was sparse in the business-class section of the wide-body aircraft, so why on earth had they seated us together? I really wanted to be alone. I smiled politely and apologized in advance that I wasn't feeling well and wanted to sleep the entire flight. I hadn't cared if I offended the pleasant stranger, which was totally out of character for me. He was perceptive enough, simply smiled and said he'd make sure the flight attendants knew not to disturb me. He'd taken on the role of my protector. Daddy always said to treat everyone the same because you never knew when you might be entertaining angels. I guess he was right.

Physical and emotional exhaustion overtook me quickly, and I slipped into a dream-filled slumber where faces and scenes changed quickly before I was at my mother's funeral. Daddy had such an empty look in his eyes as we sat in the front pew. He stared straight ahead. We sat next to Daddy in birth order from oldest to youngest. I remembered someone had lined us up. Renee was fourteen and said she was going to be strong for the rest of us. She held my hand and pulled me along as fear gripped my soul when I saw the long white box with pink trim where my mother lay sleeping. How could a nine-year-old understand that her mother would never wake up again?

Collette had started sucking her thumb the night the police had rung the doorbell after Mama hadn't picked us up from school. In all of her six years she'd never sucked her thumb. That fateful night she would start a habit that would take her well into adulthood, when her thumb had been replaced by cigarettes. Daddy held two-year-old Dawn in his arms as he spoke to the police officer, who said there had been an accident. A man had run a red light and hit Mama's car on her side, and she had died on the way to the hospital. The man in the uniform told my daddy he had to come down to the morgue to identify the body, even though the car was registered to Edward and Lorraine Naylor at this address, and the purse on the front seat of the car had a wallet that held a driver's license of Lorraine Marie Naylor. There was little doubt that it was his wife.

Then my dream turned bizarre. Mama sat up in her white box with the pink trim and called to Daddy. "Eddie, come on over with me. I need you, Eddie. I have waited long enough. Come on home with me."

Daddy left the front pew and was climbing into the box with Mama when I heard myself screaming to Daddy, "No, don't go. I need you to stay here with me. Please, Daddy, don't leave me." I woke up with tears streaming and a flight attendant touching my arm and my seat neighbor looking quite concerned.

"Are you alright, miss?" asked a young Asian flight attendant who was wearing an apron with the name Ian embroidered on it.

"Oh, I'm sorry. Was I talking out loud?" I felt groggy from the little yellow pill.

"You were in a very troubled sleep, and the gentleman here was concerned. Are you sure you're okay?" Ian took a beverage napkin from his apron pocket and handed it to me to wipe my tear-streaked face.

"Yes, I'm so sorry. Thank you for your concern." I wasn't ready to tell anyone that I had dreamed that my dead mother had come and taken my daddy from me. They would've thought I was nuts for sure.

"May I get you something to drink?" Ian was showing his perfectly aligned teeth as he smiled the rehearsed customer-service smile.

"Just some water, please," I managed to whisper.

"Are you sure you're alright? You were calling to your father," asked my concerned seatmate.

"I may never be alright again. My daddy died this morning."

"I'm so sorry. My name is William. Here's my card. I'm a psychologist. If you ever need to talk, just call me."

I stared down at the card of William Barnett, Ph.D., Grief Therapist. Now I knew why I had been seated next to this man. He *was* my angel.

I hadn't realized I'd slept so long. We were only twenty minutes from landing. I was glad the flight was almost over. Dr. Barnett would look over at me and smile occa-

sionally, but he didn't intrude on my thoughts. I was relieved.

As I gathered my things to deplane, Dr. Barnett touched
my shoulder and simply said, "Don't expect too much
from yourself. Leave the strength to others."

"Thank you." Despite my best efforts, tears filled my
eyes again.

3

Home Sweet Home?

I could see Uncle Thomas, Dawn, and Estelle standing just on the other side of the security checkpoint. I looked for Renee and Collette, but they were conspicuously absent. Estelle's flushed face and swollen eyes spoke volumes. She had shed more than a few tears. Dawn extended her arms, and I gladly ran into them. I could feel Estelle's hand on the center of my back. It brought me minimal comfort.

"Hey, Sissy." Uncle Thomas extended his arms as tears streamed down his rugged cheeks. Other passengers pushed their way past us, and I realized our family reunion was blocking the main walkway. Flower- and balloon-carrying, picture-snapping family and friends greeted those who had shared with me the past four hours and twelve minutes in the skies far above the earth. Had I been closer to Daddy up there in the heavens?

"Uncle Thomas," I said as I reached for him, feeling as if I was falling from a cliff.

"Come on ovah here and give yo' Uncle Thomas some love." We moved out of the flow of arriving passengers, and the four of us stood embarrassing one another. Tears and pain were our common denominator.

"Where are Collette and Renee?" I couldn't believe my sisters weren't here. Maybe they were at the car. If

Collette drove, for sure she would not want to pay to park.

"They'll meet us at Daddy's." Dawn shot a glance to Estelle, and I knew that meant they hadn't wanted to come with Estelle. What did they have against this woman? She had never been anything but wonderful to all of us. And Lord knows, Renee and Collette had given her plenty of cause to act differently.

"How are you doing, Estelle?" I hugged her and held her close.

She just simply waved at me and began to cry afresh.

"Let's git yo' bags and git ovah to Eddie's place, I knows yo' sistahs are waitin' ta see ya." Uncle Thomas smiled.

We walked in silence to baggage claim. Dawn and I walked hand in hand like two little girls. We followed Uncle Thomas blindly, hoping he'd lead the way; for surely we felt lost. Estelle was off a little to the right walking alone. She, too, looked lost. The walk seemed endless. When we arrived, the bags were already circling on the carousel.

"Jus' point dem out to me and I'll git 'em, Glynda. I know dey's da fancy ones, ain't dey?"

"They're not all that fancy, Uncle Thomas." I tried to fake a smile.

"I loves ya a whole bunch, Glynda, just like I loves Dawn and Renee and Collette. We gonna make it thu dis here, I promise ya dat." Uncle Thomas wasn't convincing.

"Promise me we will, please. I don't know if I can do this. I just don't know!" Before I knew it, I was wailing right where I stood in baggage claim, across from the car rental counters and ground transportation booth. People were starting to stare, but I didn't care. My daddy was dead. These people who stared obviously didn't know what a great and wonderful man my daddy had been, for surely they, too, would be crying.

Estelle moved in close to me, and I buried my head on her shoulder. She patted and rocked me as though I were a newborn baby. "Glynda, Thomas is right, we'll make it through this, but only if we have each other. Renee and Collette don't really want me around, and I'll respect that. But I loved your father with every cell in my body. I lived my whole life not knowing true love until Eddie started loving me. I'll be there for whatever you need, whenever you need it."

Uncle Thomas gathered my bags, and we headed in silence for the parking lot, where his brown Taurus station wagon, in immaculate condition, awaited. As he put the bags in the back and closed the hatch, I realized that coming home would never be the same again.

"I'll be over to Eddie's a little later. I just want to give you all time to be alone," Estelle finally said.

"Okay, Estelle, I'll talk to Renee and Collette. Everything will work out. I promise you."

Estelle only smiled. She knew I had my work cut out for me. As she walked away, her normally straight posture was low and her shoulders slumped. She felt crushed, and I truly empathized.

"You want to sit up front, Glynda?" Dawn asked.

"No, I'll just stretch out back here," I said, slipping into the backseat.

"Why didn't Renee and Collette come with you?" I was more hurt than angry.

"They're trippin', as usual."

"What happened?" My sisters need no excuse at all to trip, so there was no telling what the trauma of Daddy dying had brought out in them.

"We stayed over at Uncle Thomas's house all morning. He made us breakfast and we started calling relatives. It was so hard saying over and over and over again that Daddy had died. Of course, everyone had the same questions. It took until about two o'clock to get through Uncle Thomas's phone book. In the meantime I'd been calling Estelle every thirty minutes or so because it had been almost twelve hours since Daddy died, and the woman he was going to marry didn't know. And I don't care how much you dislike a person, that just ain't right."

"They had something to say about you calling Estelle?" I was stunned.

"They just kept saying why was I putting so much effort into trying to reach her. I finally reached her around two forty-five and told her I wanted to stop by. She knew something was wrong and pressured me, but I just couldn't bring myself to tell her without being face-to-face to comfort her. You know Eddie Naylor was the starch in her apron!"

"You're a mess, gurl!" I said. Dawn had drawn a genuine smile from me.

"Well, you know he was! Anyway, I begged, I do mean begged them to go with me to Estelle's. They flatly refused. So Uncle Thomas agreed to go, and we told them we would be leaving Estelle's and coming to pick you up. Silly me, I thought that would change their minds. Obviously it didn't." Dawn gestured with her hands as if to say, Look around.

"Ya know all of dis here mess is gonna to be hard 'nuff wit'out yo' sistahs showin' dere behinds," Uncle Thomas interjected.

"Will you talk to them, Uncle Thomas?" I pleaded.

"I'll try, but dey don't be listenin' ta me."

"I know." I sighed deeply.

"Dat po' woman is hurtin' as bad as y'all. I thought she was gonna have a heart attack when Dawn tol' heh. She clutched heh ches' 'n' fell backward. It plum scared me. But even wit' all of dat she said she had ta come ta da airport ta git chu." Uncle Thomas's voice was cracking.

"I just don't understand what Renee and Collette's problem is. Do you have any idea, Dawn?" I leaned over the front seat to look into her face.

"I'm not sure, but I think it would be that way with any woman Daddy wanted to marry. You know as long as he and Estelle were just friends, they had no problem with her. But the minute they started dating, all hell broke loose." Dawn had turned so that we made eye contact.

"You know Daddy spoiled us. We had him all to ourselves for all those years. I know he dated on the down low. Hell, he had to. He may have been my daddy, but he was still a man. But I guess there was no one worthy of meeting his little girls, until Estelle. And that can only mean that he really loved her. I will not let Renee and Lette dishonor his memory by showing their natural ah . . . behinds." I corrected myself as I shot a glance at Uncle Thomas.

"Well, gurl, you know they don't listen to anything I have to say, so good luck."

I sat back and pondered the task ahead of me. There's no way I should have to worry about the manner in which my sisters were treating my father's fiancée. We still had the task of picking a funeral home, burial clothes, the obituary, the day, and the cemetery. All of this was making my body feel heavy again. I decided to just stare out of the window, mindlessly watching Interstate 695 roll under the wheels.

Uncle Thomas pulled into Daddy's driveway behind the almost-new Lincoln Town Car. My daddy had been a big man, both in stature and character. He always said he was not going to try to squeeze his six-foot-six-inch frame into a car made for a man five foot ten. Most of his 250 pounds was heart. The Bethlehem Steel third-shift crew Daddy had managed for as long as I could remember was going to be devastated. He'd been voted manager of the year seven out of the past ten years. I wondered silently if anyone had called his job.

He had been a very active member of the First United Church, where we'd all attended from childhood. He headed up one of the Big Brother/Big Sister chapters and had been responsible for the largest volunteer sign-up drive in the organization's history. He said we couldn't give up on our young people. They were all we had. He would've been a wonderful teacher. For sure they would have made a movie of the week about him. He organized young people from the after-school program to adopt senior citizens. They would read to them, give them gifts on birthdays and holidays, and basically just show them love. It gave the young people a sense of purpose and the seniors a sense of belonging.

His friends, though few, were like his brothers. Daddy and his long-time buddies spent many hours watching sports, mostly baseball, shooting pool, playing dominoes, and telling harmless lies. I saw familiar cars on the street. I couldn't remember who owned the majority of them, but Mister Willie's pimpmobile, as Daddy called it, caught my attention first. Daddy had teased him when he bought the new candy apple–red Z-28 Camaro with the T-top. Told him he was in old-age crisis and that those young girls he was chasing were going to be the death of him. How little did any of us know . . .

How could one man have affected so many lives? How would any of us survive without Eddie Naylor?

Uncle Thomas opened my door, and my thoughts returned to the present. "Lemme hep ya outta da car, baby."

"Uncle Thomas, did Daddy die in the house?" I stared into eyes heavily laden with sadness.

He shot a glance to Dawn and then back at me. "Yeah, baby, he did."

I felt as though my feet had been cemented to the ground. I couldn't go in that house. This was the house where my daddy had died! How could any of them think that I could do this! Dawn recognized the absolute horror on my face.

"I know what you're thinking, Sissy. You can do this. I'll help you. We don't have a choice."

"Please hold my hand, Dawn." The fear of a five-year-old headed for a haunted house gripped me.

Uncle Thomas walked ahead of us and the door swung open before we were even on the first step. Collette ran down the steps to greet me. Her eyes were bloodshot and swollen, the eyes of someone who had shed tears a very short time ago.

"Sissy, I'm so glad you're here. We are finally all together! Renee is on the phone with Daddy's job. They have been calling all day. Every time someone new finds out, the phone rings. They're all crying and asking what can they do." We walked hand in hand up the steps, and, as I reached the open doorway, I felt the paralysis of the early morning hours in my bedroom return. Collette turned to see why I wasn't still moving in sync with her. She saw the trepidation on my face.

"Sissy, you can do this. We all felt the same way at first. But remember we were all here when they brought him out of the house. That was the absolute worst. If we

can survive that, then for sure you can go into the house."
I wasn't sure, but I thought I sensed anger in Lette's
voice.

"I don't know why I can't move. The same thing happened this morning, too. Then I fainted." I felt as though
I needed to explain myself.

"You fainted? Are you pregnant?" Collette asked.

"No, gurl! Rico said it was post-traumatic stress related. My body just shut down rather than deal with the
trauma."

"How is the good-doctor-married-to-the-deliveryman?"
Collette inquired snidely.

"She's wonderful and extremely happy. They'll be
here on Thursday. And you'd better be nice to my
friends. I mean it, Lette!" I wasn't taking any chances
that Collette would be her normal envious self with
Rico.

It was no secret that Collette envied Rico's success in
her career and her personal life. Though Collette enjoyed a very handsome six-figure income, Rico's income
was higher. The house Rico and I had shared was twice
as large as the home that Collette owned in the well-to-
do Reisterstown neighborhood. Collette definitely envied Rico's happiness with Jonathan. Collette's second
marriage of four years, four years longer than the first,
had ended with a bitter divorce and a beastly property
settlement battle. Collette was the one who had to pay
alimony. Her ex-husband received a nice check from her
each month. Rico's loving, caring, and sharing relationship with the handsome, strong black man named Jonathan made sistahgurl more than a little green.

"Oh paleeze, I'll be very civil to the perfect little couple. Just don't let her cross me, though. Coming up in
here thinking she running somethin'." Collette rolled
her eyes.

Focusing on protecting my friend had changed my anxiety about walking into Daddy's house, and before I knew it I was standing in the small contemporarily furnished living room watching Renee try to end her conversation with the shift supervisor from Daddy's job. As I looked around the room, nothing seemed to have changed. The overstuffed gray sofa and love seat looked as inviting as ever. A single exquisite silk plant graced the lacquered mahogany coffee table. Matching crystal lamps reflected the sunlight, casting a rainbow of color onto the matching end tables. Everything was just as I had remembered. But everything was different. How could everything still look so familiar, yet feel so strange? The only evidence that something horrible had happened in this house less than twenty-four hours ago was the new door and jamb that remained unpainted. Apparently the paramedics had used their ax quite liberally in their efforts to get to the man who lay dying inside.

"Sissy!" Renee leapt into my arms and began to wail.

"Oh, Renee, what are we going to do?" Of course I could not let her cry alone.

As our guests heard that a new family member had arrived, they felt it their duty to greet me. Mister Willie was the first to emerge from the den. "Glynda, God love you, baby. How you holdin' up? My buddy done up and left me. What am I gonna do?" Tears filled his already red eyes. Mister Willie was known for his cooler-than-cool manner, never affected by anything or anyone. To see tears in his eyes only made mine flow more freely.

Johnny Bea and Sister Greene followed him and hugged me close and echoed Mister Willie's sentiments. Sister Greene spoke first. "Babies, we gonna leave y'all so you can grieve in private. I have to go to Giants and get some chicken for some chicken and dumplin's, about twenty-five bunches of greens, and some sweet potatoes. I may as well make a pound cake since I'll be cookin' anyway. I'll bring it all by tomorrow 'bout noon. Y'all got enough to worry about besides what you gonna be eatin'."

"I bought some coffee, cream, sugar, cups, and a bottle of brandy for y'all. I made a fresh pot while Renee was on the phone," Johnny Bea whispered.

"Now why you gonna bring them some liquor, Bea?" I thought Sister Greene was going to lay hands on her and start to pray for her repentance.

"A little brandy to calm the nerves," Johnny Bea responded as though she were prescribing medication.

"Well, the Lord gonna help them through this, they sho' don't need no devil's elixir!"

The two friends were about to go at it as they had on many occasions in the past when Mister Willie interrupted. "Come on, ladies, let's get out of here and leave them to talk. They got a lot of business to handle. You girls need anything, anything at all, you call on ole Willie, you hear me? And I know I don't need to say this, but I want to be a pallbearer. God knows Eddie has carried me enough in this life. I would be honored to carry him in his death." Tears fell onto his full, perfectly manicured salt-and-pepper beard.

"Thank you, Mister Willie. We had planned to ask you if you wanted to be an actual pallbearer or an honorary one. We'll call you as soon as everything is set. Please come back tomorrow. I'm sure we'll be in and out, but someone should be here all the time. You still have your key?" Dawn was holding his hand the way she did as a little girl when he'd walk her to the corner store. Dawn was his goddaughter and clearly his favorite.

"No, baby girl, I gotta carry my man to his final resting place. That is where the true honor is." Mister Willie hugged Dawn. He then hugged each of us, including Uncle Thomas.

"We'll see y'all tomorrow." Sister Greene followed Mister Willie with the hugs.

Of course, Johnny Bea would not be outdone. But she had no words. The pain in her heart clearly showed on her ageless face.

Johnny Bea and Sister Greene had been friends of our mother. Sister Greene and Mama were ushers at the church and prayer partners. They had been closer than close, and when Mama died, Sister Greene had stepped in to help Daddy in any way she could with us. Dawn was a toddler, and Sister Greene said she needed a mother to nurture her. Renee and I suspected that the good sister wanted the mother to be her. But Daddy always kept his distance. She was a wonderful friend to him and an auntlike figure to us. We aren't sure when she stopped pursuing Daddy, but one day they were just good friends.

Johnny Bea had been a teacher's aide in Mama's class when she was killed. She had come by the day after the funeral and promised that she would do whatever she could to help with us and had done just that until Dawn graduated from high school. She would come by every morning to comb our hair until Renee assured her she could handle it. She attended all of the mother-daughter functions at school. She'd stay with us when Daddy's job sent him out of town for training, which occurred regularly. She'd never been married and shared her small but impeccably maintained home with another woman, who never came around us. It wasn't until we were adults that we figured out the two women were far more than roommates.

"Thank you all for coming." Renee spoke softly.

"We love y'all so much. We'll call you as soon as we make the arrangements." Dawn's voice cracked, and the word "arrangements" seemed fragmented.

We quickly said our good-byes and turned to one another as they started down the steps.

"I don't want to do this, Sissy. I just don't!" Renee hugged me again. "Now that we're all here, we have no excuse not to make the arrangements. The coroner should release the body early tomorrow morning." Renee stepped back but didn't let me go.

"All of this makes no sense to me. How could Daddy just up and die? How could this happen to a man who was so full of life? Less than twenty-four hours ago he called each of us; now we're talking about coroners releasing his body." I shook my head sadly.

"I know, Glynda. Estelle said she talked to him, too. He'd made plans for them to go away this weekend before they got heavy into the last-minute wedding preparations. She said he had a real surprise for her. She's so sad." Dawn's voice trailed off.

"Well, she is no sadder than we are, and we're his family," Collette spoke up.

"You can believe that!" Renee added quickly.

"Now listen, Estelle was not only Daddy's fiancée but his dear, dear friend. She's like family, and I personally think we should make her a part of our decision making. She loves him as much as we do. She's all torn up inside, too. And if you two hadn't been so damned selfish and had gone over there with Dawn, you'd have been able to see that for yourselves. This isn't a time for division. We should be clinging to anyone who feels the way we do!" Like a balloon being overfilled with helium, an emotional outburst welled up inside me.

"Well, be that as it may, she wasn't married to him

yet, so all of her imagined rights are nonexistent," Renee said, very matter-of-factly.

"I don't believe you're saying that, Renee. Daddy would be so disappointed in you!" Dawn spoke before I had a chance to voice my opinion.

"And you know he would," I added.

"Don't tell me what Daddy would be disappointed in. What he would be upset about is we can't even decide on what funeral home to call to come get him from the morgue. You know he hated indecision." Collette lit a cigarette.

"Put that thing out. You know Daddy didn't allow anyone to smoke in here!" I was livid at Collette's obvious disrespect.

"The way I see it, this is now our house and as I do in my own house, I choose to smoke!" Collette blew smoke in our faces.

"If, as you say, this is *our* house, I don't allow smoking in my house, so put that disgusting thing out," Dawn spat.

"Alright! Alright! Y'all stop it now. Ya jus' fightin' 'bout anythang so ya don't have ta deal wit' da matters at hand." Uncle Thomas had the coffeepot in his hand. "Come on in here in da dining room 'n' let's have some coffee 'n' make some decisions. Collette, put dat cigarette out. Ya knows yo' daddy wouldn't have it."

"Yes, Uncle Thomas." Collette gave me the I'm-gonna-get-you look like she did when we were kids and I'd gotten her in trouble with Daddy.

We slowly gathered around the dining room table. Uncle Thomas sat in Daddy's chair, looking so much like Daddy sitting at the head of the table. Many had mistaken them for twins throughout the years. The eleven months separating their births made that an impossibility. Uncle Thomas was two inches shorter. Seeing the familiar dark expressive eyes and olive skin they shared brought me sadness and relief at the same time.

"Now, I undastan' y'all couldn't decide on a fun'ral home dis morning. So what chu thank we should do now?" Uncle Thomas wasted no time getting to the point.

"Well, I think the first thing we should do is set a budget. We don't want to just go into a funeral home with a have-Mont-Blanc-will-write-check attitude. They'll take full advantage of us." Collette was quick to voice her opinion.

"I should've known that money would be the first thing out of your mouth!" I wasn't going to stand for this madness from my penny-pinching-wannabe-buppie sister.

"Well, it's not a pleasant topic, but a necessary one." Renee had taken Collette's side—big surprise.

"Okay, okay. How much life insurance does Daddy have?" Dawn was trying her best to bring accord to the situation.

"I have no idea. But I know he has a good policy, plus the one at work. He mentioned that to me when I asked him if he had a will." The lawyer in me was starting to show.

"You and Daddy talked about a will without the rest of us?" Collette was visibly upset.

"No, we didn't *discuss a will*. I asked him if he had one; he said no but he'd draw one up. He thought it was a smart idea." My patience was about as short as Jada Pinkett Smith's hair.

"And when did this nondiscussion take place?" Sarcasm dripped from Renee's every word.

"About a year ago, I'd imagine. It was before I finished law school."

"So did he write a will?" Collette was salivating.

"Yeah, he wrote one. He tol' me 'bout it," Uncle Thomas interjected.

"What's in it?" Collette had no shame.

"Damn, do you mind waiting until his body is cold!" I was on the verge of tears.

"He has copies of his insurance papers in his file cab'net in da den. A copy of da will prolly be in dere, too. He tol' me all of dis 'bout six months ago. He said fo' me ta tell y'all in case somethin' evah happened ta him. I joked and said da paper would be yellow befo' we'd need to go in dat drawah. I sho' was wrong." Uncle Thomas's words trailed off.

With no regard for Uncle Thomas's state, Collette and Renee headed for the den. Dawn and I only stared at each other. The lines were clearly drawn. I'd never noticed how different Dawn and I were from Collette and Renee until this very moment. It went so far beyond the physical.

Renee at five foot four was the shortest of the sisters and also the heaviest. She'd had issues with her weight for as long as I could remember. She still hadn't learned that sexy doesn't have a dress size. She had shoulder-length medium-brown hair and dark eyes that sparkled like Daddy's when she smiled. I personally thought she was absolutely gorgeous the way she was, as did her husband, Derrick.

She married Derrick, her junior-high-school sweetheart, shortly after high school. She loved her family more than life itself and believed that she had to do and have it all. When she went to college after her second child was born, she almost had a nervous breakdown, trying to be the perfect wife, mother, and student. She used her business degree to start an African import business that developed into one of the most in-demand interior-decorating concerns in Baltimore.

Collette, on the other hand, had always been the center of her own universe. Being dealt Daddy's genes, she was the tallest and had a strong five-foot-eleven build. Though she never ate, worked out five days a week, and had liposuction (she didn't know that we knew) she tipped the scale at 160. Her olive skin, jet black hair, and knockout body had caused more than a few men to bow down.

She was as obsessed with her appearance as she was with her money. Money for anything to enhance her outward appearance was the only area in which my frugal sister would spend with absolute abandon. Despite her first marriage, which was a joke after she eloped on prom night and which ended shortly thereafter in an annulment, she married the pretty frat brother she dated all through college, even though Daddy adamantly disapproved. She had to have someone who complemented her in every way, as she'd told Daddy. Daddy warned her that Calvin was too lazy to pick up his own feet. He was a playboy who'd use her until he used her up. Notwithstanding the rocky marriage, Collette excelled as a financial planner and became independently well-off.

Money meant everything to her. The only people she really cared about were her clients. She was much too selfish to ever have children. Besides, she'd become fat if she got pregnant. She claimed to care about us, and true enough she loved us, but that was a condition of birth, not of her heart.

Dawn was the one who had inherited Daddy's heart. She was so kind and full of love. She and I wore our five-foot-eight bodies proudly. Dawn's 155 pounds had me beat by fifteen pounds, and it was all in her chest. We could never figure where she'd inherited those thirty-eight triple Ds. She jokingly said she'd added new genes to the pool. Possessing the same natural beauty as our mother, she'd always played down her good looks and covered up her brick-house body with baggy clothes. She had many stories of how the parents would get into *little* discussions about the fathers paying a bit too much attention to the nurse administering to the needs of their tiny sick ones. She could never see what all the fuss was about. Though Dawn had never married, she had a twelve-year-old son who was the reason her heart beat. She got pregnant her senior year in high school and had Darryl Edward Naylor that summer. Daddy told her that the baby would make her life a little more challenging but in no way changed anything. He paid for child care when he wasn't taking care of little Darryl himself so that Dawn could attend college.

Then, of course, there was me. I wasn't as kind and selfless as Dawn, evidenced by my moving to California, but I was loving like Daddy and truly cared about the feelings of others. To say I was attractive would make me sound vain, but I liked what I saw in the mirror. Though my medium-brown hair fell below my shoulders, I liked the low maintenance of braids and the elegance of the micros. Like my sisters I had Daddy's dark eyes and my mother's smile. I was the only one of the Naylor girls to have inherited my mother's near-indigo skin. I was an overachiever and was never satisfied by what I'd accomplished. I planned to marry Anthony, but in my time. We would have two perfect little children, and I'd be senior partner in an African-American law firm by the time I was forty. My plan didn't include leaving any dead bodies in my wake.

Dawn moved over to comfort Uncle Thomas, who laid his head on her ample bosom and began to sob uncontrollably. I'd never seen Uncle Thomas break down like this. I remembered how he cried at Mama's funeral. It was a steady stream of quiet tears, and I thought, How strange to cry with no sound. This was different. Very, very different.

4

Being of Sound Mind

My thoughts were interrupted by shrill sounds from the den. What in the world? Dawn, Uncle Thomas, and I quickly made our way toward the awful noise.

"What in the world is wrong with you?" Dawn asked Collette, from whom the horrendous noise was escaping.

"Daddy has included Estelle in the will and made her an insurance beneficiary!" Renee answered for Collette.

"Why is that so strange? He was going to marry the woman." I didn't know what I felt at that very moment.

"Y'all, let's gather all da papers and go sit back at da dinin' room table to figure all dis out. We needs to call Estelle now fo' sho'." Uncle Thomas was almost smiling.

"Why do we need to call her? She still has no say-so. And we may contest this anyway." Collette was relentless.

"Get a clue, Lette," I said. "We can't contest Daddy's will or insurance policies. He was very much in his right mind. Get it through your head, he loves, or I guess I should say loved, Estelle. Now you can accept it, cherish our wonderful memories, and help the rest of us get through this grievous experience, or you can try to do whatever you can to bring us down to your subterranean level."

Collette took steps toward me, which made everyone

believe she was going to hit me. Uncle Thomas stepped between us. "Come on, babies, don't start fightin'. Let's go sit in the dinin' room 'n' read all of dis ovah. We'll call Estelle lata."

Uncle Thomas took both of us by the elbow, but Collette snatched hers away. My immediate thought was, *Oh Daddy is going to get in her stuff.* Then I realized he couldn't do that anymore. I started to cry again. Dawn and Renee came to my side.

"Uncle Thomas is right, we shouldn't be fighting. Let's just take all of these papers and sit down to figure all this out." Renee was finally making sense.

As we were about halfway back to the dining room, the doorbell chimed. Before any of us could get to the door it flew open, and Roberta, Renee's lifelong friend, came barreling into the house, screaming and crying.

"I just got your message and I rushed right over. My daddy is gone, my daddy is gone!"

Her daddy? Who was this foolish woman? Of course I knew who she was, but how dare she intrude on us at this moment talking about *her* daddy!

We stood in the short hallway, the walls lined with African-American artwork. "Roberta," I said, "thank you for coming by to pay your respects. We're just going over some family business so we can make the arrangements. Would you like some coffee and maybe have a seat in the den until we're done?" I was as polite as I knew to be in this situation.

"Oh then, I'm just in time. That man treated me like his daughter, and I know he'd want me to be a part of this. Am I right, Renee?" Roberta looked to her best friend for affirmation.

"He did love you, Roberta, but we just need a little time to sort some things out. You need to deal with your grief for a while first anyway. We've had several hours to comprehend what's taken place." Renee was looking at us as if to say, What do you want me to do here?, as she dropped her head and moved toward the dining room.

"Oh I know he loved me, too. That's why I should be included in making the arrangements, and my name should go in the obituary." It was as if Roberta heard nothing Renee said. And what in the hell did she mean her name should go in the obituary?

Roberta pulled an armchair away from the eight-foot mahogany dining room table.

"I'll just get myself together right here. I can listen and drink my coffee." It was obvious she was not going to be left out unless we got outright cruel.

"Very well then, have a seat, Bert. We were just about to go over the will and insurance policies." I couldn't believe Renee invited this nonfamily member to be a part of the most intimate discussion ever to take place in our family. Yet she didn't want the woman Daddy was going to marry to be a part of this? Oh! Now we'd just stepped into the Twilight Zone.

"I just want to go on record as saying only those named in the will and/or insurance policies should be present. And furthermore, I think we should call Estelle over here." Anger had been my constant companion all day.

"Just sit your lawyer ass down and shut up. Ain't nobody calling Estelle, and Bert can stay. She *is* family. She has been my friend since high school. Daddy loved her like she was one of his own. We haven't looked at the entire will. She is probably mentioned somewhere."

For reasons unknown to me then or even now, I just sat in silence, staring at my reflection in the mirror at the back of the beautiful china cabinet that matched the table around which we'd shared meals for the past fifteen years. This house had never known such discord.

As we looked through the small mound of paperwork, it appeared that, if all policies were current, my daddy had $1.8 million in life insurance. There were seven policies worth a quarter of a million dollars each. Each policy bore the name of a different beneficiary. We recognized all of the names except one: Nina Blackford.

There was one policy worth fifty thousand dollars with six beneficiaries. The name Nina Blackford was missing from the smaller policy. My daddy was a very astute man. He knew what it would be like making his funeral arrangements, so he made his wishes perfectly clear. We were all to have equal say. It was very apparent, however, Ms. Roberta Maxwell was not named anywhere in the insurance papers.

"Who the hell is Nina Blackford?" Renee and I said in unison.

We all looked at Uncle Thomas. He only shrugged his shoulders and lifted his hands, as if to say he didn't know either. But I wasn't entirely sure I believed him.

"I can't believe Daddy got each of us an insurance policy!" Collette said. I may have been wrong, but I thought I saw glittering dollar signs in her eyes as she spoke.

"This policy for Nina Blackford was taken out ten years ago, when all the others, except Estelle's, were written. Uncle Thomas, are you sure you don't know anything about this Nina Blackford person?" Dawn eyed our uncle suspiciously.

"But she isn't named on the fifty-thousand-dollar policy with the rest of us." Collette was thumbing through the smaller of the policies. "This is so bizarre!"

"That *is* pretty incredible. But please note that there's a policy here for Estelle. Like I said before, she should be here in all of this decision making." I was getting up to dial Estelle's number.

"I don't care how many insurance policies name her.

She will not make any decisions to bury my daddy! Who do you think you're calling?" Renee was following me to the kitchen, where the old-style beige phone with the rotary dial had hung on the wall near the back door since I was a little girl. Daddy never changed the old phone when he remodeled the kitchen. The rich cherry-wood cabinets with gray Formica countertops made the phone look even more outdated.

"I'm calling Estelle, and you can't stop me!" I spoke with such authority Renee actually cowered back.

I realized after I picked up the telephone I couldn't remember Estelle's number. What was happening to me? I knew Estelle's number as well as I knew my own. I gently replaced the receiver and stared at Renee. I saw her face soften as she stared into my eyes. Why were we acting so ugly?

"Come on, Sissy. We can call her together later. I promise," Renee said softly.

Uncle Thomas met us in the doorway. "Ima makes some fresh coffee. Y'all need to go sit down 'n' collec' yo' nerves."

As we entered the dining room Dawn had already started reading through the will. All eyes were intent on her. "Daddy has left very specific instructions for his funeral: how much is to be spent, what funeral home. Everything is written out. He's purchased two plots— one for him and one for Estelle. He also said that the fifty-thousand-dollar policy is to cover his burial expenses and the balance is to be split between all of us to compensate for any out-of-pocket money we may have spent, missing work, etc. There's one more policy that he has at work, which is equivalent to two years' wages. He wants each of the supervisors to receive ten thousand dollars, along with Roberta and Rico. The balance is to be donated to the boys' and girls' club in his name."

"Did Daddy know he was dying and not tell us? This is all so detailed." I was surprised Daddy had gone into every conceivable element based on the one conversation we'd had.

"Well, he contacted dat dere lawyer afta he talk ta you, Sissy. Da lawyer tol' him ta write down all his requests 'n' he'd make him a will. Dat way when he died dere could be no confusion ovah what he wanted." Uncle Thomas blew on his steaming cup of coffee.

"What does it say about the house and its contents?" Collette's mind was working like a Texas Instruments calculator.

Flipping through the pages, Dawn whistled through her teeth. "Daddy was loaded! He has a huge stock portfolio and a fair amount of cash in the bank. It's all to be divided among us equally. The catch is that the 'equally' includes each of the grandchildren."

"So are you saying that Renee gets a five share and you get a two share? Well, that ain't right. Why should Renee get so much of the money just because she got a house full of children?"

"Collette, for God's sake lighten up. You're going to begrudge your own nieces and nephews a part of Daddy's money?" This woman never ceased to amaze me.

"I just don't think it's fair that Renee gets to manage so much more of the money than the rest of us." Collette wasn't even embarrassed by her own selfishness.

"You mean than you, don't you? You don't give a cat's fur ball about the rest of us!" Dawn was livid.

"So how many ways do we have to split the assets?" Collette didn't know when to quit.

"We're all named, the grandchildren, Estelle, Uncle Thomas, and this mysterious Nina Blackford. Uncle Thomas, Daddy told you everything. Are you sitting there trying to tell us you don't know who this person is? She was made beneficiary ten years ago on an insurance policy and now in a will written six months ago." Dawn eyed Uncle Thomas over her reading glasses.

"How do we find out who the hell this Nina person is?" Collette asked.

"Maybe the lawyer knows. This is only a copy of the will. The lawyer probably has the original. Maybe he'll know who she is and how to get in touch with her. How could she be someone important enough for Daddy to leave her an equal share of insurance money and we not even know who she is?" Dawn said, as she stared at the documents.

"See, I told you he loved me and would name me in the will." Roberta was wiping her crocodile tears.

"I know he loved you, Bert." Renee was trying to comfort her friend, but avoided eye contact with us.

"I think I should ride in the limo with y'all." Roberta spoke with indignation.

"Who in the hell do you think you are? You're not riding in the limo. You're not sitting in the front pew. You'll sit where all the other friends sit. Is that clear?" Collette didn't give Renee a chance to intervene on her friend's behalf.

"We can discuss this later," Renee said, looking at Roberta.

"I just know that Papa Eddie would want me to be treated like y'all. I'm like your sister."

"But you're *not* our sister." I couldn't believe the icy tone in my voice.

Roberta started to cry, actually started to wail!

"Look, y'all, we'll work all of this out. Let's call the funeral home and tell them they need to pick up his body. We'll deal with all of this when we're less emotional." Dawn was the incessant peacekeeper.

"And when do you think that will be, Miss Dawn?" Collette asked sarcastically.

"Who's going to make the call to the funeral home?" I said. I knew that a brawl was in the making.

"I think Renee should do it, since she is the oldest," Dawn whispered.

"What does that have to do with anything?" Pure dread showed on Renee's face.

Uncle Thomas spoke up. "I'll make da call."

"I know the call I'm going to make is to this lawyer. We need to know who in the hell this Nina Blackford is!" Collette added.

"Well, I have to admit I'm more than a little curious. But Renee promised we could call Estelle. I think we should do that first." I wasn't letting my oldest sister off the hook.

"Okay, okay, let's call her. I guess there are no real decisions to make. Daddy did it all himself. I wonder if Estelle knows who Nina Blackford is?" Renee had acquiesced, but I was sure it was to get to the bottom of the Nina mystery, not to show some concern for Estelle, our almost stepmother.

Estelle seemed pleased that I'd called her, and she promised to be right over. She'd baked chicken and made mashed potatoes. She was thawing green beans and would be over within the hour. We told her we'd found Daddy's will and insurance papers and we had some questions for her. She didn't seem at all ill at ease. I didn't know what to make of it. Perhaps Daddy had shared all of this with his soon-to-be wife. She may have known who the mysterious Nina was and what she had meant to our father.

Uncle Thomas made the second call to the funeral home and instructed them to contact the city coroner's office for a release date and time. The funeral director on duty at Brown's Funeral Home was dispatching a representative to our home to make the arrangements. Uncle Thomas made an appointment for nine o'clock the next morning.

"That'll give us a little time ta git some rest and git owah nerves t'getha befo' we have ta talk ta 'em," Uncle Thomas said, holding his head in his hand.

"Give me the phone so I can call this lawyer. He has to be able to shed some light on all of this madness, this strange woman in Daddy's will and insurance papers." Collette took the cordless phone from Uncle Thomas.

"Lette, you know the lawyer's office is closed this time of night." Roberta didn't have the good sense to be seen and not heard.

"I'll leave an urgent message, and he can call us back. I really need to get to the bottom of this. You know, Bert, it would be nice if we could be alone for a while. We've all been up all night, and my sister has flown across country." For once Collette mirrored my own sentiments.

"I don't think I should leave. It was apparent that Papa Eddie thought of me as one of his own, and Renee is my sister as much as she is yours. I want to stay." Roberta was starting with the waterfall tears again.

"If I speak now, I'm going to say way too many things I know I'll regret. But Renee, you betta deal with your friend. You see, when I was born Renee was my sister and when I die, she'll still be my sister." I got up to make more coffee.

Renee hugged Roberta and whispered something to her that seemed to soothe her. Why is it that when some-one dies everyone wants to be related to them? I would have gladly given Roberta my spot as the daughter of a dead man. This wasn't a prize on *The Price Is Right*. This was the worst pain I could ever imagine. Why would someone want to volunteer for this tour of duty?

Just the thought of "tour of duty" caused me to miss my Anthony so much. I needed to feel his strong arms around me to tell me I would survive these tumultuous times. I needed to fall asleep to the sweet sound of his baritone voice. He'd asked me to marry him twice, but I decided I needed to pass the bar before I made any other major commitments. Anthony never understood what one had to do with the other. He promised that he wouldn't ask a third time. If we were ever to be married, I'd be the one to do the asking. If I'd been able to speak to him tonight, not only would I ask him, I'd marry him on the spot. My longing for Anthony suddenly made me tired. The heaviness from earlier in the day had returned. I needed to lie down in Daddy's bed. I was sure that desire was going to be further cause for discussion among my sisters.

"I really need to lie down. I'm going to lie across Daddy's bed." I braced myself for the assault of expletives.

"Gurl, you gonna sleep in *that* room? Are you sure?" Collette asked with a curious look in her eyes. Not the anger I'd expected.

"You're better than me. I love Daddy and all, but if he forgot something, he may need to come back! You know what I'm sayin'?" Dawn was making light of the situation and drew a laugh from all, including Uncle Thomas.

"I think I should stay with you all tonight. After all, I'm like one of his daughters," Roberta said as she slipped off her shoes.

"Oh no, she didn't go there!" Collette whispered loud enough for all to hear.

"Roberta, perhaps you should go home, get some rest, check on the kids, and come back in the morning." Renee's eyes pleaded with us to be patient with her friend.

"I thinks dat'd be a real good idear, Bert." Uncle Thomas wasn't sure how much longer he could keep Collette, Dawn, and me off Roberta's behind.

"Well, I do need to get the kids settled for the rest of the week since I'll be with y'all from tomorrow on." She was clueless.

"Roberta, I don't want to appear rude or insensitive," Dawn said, "but Edward Zachary Naylor was not your daddy. He was our father, and nothing you can make up in your little mind is going to change that. He loved you, true enough, but a friendly love doesn't make you his child, or Renee's sister. We're under enough stress, and we don't need outsiders adding to it." Dawn was so kind and thoughtful of others' feelings, and I had to admit she definitely mimicked what I felt.

As I thought back over the years, memories of Roberta intruding on our special family moments flooded back to me. Five years before we had dressed in our after-five black finery and marched down to the Expressly Portrait, taking the Security Mall by storm as only Naylor divas could do. I'd flown in for a Father's Day celebration, and a sixteen-by-twenty mounted photograph of the four of us had been our gift of choice. We'd decided to make it an occasion, hired a limousine, made dinner plans at the exclusive Pisces at the top of the Hyatt Hotel overlooking the Inner Harbor, to be followed by dancing under the stars on one of the harbor-cruise-party boats. The limo picked up Dawn and me first. After our stop at Collette's we arrived at Renee's right on schedule. You can imagine our absolute astonishment when the driver opened the door and Roberta entered in front of Renee.

As we stared from one to the other, Renee made small talk and finally said that Roberta really wanted to join us for our special outing. Though I resented her presence, I decided not to let anything or anyone ruin our day. Well, when sistahgurl insisted that she be a part of the photo shoot, we all lost it! There was nothing Renee could say that could appease us. After much discussion it was decided that if Roberta insisted on being a part of our family photos, she would have to pay for her own shoot. We would gladly be a part of *her* pictures.

Now here she was again imposing on our family moment. Somebody needed to put this woman in check. Collette picked up the key ring and jingled it as she would in front of a fussy six-month-old infant. "Roberta, I got my keys because I'm about to open the doors of the library and read your ass! We've tried to be nice and let you stay here tonight, though we told you we had business that needed to be discussed. But my sister with the big heart insisted it was okay that you stay. So you were mentioned in Daddy's will, but so were Rico and this Blackford person. Now we all know I have issues with Rico, but I do know this about the good doctor, she would never intrude on our private moments. She knows her place, and your place is right next to hers. Daddy has loved Rico since the very first moment she stepped through that door. But she's never tried to meddle where she shouldn't. You could take a lesson. Of course we want you at the services, we want you to visit with our friends; but you're not family. You may not have your own family and for that I am sorry, but we are not the ones. You and my sister may be that close, but believe me that's where it stops."

"That's enough, Lette!" Renee was comforting her friend, who could muster up tears at will.

"Well, you don't have to worry about me anymore. Papa Eddie would not be happy at the way you are treating me. But I can take a hint. I'll see you at the funeral."

"Bert, you're welcome here," I said. "Collette is just trying to say that we need some time alone. I just got here, and we need some time for us to spend together to make some decisions and to settle some of this unpleasant business." Though I agreed with Collette, I guess I had enough of Daddy in me to feel compassion.

"We do want you here, Roberta, just give us a little time to settle things." Dawn was touching her back.

"Y'all gonna be sorry. Watch what I tell you," Collette mumbled under her breath.

"Are y'all sure? I don't want to be any bother." Roberta was sniffling like a three-year-old after an encounter with the strap.

"We need you. There's so much we'll need you to take care of once we make all of the arrangements. Since you have a van, do you think you'll be able to make a few airport runs for us?" Renee said, as she finally stopped staring at Collette with disbelief.

"Oh, of course, I'll do whatever needs to be done. Just let me know. I'll take the rest of the week off. I have plenty of vacation time." Roberta was forcing a smile.

"See, that is my point, we have bereavement leave," Collette countered.

I spoke up this time. "That is enough, Lette!"

"I'll get my things and go. I'm sorry if you thought I was intruding. I just wanted to make sure that you all knew I was here for you. I loved Papa Eddie so much. He showed me fatherly love, unlike anyone else. Again, I'm sorry." The tears started up again.

I wasn't sure, but I think I felt pity for her. We had only known the love of a good strong black man since our birth. He was absolute perfection to us. We were too pompous and assumed that all little girls had what we had. It was truly to be coveted.

If I was tired before, I was on the verge of collapse

now. I just really needed to lay my body down. I hugged
Roberta, Uncle Thomas, and then all of my sisters. I excused myself and felt I needed to run into Daddy's room.
Once I was inside the room I closed the door quickly
and put my back against it to prevent anyone or anything from disturbing my sanctuary.

5

Discovery

The room was immaculate. Everything was in its place. The north wall was filled with pictures of us throughout the years. We each had our own quarter of the available square footage of white space. I hadn't looked at these pictures in years. He had started a similar shrine of photographs for his five grandchildren on the east wall. On the south wall above his bed were pictures of family friends. I chuckled as I stared at the family portrait of five years ago that had been the subject of much controversy. There the five of us stood, my three sisters, me, and Roberta. The beaming face of Renee's best friend wore the only natural smile in the photograph. Roberta would be so thrilled to know that her photo hung above my daddy's bed. She'd never even consider that the photos that hung on the other two walls could be viewed as Daddy drifted off to sleep and greet him as he woke each morning. Unlike Collette, I wouldn't bring that to her attention. Edward Naylor had been a man who truly loved his family and friends.

The king-size bed was perfectly made with a gorgeous velvet patchwork-patterned spread that brought out the natural beauty of the mahogany four-poster bed. The matching burgundy patchwork rugs on each side of the bed had been Christmas gifts from Anthony and me two years before. The gray carpeting, which had been installed at least fifteen years ago, was spotless. The massive walk-in closet and bathroom shared the east wall with the grandchildren's pictures.

I sat in his burgundy leather La-Z-Boy recliner, which had been a gift from Collette the same Christmas he received the rugs, and looked at the dresser top filled with several fragrance sets. Anyone looking at this room would have sworn a woman had been in residence, but that was just Eddie's way. The leather felt cool on my bare arms and somehow soothing. This was where my daddy had slipped away from me. Why did you have to go and leave me like this? You never even heard my first court case. Tears began to fall. Silent tears, the kind I used to not understand as a child.

I was certain Sister Greene had cleaned up the mess left by the paramedics. She had spent the hours at the house while the repairman fixed the front door. I was confident the laundry folded neatly on the dryer in the room off the kitchen had also been her handiwork. The thought of the kitchen made me realize I hadn't eaten in almost twenty-four hours. The thought of food also reminded me that Estelle was on her way over. For sure I needed to be out with my sisters when she arrived, if only to run interference.

I felt so tired and heavy. What was with this heaviness? Maybe if I just washed my face I would feel better.

The track lighting Daddy had installed a few months before cast beautiful prisms on the walls of the small bathroom. Daddy had coordinated the bathroom with his bedroom and all of the rugs and towels were burgundy and gray. A huge fern hung from a ceiling hook and unburned candles were everywhere. Renee had for sure inherited her decorating talent from Daddy.

I opened the closet that was recessed in the wall opposite the bowl to find a face towel. The closet, like everything else in the room, was neat and perfectly organized. Much to my surprise, the top shelf was lined with over-the-counter remedies for everything from athlete's foot to diarrhea, several bottles of herbs and vitamins, and three prescription bottles. I had never known Daddy to need prescription medication for anything more than an occasional bronchial infection. As I took the bottles down to read the labels, I felt my palms start to sweat. Had my daddy been sick and never told us? Did Uncle Thomas know something he had not shared? I felt a constriction in my throat and chest at the thought of Daddy suffering in silence. Tears began to fill my eyes, blurring my vision.

I spoke out loud to myself. "Gurl, get yourself together. This is medication for the flu." The first label confirmed my suspicions. It was a simple antibiotic that had long ago expired. The second bottle was an anti-inflammatory that he had taken for years when arthritis flared up in his hands. I began to relax. There were no surprises here. As I turned over the last bottle to read the label, I thought my vision had once again betrayed me. I surely could not be holding a bottle of the popular sexual performance enhancer in my hand with the name Edward Z. Naylor on the label. I thought my legs were going to abandon me, so I quickly sat on the well-cushioned toilet seat. I continued to stare at the bottle.

My daddy was a strong, handsome man with the body of someone twenty years his junior. The idea that he would have sexual performance issues was unthinkable. He and Estelle seemed so happy. Upon further examination of the label I saw the prescription was three weeks old. Was this his first prescription? The label stated zero refills. Oh my God; we had all heard stories about men who had taken the medication dying of heart attacks. Had this medicine killed my daddy? I had to show this to my sisters. I couldn't stand. I tried calling their names, but I couldn't speak.

I'm not sure how long I had been sitting in a trancelike state when I heard a faint knock on the bedroom door. When I didn't answer, Dawn slowly entered the bedroom calling my name.

"I'm in here," I managed in a voice that seemed to belong to someone else.

"Gurl, what're you doing sitting in here? The bed doesn't look like you've laid down at all. Estelle is here." Dawn stood close to me stroking my braids.

"How long have I been in here?"

"About forty-five minutes. What's that?" Dawn was pointing at my hand.

I passed her the three bottles and waited for her reaction.

"Oh my God! Daddy was taking Viagra?"

"It certainly appears to be that way." I looked at my baby sister with tear-filled eyes.

Dawn looked as though she needed to sit, but I occupied the only seat in the room. "Daddy?"

"I never even thought about him having sex, though I'm sure that he and Estelle must have. They've been together forever. They've been away together several times. Maybe she told him he wasn't satisfying her. She must have made him get these pills. Do you think they killed him?" I was praying for Estelle's sake that this was not the cause of his death. Even I, who was her strongest ally, couldn't fathom that Daddy's trying to please her would take him from me.

"Oh Sissy, so many men have died either directly or indirectly from taking sexual enhancers! They put a lot of strain on the heart and the blood pressure. Daddy didn't have any history of problems with either, so a doctor would have no reason not to prescribe this."

"We shouldn't jump to any conclusions. We'll have to wait for the autopsy report." Dawn seemed to get strength back in her legs as she stopped leaning against the face bowl and extended her hand. "Estelle is waiting to see you."

"I really love Estelle, but if this is the cause of Daddy's death, I just don't know . . . I just don't know what to think!" I took the small bottle of pills and began to shake them in Dawn's face.

"Look, Glynda, I don't like the idea of these being the cause of Daddy's death either. But Daddy was a man. He was a man before he was our daddy. He was a good man, not unlike Anthony. And you know Anthony loves your stubborn butt so much that if you want a hamburger, somewhere there's going to be a cow dead. The doctor told Daddy all of the risks involved, and he was willing to take them. That is no one's fault. That is just the kind of man Eddie Naylor was. Hell, if there was a pill to make him a better father, he would have taken that too!" Dawn had turned me to face her and had her hands on my forearms.

"I know you're right! How did you get so wise?" I was smiling through tears.

"Gurl, I ain't wise, I just been doing this kinda counseling too long. I have to talk to the parents of sick and dying children all the time. But now you know Collette and Renee aren't going to take this news so well. Should we say anything or just wait until the autopsy report comes in?" Dawn said, putting her arm around my shoulder and nudging me toward the door.

"Oh my God. I hadn't even thought of how they would react to this news. I don't want to withhold information, but I just don't want to cause a scene with Estelle. That poor woman has been through as much as we have and at least we have each other. She has no one who feels the way she does. We can tell them in the morning. Are you ready for their outrage when they find out we knew and didn't say anything?" I was wiping my face preparing to greet Estelle.

"It won't be anything I haven't been on the receiving end of before. Remember, I live here with them. They're on their best behavior when you come to town."

"Best behavior! Damn! You could've fooled me!" We laughed and hugged each other. We held on tight as though we were all we had to cling to. Perhaps we were.

"Well, let's go see Estelle. We've left her alone way too long with those two. Hopefully Uncle Thomas has them in check. But you know he has never been able to handle Collette." I was feeling a little better. I can't explain why, but Dawn had renewed my strength.

"Gurl, Daddy could barely handle Collette!" Dawn and I slapped high five.

As I entered the dining room, Estelle leapt to her feet and ran to hug me. Her face was still red and her eyes swollen. There was such a desperate look in her eyes that pleaded for me to rescue her. She held on to me so tight I felt as though she was going to wrench my back. But I fully understood and hugged her in return.

"I'm so glad you came, Estelle. We need you here with us," I managed, breaking our embrace. My mind momentarily slipped back to the prescription bottle I had left on the counter in my daddy's bathroom.

"We've been asking Estelle if she knows anything about this Nina Blackford. She tells us she has never heard Daddy mention anyone named Nina." There was a hint of cynicism in Renee's voice.

"Well, I don't know, Renee, I didn't think Eddie and I had any secrets." There was clearly hurt in her face.

"This is all very suspect, that neither you nor Uncle Thomas knows about this Nina person. I guess we'll just have to wait for the lawyer to call back." Collette didn't look up from the documents she was reading.

"Can I get anyone something to eat?" Roberta called from the doorway of the kitchen.

"I brought baked chicken and mashed potatoes and green beans. Marilyn brought the cake, coffee, and tea. She didn't want me to drive myself, so she came with me. I told her I was okay to drive. But she knew that wasn't true when I didn't know that my credit card was supposed to go back in my wallet after I bought gas." Estelle managed a weak smile.

At least Roberta is making herself useful, I thought to myself, but instead I said, "I'll have a little something with tea, please."

"Let me help you, Roberta. I think all of you could probably use a little something to eat." Marilyn made her way to the kitchen. She had blended into the background from the moment she arrived. She had hugged each of my sisters and Uncle Thomas, expressed her sympathy, and took a seat in the den, pretending to watch television. Roberta could have taken a lesson from Marilyn.

Marilyn was Estelle's oldest daughter, whom I had met a few times over the years. She was a strong sister who was really in touch with her African heritage. She had spent two years in Kenya while working on her doctorate degree in Pan-African studies. She now taught at the University of Maryland. With her mother's down-to-earth demeanor and warmth, she was quite easy to like. Marilyn was her mother's double. She was petite, with an almond complexion and light-brown eyes. Her natural good looks were always highlighted by the slightest hint of makeup. Like her mother, Marilyn's ample body was always impeccably clothed. Her designer business suit fit her like it had been custom tailored. As she removed her jacket to help Roberta in the kitchen, it revealed a bosom that you could lose a small child inside.

Estelle had three children. Jimmy was a dancer with a local dance troupe that had received international recognition. Jimmy was so far out of the closet that the door's hinges had been removed. Daddy had been the first one to defend Jimmy as a teenager. When his sexuality was the subject of more than a few round-table discussions, he had simply said, "The boy is doing well in school, never gives his mama any trouble, and unless one of y'all want to date him, it ain't none of your business." But it never stopped us from whispering when Daddy wasn't around. As we grew up and I realized there wasn't a kinder and more sincere person on the planet than Jimmy, or Jamaica, as he liked to be called, I began to love him like he was my own brother. We were in constant contact by phone or e-mail. I wondered if he would fly home from Paris for the funeral.

Maxine was the youngest and lived in Los Angeles. She worked for one of the sound stages and none of us really knew what she did. Though she and I lived in the same city, we had virtually no contact. She'd been caught up in the Hollywood crowd and didn't associate with anyone who wasn't in the business. I was sure she couldn't break away from her get-us-some-more-donuts duties to make it to her near stepfather's funeral.

"Did you git a nap, Sissy?" Uncle Thomas looked very old to me at that moment.

"No, I was just looking at all the pictures and remembering the times when they were taken. The time just slipped away." I shot a glance at Dawn, who looked away.

"Back to the business at hand." Collette really knew how to step on my last good nerve.

"Can't we at least eat first, Lette? Damn!" Much to my surprise, Renee was the one to shut her down.

"Yeah, I guess. But we have to deal with this. We have to settle what we'll spend and how the fifty-thousand-dollar policy will be divided. We have to agree on what to spend because what is left is to be split between us equally." How was this woman the product of the same parents as the rest of us?

"We will not, and I mean will not, cut a corner. We'll pick out the casket Daddy wanted, get the flowers we want, have limos for all the family and near family. The programs will be professionally printed. The food will be catered. Are you feelin' me?" I felt like slapping Collette.

"Why do we have to cater the food, you know the church will provide the food!" Collette said, throwing her hands in the air.

"Because I said we will." I moved closer to Collette.

"Girls, girls!" Estelle was trying to keep the peace.

"Well, I'm glad to hear that near family will get to ride in a limo, too!" Roberta had a plate of food in each hand.

"Shut up, Roberta!" Collette and I said at the same moment.

"Well, I was just saying."

"For the record, near family are Estelle and her children. They would have been our stepbrother and -sisters." At least Roberta had diverted my attention from Collette and the impending stomp-a-hole-in-her-ass she was sure to get before this was all over.

While we'd been arguing, Marilyn and Roberta had brought in from the kitchen food-filled dishes for the group. We took our places at the table.

"The food looks wonderful, Estelle. Let's say grace." Dawn took my hand and then Estelle's.

The others did the same, and we were standing in a small circle when Uncle Thomas began to speak. "Heavenly Fatha, we thanks Ya tonigh' fo' Yo' savin' grace. Fo' Yo' mercy 'n' power ta heal even da heart dat seems brok'n beyon' repair. While we don't undastan' why Ya took mah brotha, we accepts Yo' will. We ask dat You brang peace to dis here house and undastandin' and tol'rince. Thank You fo' Yo' travelin' grace fo' Sissy. We thanks Ya fo' dis here food prepared fo' our bodies by da lovin' hands of Estelle. We ask Yo' blessin' on da food, da cook, and da eaters. Amen."

"Amen," we sang in unison.

There was little conversation as we ate. The food was excellent. I had forgotten how Estelle could throw down in the kitchen. The red-skin mashed potatoes with garlic were the best I had ever eaten. And the green beans made me want to slap Collette . . . no wait, I already wanted to do that.

"Thank you, Estelle. I didn't even know I was hungry until I started eating." Renee smiled genuinely at the matriarch.

"Chile, I just had to do something today. I can't believe my Eddie is gone!" Estelle put her napkin to her face, as if she could possibly hide her tears.

Marilyn put her arms around her mother, patting her gently. It was all the reason we needed to start our own personal pity parties. Within seconds everyone around the table was crying, but, of course, Roberta was the loudest.

"Let's clear the table. Someone start a shopping list. We need paper plates." As she got up from the table, Collette barked out the order as though we were her employees.

"Jimmy's flying home tomorrow. He is so broken up,

poor thing. You know he always said Eddie loved him more than his own father. As soon as you set the day for the funeral I'll let Maxine know and she'll fly in the day before. They're in production. At first she wasn't coming, but I had a come-to-Jesus meeting with her, and she saw things a little differently when I was done. Do you ever get together with her, Glynda?" Estelle cleared plates as she talked.

"No, Estelle, we have never even spoken on the phone since she moved to L.A. I thought she would have come to my law school graduation party, but . . . oh well."

"I don't know what that chile's problem is. I sure raised her better. She got out there in Hollywood and just lost her mind." Estelle shook her head.

"When can we expect to hear from the coroner's office?" Collette said, wiping her hands on a burgundy dishtowel.

"Probably tomorrow afternoon. They will at least have a preliminary cause of death. They'll have to wait for the toxicology report for a day or so," Dawn said very matter-of-factly, walking to the kitchen with an armful of dishes.

"So the funeral home can pick up the body then?" Estelle's eyes filled with tears as the room filled with her words.

"Yes, that's the way it works. Daddy wanted Brown's on North Avenue. He wrote it all out, Estelle." I was fighting back tears of my own this time.

"He told me when he did that. He said that he didn't want there to be any trouble between y'all and me. He said he didn't want y'all to have to worry about the little details or try to overrule my wishes. He said he knew y'all would never agree on anything. So he was just going to make it easy on everybody. But I never thought we'd be dealing with all of this so soon. He only drew up his will and wrote out his last wishes a few months ago. He said since we were getting married he wanted everything to be right. All the details handled. That was my Eddie. Look at this house. Not a paper clip out of place." Estelle buried her face in her hands and started sobbing.

"I guess we need to decide what day the funeral will be. Do we do a night funeral and morning burial or all together?" Renee picked up the files that held all of the insurance and will information.

"I think we should have it in three days. Just get it over with." It didn't come out at all like I meant it. I braced myself for their wrath.

"What in the hell do you mean get it over with? We're sorry that this has interrupted the big-time lawyer's schedule." Renee spat the words at me. "Gotta get back to those billable hours? But we're not rushing my daddy into the ground to please your time-is-money schedule."

"Renee, I didn't mean it like it sounded. I just don't want to have to wait five or six days, putting off the inevitable. It is so hard on everyone."

"Well, maybe that is the way you black folks do it in California, but we black people here in Baltimore believe in a decent grieving period. Besides, Daddy's aunt Ida Mae is coming from Alabama, and she is not going to fly. She is taking the Greyhound tomorrow, so three days is out. It means the funeral would be the day she got here." Collette surprised me by siding with Renee on this issue.

"Why is Aunt Ida Mae taking the bus? Lawdhamurcy, ain't she like ninety-two?" Dawn had returned with the coffeepot in her hand, along with three coffee mugs.

"She refuses to fly. Junior wants to rent a car and drive

up here with her. But she said, and I quote, 'I am not going to get in a car with his alcohol-drinking butt to end up dead before I get there.' I recommended she at least take the train. She said the bus has been good enough for her all these years, and she don't see any reason it can't do now. I hushed." Renee was slicing cake.

"Uncle Thomas, how old is Aunt Ida Mae?" Dawn asked.

"She least eighty-five. I thank she 'bout three years olda than Mama woulda been. But she may be olda. Ya know ol' folks don't tell ya how ol' dey really is."

"Okay, so does that mean the funeral will be Monday? We can't have a funeral on Sunday." Roberta, with the cake and plates in her hands, spoke up for the first time since we told her to shut up.

"Oh please don't make it that far away, that will be a week. That is too long. Can we do it Saturday?" I couldn't stand to go through this madness for six more days.

"Well, Saturday would be good. Our shift is off, and I know everyone wants to come," Estelle added.

"Don't we have to pay premium at the cemetery on Saturdays?" Collette had no shame.

"So what?" Dawn screamed at Collette.

"Well, I don't think we should spend money we don't have to. I say Monday and we do it all in one day. It will cost less."

"If you mention money one more time, I'm going to go stone projeckish on your ass. Do I make myself clear?" I was fed up with Collette's money grubbing.

"Ladies, ladies, let's not lose our cool. Can I make a suggestion?" Roberta was treading on thin ice and the sun was rising.

"Hell no, you can't suggest anything. Does the concept 'seen and not heard' mean anything to you?" Collette spoke before I could.

"Wait a minute, let's hear what she has to say. We can't agree among ourselves." Of course Renee would say that!

"Thank you, sis. I was going to suggest a Friday night service with a Saturday burial. That way all of the people from the plant who want to attend can make one or the other, if not both. Aunt Ida Mae will be here and by Saturday afternoon Papa Eddie will be laid to rest and everyone can get back to work or whatever they need to get back to by Monday, with a day to rest in between."

"Da gurl makes sense." Uncle Thomas smiled at me.

I rolled my eyes, despite thinking it was a good compromise. "Well, if the others agree, I think it'll work for all the reasons you mentioned."

You would have thought Roberta had won the lottery. She was grinning and prancing like a peacock around the dining room. "I'm just trying to help wherever I can."

"I think it is a good idea, too. I know all the employees down at the plant will be happy. Most of them were afraid they wouldn't be able to come to the services. Most of the people who work Friday nights are new and don't really know Eddie that well. I heard that they are sending someone from the head office, too. The union is sending a representative. I'm telling you everybody loved and respected my Eddie."

"All in favor of Friday night service and Saturday morning burial, say 'Aye,' " Ms. Diplomacy said.

Everyone raised his or her hand and said, "Aye."

"Don't we have to see if the funeral home has that time available?" Even though it was the best idea, I just didn't want Roberta to have the victory. And yes, I know that this wasn't a good Christian attitude. I would repent later.

"I'm sure they'll make it work. We're going to be spending some tall dollars with them." Collette cowered back as she realized she'd mentioned money again.

I was almost amused.

As I took my last bite of cake, exhaustion surrounded my body like a handmade quilt on a cold winter night. The adrenaline that had fueled all of my movement since that first phone call was suddenly gone. The heaviness once again took over my body to the point that I didn't think I could stand. I wanted Eddie Naylor to hug me. I wanted him to lift me off the floor and spin me around the way he did every time he picked me up from the airport. No matter what the weight of my burden, I knew Eddie Naylor could lighten my load.

Like a lowly thief approaches his next victim, reality crept its ugly way back into my psyche. Eddie Naylor couldn't lighten my heavy load. Eddie Naylor's death *was* my burden to bear.

"Glynda, you look so tired all of a sudden. You need to get some rest." Estelle rose from her seat at the table and started toward me.

"Sissy, you don't look so good. Let me take you home," Renee offered.

"Who said she was going home with you? You have so much activity at your house, how do you think she would get any rest?" Collette rose to take her dessert dishes to the kitchen. "I have the most room, and it is always quiet."

"But we're the closest, and I know she would be more comfortable with Devin and me," Dawn added with confidence.

"What the hell you mean more comfortable with you?

My house is twice as big as that roach motel you call home. Besides, it's just me. Devin plays that rap music, too. You know how much Sissy hates anything that isn't jazz!"

"See, that is your problem, Lette. *My* roach motel is a home. Your hacienda is a house."

"I want to stay here." I thought I spoke aloud, but Collette and Dawn were still going at it as though I hadn't spoken a word.

"Who the f—"

"*Stop it!* I'm staying here!" I screamed.

"Staying here?" Everyone in the room seemed to sing the same question.

"Yes, I want to sleep in Daddy's bed. I want to smell his cologne. I want to feel his spirit."

"See, your ass been living in California too long, talkin' about feeling his spirit. Only spirit I ever wanna feel is the Holy Spirit," Renee said, shaking her head.

"Are you sure this is something you want to do, Glynda?" Estelle moved in closer to embrace me. "After all, you would be here alone in the house where Eddie d . . ." The letter hung in the air like a foul stench from a dairy farm.

"I'm sure, Estelle."

"Gurl, suppose Daddy forgot something. Needed to come back and have a little visit. You're not scared?" Dawn surprised me with her superstitious nonsense.

"Daddy would never dream of hurting me when he was alive, and I know he would never hurt me now that he's dead. Besides, being in his room gave me a sense of peace."

"We'll see how peaceful your ass is when we come back in the morning!" Collette had a mean streak, and no one clearly understood its origin.

"Baby, Uncle Thomas will stay wit' chu. I feel some peace mahself here."

"Uncle Thomas, there's nothing I'd like more." I ran over to hug his neck.

"Well, y'all just peace on. And as for me and mine—we'll peace out." Renee laughed at her own attempt at humor.

"We'll help you clean up the kitchen and put the food away. Promise y'all will have breakfast before all of this funeral-planning business starts." Estelle and Marilyn cleared the remaining cake plates and coffee mugs.

"I think I'll stay with you, Renee," Roberta said. "After all, sisters need to be together. Since everyone seems to be staying in separate places tonight, I think it's best if I stay with you. We need each other more than ever now."

"Roberta, you're not Renee's sister. Don't make me hurt your feelings. I resent your implication!" Collette's nostrils flared. She was pissed.

"Come on nah, y'all don't start dis agin." Uncle Thomas seemed genuinely agitated with us.

"Uncle Thomas, I don't mean any disrespect, but Roberta has stepped out of bounds for the last time. She's implying that she needs to stay with Renee because we aren't. We've been away from our homes all day, and there are a few things that need to be taken care of. Renee has her family. She needs to be with her husband and children tonight. This woman needs to check herself before I stomp a sinkhole in her ass." Collette pulled a cigarette from her jacket pocket, placed it between her lips, but thought twice before lighting it.

"We all need to get some rest. Glyn, are you sure you want to stay here?" Dawn said, touching my arm.

"Yes, I'm sure, and if Renee wants Roberta to spend the night at her place, that is none of our concern. But please, let's stop this bickering. It's making me so much more tired than I already am."

"I just want to be here for Renee, and all of you, for that matter. I don't want to cause any confusion. I'm just going to miss Daddy so much." Roberta began to cry.

My eyes rolled to the back of my head.

"Well, let's get the kitchen cleaned and the food put away so we can all get some much needed rest. Roberta, will you come help Marilyn and me in the kitchen?" Estelle had taken charge of the situation. I was surely glad. I wanted to ask her if she wanted to spend the night here with me and Uncle Thomas, but thought better of it because the sparks would surely start to fly again.

The cleanup seemed to take hours. I just wanted everyone gone so that I could be alone in Daddy's room. Uncle Thomas had the same look in his eyes. Eventually everyone gathered their things and headed for the door. Hugs and kisses abounded, and once again it was hard to imagine how much we'd disagreed over the past several hours.

"We'll be over first thing in the morning. I want to be here before the lawyer calls. I probably won't be able to sleep wondering who this Nina Blackford is and what she meant to Daddy." Collette looked pleased, knowing she was causing pain to Estelle.

Estelle's face revealed the agony of a thousand torturous years as she spoke. "I'm sure my Eddie had a very special relationship with this woman that had nothing to do with his fidelity to me." If only she believed her own words.

"I'm sure you're right, Mom." Marilyn was doing whatever she could to comfort her mother.

Like pulling a stopper from an old bathtub, the last exchange had drained us of all remaining energy. We could only manage to exchange farewells and I love you's.

Closing the door gave me more comfort than I could have ever imagined. The house was finally quiet. I relished the quiet, embraced it. Within seconds, my haven of silence was shattered by a blaring sound from the guest bathroom.

6

The Harder They Fall

I thought my heart would beat out of my chest as my feet tripped over each other trying to get to the bathroom to see what was happening to Uncle Thomas. Uncle Thomas's body weight against the door precluded my entry.

"Uncle Thomas, what's wrong? Uncle Thomas, let me in!"

I could only hear his sobs. Anguish like I'd never heard before. Moaning and wailing so deep and pain-filled. I could only imagine this was the sound that reverberated through hell.

"Uncle Thomas, please let me in."

"Go 'way, Sissy. Ya can't see me like dis. My buddy done gone. My buddy done left me to fen' fo' mahsef."

"Uncle Thomas, please, please let me in!" I pushed harder against the door, and it finally gave way to my weight.

As he moved away from the door, I stumbled into the room, almost falling onto him. He knelt over the closed toilet with his face buried in his hands. Tears spilled onto the gray toilet-seat cover. His futile attempts to silence the horrific sounds brought tears to my eyes. I could only kneel next to him in the small room and place my arms around his shoulders. Shoulders so broad were now slumped. A back so strong was now bent in misery. Several minutes passed before I finally sat on the gray marble tile floor and leaned against the paisley-covered wall opposite the toilet. I pulled Uncle Thomas into my arms and rocked back and forth until his sobs turned to silent tears. His tears matched my own.

"Sissy, I sho' 'nuff is sorry I broke down like dis here. When I came in dis room, I 'membered how we'd fussed when we built it. He tol' me I didn't know a thang 'bout construction. And he'd go git a Mexican off da street to hep him if I didn't hush up. Pain shot thu my chest at da thought 'n' fo' da firs' time since yo' sistahs showed up on mah do'step, I knowed he'll nevah fuss at me again. He'll nevah whomp on me at dominoes, tell me how much betta his barbecue is than mine. Fo' mah whole life dat man has been da worl' ta me. When I was in da jungles of Vietnam, Eddie was right dere wit' me. His voice kep' me goin'. I'd hear him say, 'Be a man, Thomas, make me proud.' When I was shot, I wasn't so scured 'cause I knowed Eddie was wit' me.

"Where is I gonna find da strength ta be dat brave agin, Sissy? He sho' 'nuff wouldn't like me in here on mah knees cryin'. He'd say, 'Look at chu, Thomas. You pitiful!' "

"He wouldn't call you pitiful. If the fates had taken you instead of Daddy, this would be him on his knees."

"Did I evah tell ya da story 'bout when the white man at da sto' where we delivered groceries afta school called me Tommy?"

"No. What happened?"

"I think I was ele'em or twelve. Eddie was workin' at dat ole sto' for 'bout six months when he tol' me dey needed mo' hep. I went down dere and Mista Stein was his name, tol' me if Eddie reccamend me, I had da job.

He slapped me on da back and said, 'Tommy, git da broom and sweep up.' Eddie looked Mista Stein square in his eyes and tol' dat white man, 'My brotha don't like to be called Tommy. His name is Thomas.' Dat white man turn da color of da red stripes in da 'merican flag, but he called me Thomas. He would pretend to forget, but when he would call me Tom or Tommy, Eddie dared me ta answer.

"Dat's the kinda strength yo' daddy had when he was twelve. He was a man evah since I could 'member."

"Uncle Thomas, did you know Daddy was taking sexual performance drugs?"

"You mean dem Viagra pills?" Uncle Thomas laughed knowingly.

"So you did know?"

"Sissy, dere are some thangs ya might not undastan' 'bout bein' a man. No matter what a woman says, she needs good lovin'. Yo' daddy loved him some Estelle. Back in da days when she was married to dat man who treated heh so bad, yo' daddy was lovin' heh even den. He would tell me all the time dat if she evah got smart 'nuff to know she deserved betta, he was gonna be heh betta.

"When a man gits older, thangs don't work quite like dey did back in da day. Yo' Daddy was just tryin' to hold on to dat which is mos' precious to us menfolk."

"Uncle Thomas, true love can withstand anything. Even impotence. When you truly love someone, being with them should be enough."

"Sissy, baby, 'member when you first went out dere to L.A., ya tol' yo' daddy how bad ya needed a car. No real good buses runnin'. Ya tol' him ya couldn't catch no cab. No subway. When he tol' chu he thought L.A. was such a perfec' place, you tol' him dat it was almost perfect, but havin' a car would be all you needed. Well, chile, dat what love wit'out sex is to a man. It is like livin' in L.A. without a car. Sure you can survive without it, but it sho' 'nuff be a whole lot betta wit' it."

I couldn't help but laugh at his analogy. "I guess I see what you mean. I can't imagine life without a car in Los Angeles. But there are so many other things you can do besides . . ." I was too embarrassed to finish the statement.

"It'd be like takin' da bus. Like takin' a bus!"

"Okay, okay, I get your point. How long had he been taking the pills?"

"I don't even thank he'd took one of dem. He was saving them for the honeymoon. Estelle tried ta talk him out of gettin' 'em. She tol' him she knowed she'd be plenty satisfied and dat he was gonna kill her wit dem pills. But yo' daddy knowed betta."

"Estelle tried to talk him out of even getting them?"

"Yessah, she did! She even call me ta talk some sense inta him."

"I got angry at her tonight when I found the prescription. I blamed her for taking my daddy from me."

"Sissy, Edward Naylor was his own man! Plain 'n' simple. Estelle couldn't say a thang dat would have changed his mind. In his mind he needed to perform as a husband in all ways. Chile, let's get up off dis here floor." Uncle Thomas helped me up and we moved into the den.

"I knows ya tired, but would ya mind sittin' in here wit' yo' ol' Uncle Thomas fo' a spell? Ya can even lay on mah lap da way ya use ta when ya was upset wit' Eddie cuz he tol' ya ya couldn't do dis or do dat."

"Oh, I'm too old for that!"

"Chile, I was just layin' in yo' arms like I was a newborn baby. Come on ovah here and lay on yo' uncle. I needs ta feel useful."

I grabbed the afghan from off the back of the couch and nestled under the arm of the man who would now have to substitute for my Eddie Naylor.

7

By the Dawn's Early Light

The shrill of the old rotary phone on the kitchen wall shook me from a sleep so deep I didn't recognize my surroundings. Golden sunlight streamed through the skylight, giving the room a warm glow. My head rested on a down pillow that smelled of Hugo Boss, my daddy's favorite cologne. I still wore the stretch pants and T-shirt Rico had chosen for me the morning before. My feet were bare, and I was covered in a burgundy comforter. Pain shot through my chest as the memories of the previous day's events flooded back.

I was lying on the burgundy leather sofa in the den of the house where I'd grown up. I was on this sofa with the deep soft cushions because a little more than twenty-four hours previous, Edward Naylor had decided that his time on earth as my daddy was done. I just had to make it in this life without his strong shoulders to lean on.

I could hear Uncle Thomas in the kitchen whispering. "She still sleepin'. We had a long talk when y'all left 'n' when she laid down in mah lap she jus' fell right ta sleep. I took off heh shoes 'n' covered heh up. I knowed she wanted ta sleep in heh daddy's bed, so I put his pillow under her head. What time you comin ovah here? . . . You shouldn't make dem chirren go ta school. Dey grandpa is dead. . . . Well, you dey mama, do as you please. I'll see ya 'bout eight thirty then. . . . I loves you, too."

I knew from the conversation Renee had been at the other end of the connection. I tried to sit up, but my head hurt as if I had drunk several shots of vodka the night before. Uncle Thomas peeped in just as I managed to get myself upright.

"Good mornin', Miss Sleepyhead. Yo' sistahs on dey way ovah ta git on wit' dis here funeral-plannin' bizness. Ya want some coffee?"

"Good morning, Uncle Thomas. Thank you for covering me up. I don't remember anything except lying down on your lap last night. I'd love a cup of coffee. My head really hurts."

"It's all dis here stress."

"I guess you're right. I'm going to shower and change while you make coffee. You want me to help you cook some breakfast for the gang?"

"No, chile. I got dis kitchen unda control. You go take yo' time doin' what evah it is y'all womenfolk do ta make yo'self look so pretty. Ya want some Tylenol or sumin for yo' headache?"

"I have some in my bag. Uncle Thomas . . ."

"Yeah, baby?"

"Thanks for last night. You shed a new light on Daddy. I guess I always knew he had a love life, but I never wanted to think about it."

"I should be thankin' you. Ole Thomas jus' let it all go las' night. You know a man ain't suppose ta be breaking down like dat. But I sho' 'nuff feel betta dis morning. Some of dat pain done ease up outta mah chest."

"Uncle Thomas, who wrote that stupid rule about a man not crying?"

"Dunno. Jus' know dat's how it is. Now go showah

and change b'fo' yo' sistahs git here. Ya know da first thang on da list is da call ta dat lawyer fella."

"Well, I'm a little more than curious what he has to say about this Nina person."

"Kinda curious, mahsef."

As I folded the comforter, I wondered what secrets would be unveiled. Did Daddy have a life that none of us knew about? Was he a man different than the one we all knew and loved? Was Nina Blackford another woman? Poor Estelle must be in pure torment wondering if the man she was about to marry loved another woman. A woman he loved enough to make a part of his will and the beneficiary of a rather sizable insurance policy. He bequeathed the same share to her as to the rest of us.

I decided to shower and change in the guest bathroom. I didn't want to face all of the memories in my daddy's bath. I dressed quickly and added only enough makeup to put some color back in my cheeks. Just as I began hanging my clothes in the guest room closet, I heard Dawn yelling greetings from the front door.

"Good morning, we're here!" Devin's voice had changed since the last time I'd spoken to him.

"Hey y'all. Where's everybody?" Dawn sang out.

"In da kitchen."

"Good morning, sis." I was so glad to see Dawn. "Boy, you sound like a man, Devin. Come here and give your auntie a hug and kiss. You're so tall and handsome. You sure look like your grandpa."

"Hey, Aunt Glynda. Yeah, Mom tells me that all the time. I'm real sad about PaPa, though. He was my hero."

"Baby, you ain't said nothin' but a word! Eddie Naylor was a whole bunch of folks' hero. Uncle Thomas is making us some breakfast. Renee is on her way over, too. Have you talked to Lette this morning?" I hugged Devin again.

"Yeah, she's stopping by her office to tie up some loose ends with her assistant and will be here about nine thirty. She said not to call the lawyer until she gets here."

"Why don't we just wait until he calls us?" Collette was going to really work everybody's nerves before this was over.

"Gurl, you know your sister. If money is involved, she has no patience. We talked a long time when we got home last night, and she still says Estelle will have no say. I tried to reason with her, but she won't budge."

"So does she think we are incapable of talking to the lawyer, or has she forgotten that I *am* a lawyer?"

"Auntie Glynda, don't be mad at Mom." Devin's voice had the typical young male octave variables.

"I'm sorry, Dawn. Devin is right. It's not you who is being unreasonable. But if the lawyer calls, we'll sure as hell talk to him. I'll deal with Lette on my own."

"Can I pop some popcorn and watch? That should be quite the show. Better than any movie Devin has dragged me to this year for sure." Dawn's words drew a genuine smile from my face.

"Come on in here and make yo'sef a cup a coffee, Miss Dawn. I made it jus' like ya like it. Strong 'n' jet black." Uncle Thomas poked his head around the corner smiling.

"Oh, Uncle Thomas, just like I like my man. With just enough sugar to take the bite out of it! Ooooow weeeee!" Dawn ran to hug Uncle Thomas's neck.

Everyone turned at the sound of a key slipping into the front-door lock. Eddie had never taken the house keys from us girls as we moved out one by one.

"Oh chile, them kids wore me out this morning. They

didn't understand why they had to go to school. I want to thank you very much, Devin, for blabbing that you weren't going." Renee was heavily laden with bags.

"Good morning to you, too!" Dawn was very defensive when it came to Devin.

"Oh, I'm sorry. I been up so long and done so much, I feel like it is afternoon. How y'all feeling? I didn't sleep a wink last night. I dozed off about four, four thirty, and the clock went off at five fifteen. Phone started ringing at six. People were just calling to see what they can do to help. Nobody wants to believe it. I smell food. I'm starved." Renee hadn't given anyone else a chance to say a word.

"Breakfas' be ready in a few minutes. Come git chu some coffee 'n' I can make a fresh pot. What's in all dem bags?"

"People started dropping food by the house at seven this morning. We got pastries, coffee, sandwich meat, bread, liquor, all kinds of stuff. Everybody sure did love my . . ." Renee started to cry.

"Oh Renee, why you gonna start this again?" Dawn was dabbing at tears.

"We need to organize the kitchen so we can accommodate all of this food. This is just the beginning, and we are already running out of room. Come help me, Devin." My main goal was to busy myself to the point of exhaustion. It was my only solace.

"Collette called me on my cell a few minutes ago. She is on her way. She went to the office, but she says she can't concentrate and wants to be with us. She said the lawyer should be calling soon." Dawn poured a cup of coffee.

"She just doesn't want us to talk to the lawyer without her being here. I'll lay you dimes to donuts she walks through that door before nine o'clock. If I'm wrong, I'll fly both of you to L.A. first class."

"Damn, please let her get here at nine-oh-one!" Renee high-fived Dawn.

"Well, she only has eight minutes. First class, did you say?" Dawn raised her eyebrows, which made her look so much like our daddy.

"First class!"

"Since ya done predicted Lette's soon-ta-be arrival, we'll jus' hol' breakfast. Den we need ta git ta da serious business of plannin' all dis here bidniss out. Eddie left some real good instructions so it won't leave a lot of decisions ta be made. Da funeral-home man called ta change da time he gon' git here to ele'em." The phone rang, interrupting Uncle Thomas.

"Naylor residence, Dawn speaking. . . . Good morning, Bishop Hayes. We're doing surprisingly well. Just a few tears so far this morning. . . . Yes, I guess this will be the headquarters, as you put it, for all of the activities. There'll be someone here all the time. . . . Daddy left very explicit instructions, so we'll carry out his wishes as best we can. . . . Of course, you'll be presiding. . . . We'd really like it if you'd stop by sometime today. Thanks so much for calling." Just as Dawn was about to end the call, she seemed to have a thought.

"Bishop? . . . Does the name Nina Blackford mean anything to you? . . . I just thought I'd ask. Her name has come up and no one seems to know any details about her. . . . We'll see you this afternoon. Please give Sister Hayes my love. I haven't seen her since I started attending seven-thirty services. . . . Bye now."

"What did he say about Nina?" The words rushed forth from my mouth.

Before Dawn could answer, at precisely eight fifty-eight and forty seconds, Collette slipped her key in the door. "Damn you good, Sissy!" Renee laughed.

Laughter hit each of us. We laughed so hard we were unable to speak as Collette walked in.

"May I be let in on the joke?" She wasn't amused.

"Oh lighten up, Lette. Glynda just promised to buy us first-class tickets to L.A. if you weren't here by nine. She said there was no way you would allow the lawyer to call without your being here." Dawn was still laughing.

"And just why is that so hilarious?"

"Like she said, lighten up. I wasn't wrong, was I now?"

"Come hep me set da table for breakfast. 'Cuz y'all 'bout to start, and I ain't havin' it!"

"We betta straighten up, or Uncle Thomas is gonna get a switch for us," I chided.

"Don't thank I won't now, ya hear?"

Uncle Thomas had fixed a small feast: homemade biscuits, slab bacon, grits, and eggs with fried potatoes and onions. I really don't know why seeing all of that food made me feel famished. It was only six in the morning to my body since I was still on L.A. time, and I never ate before ten. We gathered around the table holding hands, and Renee prayed the blessing. We each took the seat where we had sat as children, with Uncle Thomas in Daddy's chair. The resemblance was unsettling.

Several minutes passed before Devin spoke. "Do you think PaPa is in heaven?"

"Honey, if there is a heaven, and truly I believe there is, then Edward Zachary Naylor is up there directing traffic. What made you ask that?" Dawn leaned over to hug her son, but Devin, like the average twelve-year-old boy, squirmed away.

"Bishop says every Sunday that if we want to see our loved ones who died in the Lord again, then we better get saved. I think I'm saved. I prayed the sinner's prayer and I've been baptized. But how can I make sure?"

"Honey, you've done all you need to do. God is not like people. We don't have to keep begging him for salvation. It's a gift. A gift you accepted when you were ten. And when we pray together, you always ask God to forgive you for sins you know you committed and even for those you didn't know about. So to answer your question, yes, you will see Daddy again." This time Dawn wouldn't be denied a hug.

"See why you gonna start some mess, Devin? We were doing just fine!" I asked jokingly.

"I'm sorry, Auntie Glynda, but I had to know if I would see PaPa again."

"I sho' 'nuff undastan' what chu talkin' 'bout, Devin. I'm right pleased wit' my place in da Book of Life mahsef."

"How long has Daddy belonged to First United?"

"Gurl, since the big split off from Rehobeth back in the sixties. I was just a baby when he and Mama joined the church. Bishop was just a teenager back then." Renee waxed nostalgic.

"He sure didn't like change, did he?" I asked the rhetorical question.

"Not even a little bit."

The phone intruded on our precious moment as we looked from one to the other. It was nine forty-five, and we assumed it was the lawyer returning our call. I couldn't speak for my sisters, but I wasn't sure I wanted to know the answer to the question that seemed destined to change our lives. Devin looked at each of us before finally asking, "Do you want me to answer the phone?"

"No sweetie, I'd better get it." Renee moved slowly, trying to delay the inevitable.

8

Stranger Things Have Happened

"Hello?"

"Is it the lawyer?" Collette, of course, was leaning over Renee's shoulder.

"Oh hello, Mr. Brown. Yes, we're all here and ready to meet with you. Yes, Uncle Thomas gave us your message, and eleven will be fine. See you then."

A sigh of disappointment passed among us. We were all anxious to know the answer to the question that cast an even darker cloud over our life's parade than Daddy's death. Who is this Nina Blackford person?

"We'd better clear the table. Let's talk about the funeral services and budget before the funeral director gets here. We want to present a united front. No infighting." Collette was clearing dishes as she spoke.

"Daddy's instructions were very clear. No need for interpretation. We could, in fact, turn over that piece of paper to the funeral director and give him the insurance policy. Other than the flowers, which we'll order on our own, Daddy left no detail unattended."

"But I think we need to go over the cost of everything Daddy requested. After all, we may be able to save some money here." Collette had clearly forgotten my words of warning from the previous night.

"Daddy said it. That does it. Amen!" Renee said, possibly saving Collette from serious bodily injury.

"I just thought we should go over his instructions and see if there's anything we want to eliminate."

"And just why in the hell would we want to do that?" *Lord please help me not to whip her ass in my daddy's house,* I prayed silently.

"I'm just saying, in case there's something frivolous."

"And if there is?"

"Why do you always pick on me, Glynda? You're a lawyer. There is no profession more money-conscious than yours."

"The operative word, my little sister, is 'profession.' *This* is about my daddy."

"Give it a rest, you two!" Renee spoke with mother-like authority. "We'll sit down and go over Daddy's wishes. But it won't be to cut corners. It will be to make sure it is practical on all fronts. Collette and Glynda, I won't have you disrespecting Daddy by consistently bickering over things that didn't matter even a tiny bit to him."

"I think we should call Estelle over," Dawn almost whispered.

"Oh, here we go! She has no say!" Collette said, putting her hands on her hips.

"Wait, Lette, I think she's right. I've been thinking about Daddy's will and last wishes. It was apparent how he felt about her. He'd be really upset to see us treating her this way."

"I can't believe you! You treasonous hussy! I thought we agreed!"

"I know what I said, but right is right. I'm calling her now." As Renee reached for the phone, it rang.

Was my heart the only one that skipped a beat? As Renee answered it, I watched her face for the slightest hint as to who was on the other end of the connection.

"Hey, Roberta . . . we're making it. Just about to sit

down and go over the details of the funeral. Why don't you stop in around lunchtime? That'll give us a little more time. Of course, I'll plead your case. I love you, too."

"And just what case exactly do you need to plead for your busybody friend?" Collette wasted no time.

"She just wants to be sure she is included in all the family activites. She really wants to sit with us. Ride in the limo, walk in with us. You know, all the family stuff. She has been my friend since high school. Daddy really did love her."

"And Rico has been my friend since college. We even bought a house together, but do you see me trying to impose her on the family? Hell, she would never even ask such a thing. Daddy even flew to L.A. when she graduated from medical school, and gave her away at her wedding. How much closer do you think they could've been?"

"Neither one of them are family. Period. Case closed. Edward Naylor had four daughters. Why does everybody want to be related to him?" Collette said, rummaging through her purse for a cigarette.

"That's only Roberta. Rico will be here to assist in any way she can, but she knows her place, and no one will have to remind her to stay in it!"

"Dat's enough! I'm 'bout sick of y'all grown women actin' like little teenage gurls. Yo' daddy would be real disappoin'ed in da way y'all carryin' on. Roberta's a sweet chile 'n' she don't mean no harm. Eddie'd nevah do a thang dat would hurt heh feelin's. So we gonna jus' make do 'n' try ta keep heh happy."

We all sat quietly as Uncle Thomas chastised us for acting like children. He was right. Daddy wouldn't do anything to hurt Roberta's or, for that matter, anyone else's feelings. Daddy's death was bringing out the worst in all of us. Our true colors were waving like a flag on a windy day.

We cleared the table and loaded the dishwasher in silence. When the kitchen was spotless, Dawn spoke. "We'd better go over the details of the funeral before Mr. Brown gets here."

"I'll get the folders," Collette said quietly.

Daddy had everything so neatly arranged and labeled. The night before I hadn't noticed how orderly everything was placed in the folders. My dad had been one of a kind. "Renee, you never did call Estelle. You want me to do it?"

Collette looked at me to say something but caught Uncle Thomas's glare and thought better of it. I quickly called Estelle and asked her how soon she could be at our place, explaining that the funeral director would arrive in forty-five minutes. She said she would be at our place in fifteen. She thanked me with a sincerity that caused a constriction in my chest.

"I think we should wait until she gets here." I wanted Collette to object so Uncle Thomas could check her. But she never even looked in my direction.

"I want to read the will again. Maybe we missed something in it last night that'll give us some clue as to who Nina Blackford really is." Renee was spreading papers out on the dining room table.

"This is such a mystery. If Uncle Thomas and Estelle don't know, I'm just dumbfounded. Uncle Thomas . . . ?"

"I swear I don't know! I sho' 'nuff don't believe 'twas 'notha woman. He loved Estelle somethin' fierce. Maybe it was jus' a friend. Somebody who done somethin' for him a long time ago. Maybe a friend of yo' mama's? I just dunno."

"But if it was a friend, some of us would know who

she is. Daddy would never hide a friend. This is so unlike him!" Renee said, placing the papers in neat stacks.

"I have to agree with Renee. This is very, very strange.
So are there any clues we missed last night, Renee?" I
was leaning over her shoulder.

"I don't see a thing that gives any indication. There's
one thing that's interesting, though. According to this
insurance policy, Nina Blackford is three years older
than me. So I think that would rule out the possibility of
her being Mama's or Daddy's friend."

One possibility came to my mind, but was too far-
fetched to verbalize, so I said nothing. The conversation
was minimal as we all looked through various papers in
the folders that Daddy had left marked with all the final
details of his life. Or were these the beginning details of
his death? As I walked to the kitchen to pour yet another
cup of coffee, the phone rang. My earlier trepidation
had left me, and I answered without giving it a thought.
Had I known it was for me?

"Hello, Glynda Naylor speaking."

"How's my best girl?" The deep sexy voice on the
other end immediately brought tears to my eyes.

"Anthony! Oh baby! I'm so happy to be talking to
you. I need you here with me. Will they let you off duty?
Where're you? Are you at home or still in the desert?"

"Whoa, baby, slow down. I'm so, so very sorry about
your dad. I just got the message this morning. I'm still in
the desert. I've talked to everyone I know to talk to,
short of the president himself, but no can do. Your dad
isn't a relative. You know I want to be with you. They
let me skip maneuvers this morning to make the calls. I
feel so powerless. You so rarely need anything from me,
and the one time you do, I can't be there. I just want to
hold you, baby."

"I want you here with me, honey." My words came

out between sobs. "Rico and Jonathan should be here tomorrow morning. I haven't heard from her yet today, though."

"Ain't that a bitch. Another man can be there for my woman, and I can't." The sound of his fist pounding a hard surface made me jump.

"Baby, I understand. I don't like it, but I understand. Maybe if I'd married you on one of those dozen times you asked me, this wouldn't be an issue."

After a long silence Anthony managed, "All in your time, Glyn. So other than the obvious, how are you? You eating, sleeping, drinking less than three pots of coffee a day?"

I so appreciated him not implying he had told me something like this would happen because he wasn't my husband. I mustered up a laugh at his barrage of questions. "Funny you should ask about the coffee. I was headed to get another cup when the phone rang. I slept okay last night. I'm staying here at Daddy's with Uncle Thomas.

"We're waiting for the funeral director to come by to make the arrangements. Daddy had written out all of his final wishes. I mean every detail. He'd picked the funeral home, casket, songs, everything. I'm wondering if he was sick and never let us know. There is one thing though. Has he ever mentioned the name Nina Blackford to you?" I knew I was fishing. If none of us knew who she was, it was not at all likely Anthony had a clue.

"No. Who is she?"

"An insurance beneficiary and an equal heir."

"No kidding? And none of you know her? How about Uncle Thomas?"

"No. He doesn't know either."

"Damn! That's deep."

We continued to catch up on the events of the past

thirty-six hours. He told me he'd called his brother, John, to ask him to fly in for the funeral to represent for him. He had left a message and was reasonably certain my favorite of his five brothers would be there to offer whatever support was needed. He wanted to know if we had picked all of the pallbearers and said that he knew John would want to be considered.

I thanked him for just being the wonderful strong black man he was, and for loving me, even in my unreasonableness. He promised to call again as soon as he could. He told me to expect to hear from John sometime that day. We exchanged our normal "I love you"s. As I returned the receiver to its resting place, I knew I wanted Anthony to ask me to marry him just once more.

The doorbell ringing while I was on the phone with Anthony announced the arrival of Estelle, who looked so tired. Her face was drawn, and large dark circles surrounded her beautiful green eyes.

"Good morning, Sissy. Did you rest at all last night? Thomas told me you slept on the couch."

"Good morning, Estelle," I said as I hugged her long and tight. "I slept really deep, but not very long. Uncle Thomas and I talked a long time before I lay down. I'm so glad you could come over this morning. We only have a few minutes to go over everything before the funeral director arrives."

"Thank you for including me."

"You belong here. But in all fairness, it was Renee's suggestion we call you this morning. I'm sure we're all glad you're here. Isn't that right?"

All except Collette agreed. "May as well call Ms. Busybody, too, since we have nonrelatives involved," she muttered.

"I ain't havin' it, Collette!" Uncle Thomas had spoken in anger. Even Collette knew when to shut up.

"Well, let's get down to business. Daddy wants a burgundy casket trimmed in gold. He didn't indicate the lining color. Do we have any preference?" Renee took charge.

"My Eddie loved that burgundy and gray combination. How about a soft shade of gray satin lining?" Estelle spoke just above a whisper.

"He's wearing a gray suit," Collete said with as much disdain as she could muster.

"He didn't indicate what he wanted to wear, so why did you say he's wearing a gray suit?" Dawn asked.

"I just thought it would go nicely with the burgundy casket."

"I think we should vote on it. I think burgundy silk pajamas and robe would be really nice. He'll look like he's at rest." I put my two cents in the pot.

"Pajamas? Where in the world did you come up with that? Is that a California thing? You've been in Hollyweird too long. Normal decent people are not buried in silk pajamas. My daddy wasn't a pimp." Collette pulled a cigarette from her jacket pocket.

"Don't light that thing in here! It's not a California thing. And I don't live in Hollywood. I really don't appreciate your tone. It's only a suggestion. Daddy had such exquisite taste and style, I just think we should do something a little different. Something that makes a statement."

"The only statement pajamas would make is: 'Here lies Pimp Daddy Eddie.' Now Willie being buried in silk pajamas wouldn't surprise anybody." Renee tried to defuse the impending argument with humor.

"Okay, so maybe that was a bit of a reach. I like the idea of the soft gray liner. How about we buy a burgundy with gray pinstripe suit, soft gray shirt, and use the burgundy and gray tie and pocket square Devin gave him last Christmas? He loved that set." Dawn's bid had been placed.

"Why do we have to buy something new? Daddy has a closet full of suits. That is just throwing away money to buy him a suit to be buried in." Collette said the *M* word and indicated that we would be wasting it. It was on!

"Let me tell your uppity, money-grubbing, snobby ass something. If we spend every dime of the burial policy and then some on this funeral, that's just the way it is. I can't believe you. Despite me warning you countless times not to mention money, you have done it anyway. I'm a Brooklyn minute off you. I'll grab that weave and spin you around the room with it. You can spend fifteen hundred dollars on a weave thinking you Miss Jackson, but then try to tell us what we should spend on our father. Negress, you betta recognize." I was so angry my face was hot.

"Just because you don't care about how you look, don't be mad at me because I keep myself up. You walking around with braids, like you're some Afrocentric college student. I'm surprised any decent law firm will even interview you. You need to have a more corporate image."

"Gurl, what millennium are you in? We were set free in the nineteenth century. We can wear our hair as we please. I like being culturally in tune with my people. Besides, what does my hair have to do with what Daddy wears to his final resting place?"

"You started it, talking about my weave. No one can even tell I have extensions. That's why I pay so much."

"Gurl, please! How many sistahs you know with jet-black silky hair midway down their back? You ain't fooling nobody but your damn self."

"Ladies, please! You're missing the point, and the funeral director will be here any minute," Dawn interrupted. "I see why Daddy left such detailed instructions. I'm sure he thought we could decide what clothes he should wear. He has a solid burgundy suit that he bought a month or so ago. Devin and I were with him. He bought it to go with the tie set Devin gave him. So can we move on?"

"So why does he have to wear something that Devin gave him? You talking like he had no other grandchildren. My kids have given him plenty nice gifts, too! He loved them all the same. He didn't have any favorites. Besides, Derrick junior is the oldest grandchild." Renee rose and headed for the kitchen.

"Lord, Lord, Lord! Yo' daddy hated a disturbment mo' dan anythin' in dis world. Listen to yo'selves. Now ya arguin' 'bout who Eddie loved best."

"I'm not saying he had favorites, but you all know how much he loved that tie set. He went out and bought a suit to go with it. That says it all! It was his favorite color combination. I'm sure we can find gifts from each of the grandchildren to be buried with him. You're being so immature."

"Immature? You need to show me some respect. I'm the oldest. You need to respect your elders," Renee fumed from the kitchen doorway.

"Elders? Hell, you're my oldest sister, not my mother. Order of birth gives you no authority over me. And as far as respect goes, you gotta give it to get it. You're acting like you did when we were all little. You always thought you were my mother. Well, my mother is dead. And now my daddy is, too. So ain't shit you can say to me. Nothing!" Dawn began to sob.

"Now y'all need ta jus' calm down. And Miss Dawn, ya ain't so grown I won't give ya what fo', using dat kinda language. I been mo' dan a little patient wit' y'all.

Eddie wouldn't stand for dis, and neitha will I. I think Estelle's suggestion on the liner is perfect. The burgundy suit seems like the right choice. Renee, didn't your boys give dere grandpa a gray shirt a while back?"

"Yes sir."

"Then he'll wear that. Dey gave him cuff links, too. I think dat would round everything out right nicely. So e'erybody's child'll gave somethin' fo' da occasion. I'm just plum shamed of y'all. Educated women actin' like dat trailer-park trash on dem talk shows. Mah brotha would *not* be happy."

We looked from one to the other. It was rare for us to see Uncle Thomas mad. We'd ground our heels into the quick of his patience, and he'd had a knee-jerk reaction. We knew better than to say a word.

Estelle broke the deafening silence. "Thomas, that sounds real good. I think Eddie would be pleased."

"Now what's next? We not gonna have any more of dat bickerin'. Do I make mahsef real clear?"

"Yes, sir! Real clear," we all said together.

"I guess the pallbearers would be the next thing. We need five more. Willie already said he wants to be one. Renee, you think Derrick wants to be an actual or an honorary?" I proceeded with caution.

"What chu mean ya need five mo'? If Willie is one, den you only need fo'!"

"Uncle Thomas, I assumed you wanted to be an honorary."

"Miss Just-Passed-the-Bar is about to get what-for now." Collette seemed happy at my bad assumption.

"Sissy, baby, I dunno where dis honorary mess came from. But when ya ax a man ta be a pallbearah, it's a honor all on its own. It ain't somethin' taken lightly. Means ya takin' someone ya luv to dere final restin' place. I guess you educated folks came up wit' dat honorary mess. Y'all too good ta strain a muscle. But ya see, mah brotha sat by mah bed 'n' wiped bullet-size sweat from mah forehead when I firs' got back from Nam. He made me stay in his house wit' y'all 'til da nightmares stop comin' ev'ry night. He took care of me when I was jus' a boy when owah mama had ta work three jobs jus' ta keep us fed. He used da money he earned ta buy lunch meat for me to have food when I went ta school. And ya thank I'd dishonor him by lettin' anotha man carry him? Oh no, sweet chile. See if need be, I'd find a way ta carry him all by mahself if I could."

"Well, I guess we only need four," Collette said with a smirk.

"Make it three. I know Derrick wants to do it, too."

"Anthony can't come because he is on reserve duty. But his brother John is coming, and I'd like to ask him to stand in for Anthony. Does anyone have a problem with that?"

"I sure don't. Is John still single with his church fan foine self?" Dawn pretended to cool herself with her right hand and placed the back of her left hand on her forehead.

"No, she didn't go there! I thought you were in mourning?" I shook my head at my baby sister, who had been fiendin' for Anthony's baby brother since the first time they met while she was vacationing in California.

John had been the reason I met Anthony. We'd been in a business law class, and he'd invited me to join his study group. John was the give-you-the-shirt-off-his-back kind of brotha that I truly respected. When I arrived on his doorstep heavily laden with books for the study session, Anthony had rescued me and I realized that good looks and chivalry ran in the Sanders family. When Anthony's hands touched mine, magic happened. He told me later he had felt it, too.

"Gurl, is he single or not?" Dawn was laughing. For a brief second the pain that lay deep in her heart seemed to disappear.

"He broke up with someone a couple months ago. She was cheating on him. Can you imagine? What must she have been thinking? Brotha got it all. And she was cheatin' with a high-rollin' playa. But he isn't good prospect material. He is hurt and bitter. I've been trying to talk to him, but he's not feelin' any woman right now."

"Just my luck!"

"If we can break you two away from the dating game, can we get back to the issue at hand? Pallbearers," Collette said.

"Sorry, I guess we did get way off track. Mr. Brown is late. It's eleven fifteen."

"Like we ready for him, anyway." Collette enjoyed someone else being at fault for any transgression.

"So that's Uncle Thomas, Mister Willie, John, Derrick, and who else?" Renee was writing as she spoke.

"What about my Jimmy?"

"With all due respect, Estelle, does Jimmy consider herself a man?" Collette asked.

"Collette!" I was stunned that she would ask such a question.

"It's alright, Glynda. He really doesn't think of himself as male. But I know he'd want to do something. He said Eddie was more of a father to him than James ever was or even tried to be."

"How about if he sings one of the songs Daddy chose?" Collette had redeemed herself.

"Now, Lette, you have finally said something worth listening to. That boy knows he can blow! He can sing 'I Won't Complain.'"

The doorbell chimed, and we all turned. It must be Mr. Brown. He was nearly thirty minutes late, and I de-

tested businesspeople who showed up late for appoint-
ments. Devin showed him into the dining room, then
headed himself toward the den. The dark-suited man
addressed each of us with the rehearsed and often-used
greeting reserved for the bereaved. He spoke quietly and
held our hands in his as he spoke to each of us in turn.

"I'm so very sorry to hear of your loss. I knew your father well. He was a very outstanding man. We served on
the board of the boys' and girls' club together. That's
why I'll be handling his services personally. I apologize
for being late. We had some very pressing business that
ran over this morning. We'll be expanding our facilities
in the coming year."

My sisters and I looked at one another, none of us exactly sure how to respond.

"I think we should get down to business," I said. "My
father left very clear instructions. That's why we called
you. He's chosen the type of service he wants, casket, et
cetera. We have very few decisions to make."

"I'm sure a man of your father's means has a substan-
tial insurance policy. Only the best for my friend will
do." Dollar signs hung in the air around his head.

"We aren't spending a penny more than is necessary
to carry out his wishes, Mr. Brown." For once I agreed
with Lette.

"Oh, I fully understand. How much insurance are we
talking about, Miss Naylor?"

"The value of the policy is irrelevant at the moment.
We want to get the cost of the items he has requested,"
Collette said as she passed him the typed list of Daddy's
last requests.

After a moment the man dressed in the fifteen-hundred-
dollar Hugo Boss suit looked up and smiled. "Without
doing a detailed calculation, I'd estimate this to cost in

the neighborhood of twelve thousand five hundred dollars."

"Then we need to move to a different neighborhood." I didn't even give Collette a chance to speak. "I believe my father's wishes should be followed to the letter, but there is no earthly reason it should cost that much money."

"He has chosen the most expensive cemetery in the tri-state area. The crypt alone is four thousand dollars. The figure I quoted is discounted based on my long-standing friendship with Eddie."

"Mr. Brown, the mausoleum is paid for in full. So you can deduct that from your estimate. What in your services is valued at eight thousand five hundred dollars?" Something was terribly wrong. Now I agreed with Collette's approach.

"Miss Naylor, I assure you my prices are in line with the quality of service and are very competitive."

"I don't doubt that in the least. But please explain to me what costs eight thousand five hundred dollars," Collette continued.

He shifted nervously in his seat. When death strikes, especially suddenly, families are so overcome with grief they don't even notice those so willing to take advantage of their vulnerability. Collette had pissed me off with great frequency, but she was now working boyfriend like a personal trainer works an Olympic contender.

"I'm sure you want a top-of-the-line casket, and they run forty-nine ninety-five and up. They are fully insulated and sealed to prevent corrosion. We'll provide it at cost for my dearly departed friend."

"Excuse me, but if he is being placed in a mausoleum, why do we need all of that?" Estelle interjected.

"It's just the Rolls-Royce of caskets. Edward Naylor was a man of great style in life. I'm sure you would want nothing less for him in his final accommodations." Mr. Brown reminded me of a minister laying on guilt as he collected the third offering.

"We surely want a quality product," Renee said, "but I think we'll shop on the Net for a casket and have it delivered to you. Now, would you kindly break down the service charges for us." Renee handled Mr. Brown like she was buying drapes.

"I assure you, you'll receive the best service available anywhere for your money. We pride ourselves on top-quality service for our bereaved. As I stated previously, your father was a man of great style and class. I also assume that he was blessed to be well insured. If I may take a look at the policy, I'm sure I can put your mind at ease."

"We'll be paying cash." Everyone's head turned so quickly toward Renee, the air seemed to shift throughout the room.

"I see." There was an immediate change in Mr. Brown's attitude. He again moved nervously in his chair.

"So you see," I said, "we'll need all of the expenses broken down. I'm sure you brought the contract with you." I wanted him to understand we were a united front.

"Yes, I have the contract here. We can get right to the business at hand. Please be sure you are getting the best-quality casket. These wholesalers can be charlatans." The fox had feathers all around his lips while blaming the hens for jumping in his mouth.

From that point forward, Mr. Brown was cool and directly to the point. The services, including three cars, were reduced to just below four thousand dollars. A third of the bounty he had anticipated. We were all very pleased with Renee's handling of the funeral director.

But Collette looked as if she should've been smoking a cigarette.

Since we were paying cash, he insisted we each sign the contract to ensure our financial responsibility. He checked his calendar one last time to confirm there were no conflicts with our desired schedule and told us he would need to have the casket delivered no later than Thursday afternoon for the preliminary viewing.

We assured him we would start shopping immediately and would get back to him in the afternoon if there was any problem with delivery. Estelle showed him to the door and thanked him for his time.

I had retrieved my laptop from its travel case in Daddy's room and was settling down to look for caskets on the Net when the phone rang. Dawn answered it. "This is Dawn Naylor, how may I help you?

"Yes, that's correct, your client Edward Naylor passed away yesterday. We read a copy of his will and wanted a matter cleared up for us. There's an heir listed whom we don't know. We were wondering if you could shed some light on it. Her name is Nina Blackford. . . . I understand. When can we expect a callback? . . . Very well, we'll speak with you then." Every eye in the dining room was on Dawn as she hung up the phone.

"Well?" Collette, of course, spoke up first.

"He'll have an associate pull the file and get back to us. He couldn't remember the contents or the details of the will."

"When the hell is he calling back?" Collette asked impatiently.

"He said no later than tomorrow afternoon. He sends his condolences."

"Tomorrow afternoon?" Collette slammed her fist into the table, causing the coffee cups to bounce.

"Calm down, Lette. He'll get back to us as soon as he

can. We're real small potatoes to a law firm." Though I understood the internal operation of a large law firm, I, too, wondered why it would take so long to pull a file and tell us who Nina Blackford is and what she meant to Edward Naylor.

"You calm down! Just like your wannabe lawyer ass to defend him."

"I'm not a wannabe lawyer. I *am* a lawyer, and twenty-four hours is not unreasonable. I want to know who Nina Blackford is as much as the rest of you. Though I'm sure my motivation is not the same as yours, Collette. The only thing you can think of is how can you get your hands on her share."

"You know you really make me sick with your high-and-mighty ass!" Collette said angrily. "So what, you're a lawyer. I'm going back to get my MBA, and then we'll be equal. Daddy shouldn't have died before I gave him bragging rights the way you did. He was so proud of you. You're all he talked about." A steady flow of tears dripped onto Collette's silk blouse.

"Oh Lette, he was so proud of you! What are you talking about?" I said, trying to comfort her. "He talked about all of you to me. Hell, he has worked my nerves on a few occasions about y'all. When you got your own branch office to manage and I was still struggling with my last year of law school, I felt like I'd never measure up to your success. Your MBA or lack of one meant nothing to him. He was just proud. He told me how proud he was because Renee wouldn't give up her business four years ago when Derrick wanted her to stay at home after Krystal was born. And Dawn could do no wrong. According to Edward Zachary Naylor, you were the director of pediatric nursing. Please don't think he was prouder of any one of us. We were all his darling princesses." We all had started to cry while I was talking.

"He was sho' 'nuff proud of all four of y'all," Uncle Thomas interjected.

"So Lette, please don't think that I think I'm any better than you. Just different. There's one thing I know for sure and that is you're not up to your long curly eyelashes in student-loan debt. And do you have any idea how long it will be before I make the kind of money you do?"

"I don't know where that came from. I'm sorry." Collette never said she was sorry about anything. Grieving did strange things to folks, for sure.

9

Everybody Wants to Go to Heaven

"Renee, chile, you worked him! That was an awesome idea to buy the casket direct. I saw an exposé on *Dateline* on how funeral homes rip people off, capitalizing on people's grief. We saved more than five thousand dollars because you were so consumer savvy." Estelle was pacing.

"That was pretty cool how you handled that, big sis. I gotta give you your props. I don't want to scrimp, but I don't want to blow money to the wind either," I said, looking at Collette.

"Well, I buy for a living, so I'm always shopping with someone else's money. What keeps them coming back is that I spend it like it's my own. I'd seen the same show Estelle did on funeral homes, so I was ready for him. Now that we've got Mr. Brown out of the way, we need to get back to the pallbearers. We never finished our conversation, and we really are spending too much energy arguing."

"Dat what I been tryin' ta tell y'all. All dem wasted words. What y'all should be talkin' 'bout is what a good black man yo' daddy was!"

"He was the best, wasn't he?" I said. "You remember when Dawn told him she was pregnant? We were all so scared. Y'all were leaning against the door listening because we knew he was going to kill her." I began the tale.

"Y'*all* were leaning against the door?" Dawn continued the story. "When I opened Daddy's door, you fell into the room! I knew I was dead, too. But you know he always told us to never think a problem was so big he couldn't handle it. He said that as long as we kept a problem from him, it was *our* problem. The minute we told him, it became *his* problem.

"He listened to me intently. Never even raised an eyebrow. Asked me who the baby's daddy was and if I wanted to keep it. Fear truly gripped my heart when I told him it was Dexter Hollis, the captain of the football team. I just knew he was going to kill him and Edmondson wouldn't make it to the playoffs. He just rubbed his chin, thought for what seemed like an eternity, then slowly said, 'We need to get you in to see a doctor. Can't have anything wrong with my grandchild. Give me that Hollis boy's phone number. I need to talk to his daddy.' "

"Gurl, do you remember when Renee said she wanted to get married? Oh my God, you would have thought Derrick had kidnapped her." I smiled as I thought about the good ole days.

"He was throwing stuff and saying how I had to go to college and Derrick didn't have a pot to piss in. He must have asked me a hundred times if I was pregnant. Then told me if I was I didn't have to marry him. He never believed I was still a virgin. Said Derrick didn't make enough money to support one person, how was he going to support two? Then I told him we were in love and if he didn't give me permission, I'd elope and he'd never see me again. He pouted for about a week. Then told me to come take a ride with him. He took me to a bridal shop to pick out my dress. They sure broke the mold when they made him." Renee had a distant look in her eyes. "After we had been married about ten years he started telling Derrick how he had to talk me into marrying him."

"But that wasn't shit! When Collette eloped on prom night, oh my God! He woke up the whole house at four in the morning because you weren't home," I said. "He was pacing and at six he called the police. He knew you were somewhere dead."

"Gurl, I was so scared to call him. That fool got me drunk and drove to Delaware. I'm standing in front of the justice of the peace not even hearing him because I knew Edward Naylor was going to whip my ass."

"By noon he had the state police involved," Renee said, "and then here y'all come. I've never seen him that mad. When he knocked Kenneth unconscious, we all thought he was dead. If it hadn't been for Derrick, I think Daddy would have killed him." Renee laughed as she recounted.

"Then I ran to my room and slammed the door like I was grown. Gurl, that man came in that room with his belt in his hand and whipped me until he got tired. He was crying as hard as I was. Monday morning we were at the courthouse filing for an annulment. Kenneth brought his stupid ass around talking about how I was his wife and he didn't want a divorce. Daddy told him death would work just as well." Collette's tears were the product of her laughter.

"I think you're right, Collette wins for making Daddy the maddest." Dawn and I high-fived.

"Can I get anyone a cup of coffee?" Estelle seemed to feel out of place as we shared our memories.

"I would love some, but I want a little sumin' sumin' in mine. I need to settle my nerves," Collette said with a sly grin.

"Gurl, you betta not let Sister Greene hear you say

that. She would be rebuking you." Dawn then added, "But you can put a little, no make that a lot, in mine, too."

"We all caught hell when Sissy told him she wasn't coming back to Baltimore when she graduated. Oh man, none of us wanted to call him. He would sound so sad. He couldn't understand why you wanted to live so far from him," Dawn said, blowing on her hot coffee to cool it.

"See, y'all don't remember when she said she wanted to go away to school, period. I was already married by then, and I thought he was going to have a nervous breakdown. He never let you know though, Sissy. He didn't want to step on your dreams. He would say, 'Who's going to take care of my child way out there in California? She is too young to be that far away from me.' "

"My Eddie was a wonderful man and an even better father. After you all were grown and gone he started working with the boys' and girls' club. He made a real difference in so many of those children's lives. He got so many black men to start volunteering that they gave him an award. Someone should call the director down there and let her know he . . ." Estelle's words trailed off.

"Yeah, mah brotha was one of a kind. One of a kind."

"We still need to pick the rest of the pallbearers. Let me see, Uncle Thomas, Derrick senior, Mister Willie, foine-ass John, who else?"

"What about Deacon Kemp? They been friends since Daddy joined the church back in the sixties." Renee tapped the pencil on the table.

"He's kinda feeble. I'm not sure if he's strong enough to carry the casket. Eddie wasn't a small man." A smile found its way to Estelle's grief-stricken face.

"Yeah, the foine scale definitely tipped in Edward Naylor's favor. That brotha wore that six-foot-six, two hundred fifty pounds with such style. And when he put his clothes on. Man! Shoot, when Daddy came to my law school graduation, a couple of the grads wanted to push up on a brotha. But I was not having it! When I told them he was sixty-two, they told me I had to be lying. They were just gold diggers because he was looking so sharp."

"Pallbearahs!" Uncle Thomas chuckled.

"What about Derrick junior? He's the only grandchild old enough. Do you think he would want to do it?" Collette was fixing another cup of laced coffee.

"I know he would." Renee smiled. "Estelle, what about Mr. Lopez from the plant? He loved Daddy so much. I remember when he came to work at the plant, Daddy worked with him so hard. He had me tutor him with reading and English because he couldn't be promoted until his English was fluent."

"Oh, Renee, he would be so honored. Juan wasn't the only one, though. Your father is the cause of so many success stories at Bethlehem Steel. But I'll call now and ask him."

"That makes six. We can do the honorary thing later. I just know my Anthony has to be one of them. This is wearing me out. Oh, Bishop called this morning and will be by after his office hours this afternoon," I said, suddenly remembering the call I'd taken earlier. "He's real broken up. He has known Daddy since he was in high school. Daddy taught him in Sunday school."

"What else do we need to decide right now?" Collette said as she fiddled with a cigarette.

"We've taken care of the funeral home, the pallbearers, the casket. That leaves flowers, what we will wear, who will ride in the limos, and the actual service program." I was starting to feel heavy again.

"What about the obituary?" Estelle asked.

"Oh yeah! This should be interesting," Collette said, staring at Estelle.

"Why do you say it will be interesting?" I was immediately defensive. We'd had such a good time reminiscing. I hated to start arguing again. But I knew it was inevitable.

"Just trust me on this one. Everybody wants to go to heaven, but nobody wants to die."

"And just what are you implying?" Now Renee was defensive.

"Everybody wants their name in the obituary, sit in the front pew, ride in the family car. But nobody wants it to be his or her father, or brother. I'm not trying to argue, but you know I'm telling you the truth. But before we start to consider all of the nonfamily members, if we include one, we have to include them all."

"As much as I hate to admit it, Collette is right." Dawn was starting to get tipsy from our special coffee. "The one thing I do know for sure is that Estelle and her children will be in the obituary. Estelle will be riding in the family car. That isn't even open for discussion."

Collette rolled her eyes and sucked her teeth, but she remained silent.

"We may need to save space for Nina Blackford," Estelle said with great pain.

"Oh hell, naw. Whoever she is, she is not family," Renee said with disdain.

"Don't y'all be jumpin' to no conclusions."

"Uncle Thomas is right. We just need to wait to hear what the lawyer has to say."

"Renee, why did you make your children attend school today?" Dawn said, deciding to change the subject.

" 'Cause I'm their mama and I can!"

"See you just too smart at the mouth!" Dawn laughed.

"I just didn't want them underfoot today while we worked out all of these details. I'll keep them out the rest of the week. I sent notes with them today."

"Let's talk about something less heavy than the obituary. What should we wear? I was thinking maybe burgundy and gray?" I fixed myself another cup of laced coffee. It was amazing how much better the coffee tasted.

"Burgundy and gray? What the hell kinda mourning colors are those?" Collette was hanging out of the kitchen door, smoking.

"Those were Daddy's favorite colors, and I just think if we are matching him, it would be really nice."

"Well, I'm traditional and think we should wear black. What are people going to think if we wear red?" Dawn's Laura Ashley–loving ass spoke up.

"Who said anything about red? Burgundy is not red. You can be such a drama queen, and besides, what do we care what people think? Black for funerals is so passé." I lashed out at my only true ally.

"Since when is respect passé? I guess wearing red to a funeral is an L.A. thing?" Collette's eyes were going to get stuck in her forehead.

"If we choose to wear fire engine red with Roaring Twenties feather hats, it's nobody's business! Daddy always taught us not to follow the norm." I wasn't giving in strictly on principle. I'd rather have my bikini line waxed than disrespect my daddy in such a blatant manner. But they didn't have to know that.

"See, now you've really lost your mind. I dare you to step up in a church where Eddie Naylor is laid out, wearing red. He would get up and whip all of you. The one wearing red and the other three for letting her do it." Estelle had neutralized the situation with laughter. Even Collette had to laugh.

"You know she has a point—no matter how passé

black may be, we better seriously consider wearing it. Gray suits with burgundy accessories would look nice. What do you all think?" I guess I wanted to make peace, again.

"That sounds good to me. But a burgundy suit would look good, too. I have a gray satin blouse Daddy gave me for no reason at all. You know how he was. Called me on the phone and said, 'Dawn, I was shopping today and I know you have a tough time with that boy in private school. I bought you some uniforms for work. Why don't you come on over here and see your old daddy and pick them up?' When I got here, he had three beautiful silk and satin blouses for me."

"Dey broke da mol' when dey made mah big brother. I thank he'd sho' 'nuff like it if we wore his favorite colors. I'll wear mah gray suit 'n' burgundy tie he gave me."

"I bet if we think back, we'll each have a piece that is either burgundy or gray that Eddie gave us. It would be a great tribute to him if we each wore it," Estelle said softly.

"So you plan to wear what the family wears?" Collette said, sneering.

Lawdhamurcy, I thought we had prayed some temperament into Collette's tongue. "Why don't you just stop it!" I had lost all patience with her and was not afraid to show the ghetto girl that Daddy had always forbidden in his house. "Collette, she is family. Case closed."

"She may be—" The doorbell interrupted her.

"I'll get it," Devin yelled from the den.

Entering on Devin's heels was Roberta with grocery bags in both hands. Devin pulled a carry-on bag. My initial thought was, Oh, she's leaving town.

"Whew, I don't think I've forgotten anything. I stopped to get plenty of breakfast food. We're going to need our nourishment in the days to come. I brought a couple dresses. What color are we wearing? I brought black and white. Devin, baby, put that bag in the guest room."

We looked from one to the other. None of us could speak. The focus of our anger had definitely shifted.

10

And the Truth Shall Set You Free

"Roberta," I said sternly, "have you considered that the guest room may be reserved for those coming from out of town? How *dare* you assume that you can just move into my daddy's house uninvited. I tried to be nice to your pushy ass last night for Renee's sake, and I was bone tired from flying all day, but I'm not tired now and if Renee doesn't understand then f—"

Renee cut me off before I disrespected Estelle and Uncle Thomas. "Sissy, that's enough!" I'd truly lost control. Everyone was working me to the core of my soul. Daddy would be sorely disappointed in my behavior.

Oh, where was that strong black man who had a kind encouraging word for everyone, the man who never met a stranger? The man who opened his home to anyone who was down on his luck? In the more than twenty years Daddy had worked at the Bethlehem Steel plant, he had been responsible for in excess of fifty people being hired. When those whose luck was on hiatus came to him, he would provide food, shelter, and an opportunity to go to work. Although a few weren't interested, most pole-vaulted at the chance. Most of those who'd been hired on Edward Naylor's recommendation were well on their way to retirement.

"Roberta, you know I love you, and though I wouldn't put it as crudely as Glynda, I have to agree that we need to have any available space here for those coming from out of town." The plastic customer-service smile on Renee's face indicated that she was trying to spare everyone's feelings. "Actually, what would be better is if you could open your home for some of those coming from out of town. Mr. Fred Bowman, Daddy's old army buddy, called this morning to say that he'd be here with his wife. Maybe they can stay at your place. We sure don't want people to have to stay in hotels if we can avoid it. Buying last-minute airline tickets is enough of an expense. So what do you think?"

"Well, I'd rather be here in the heart of everything to help wherever I can. I can sleep in the den on the sofa bed. Mr. Bowman and his wife are welcome to stay at my place, though." It was clear that Roberta had no sense of appropriate behavior.

I felt it my responsibility to open the doors of the library's main branch to read her ass. "I'm saying this only once," I began, "and I really don't care if you ever speak to me again because I've only tolerated you all these years for Renee's sake. We don't want you staying here. You can visit like all of the other family friends. You may stay as late as you like, arrive as early as you please. Understand me when I say, you don't have to go home, but you gonna get the hell outta here!"

Crocodile tears flowed freely onto Roberta's red sweatshirt with the Delta sorority logo. "Why do you begrudge me being with my sister in her time of need? I just want to pay my respects and do what I can."

I couldn't understand why Roberta wanted so badly to be one of us. She and Renee had met in high school their senior year. As was Daddy's way, he'd welcomed Roberta into his home as if she were family when Renee invited her to one of his famous cookouts. He had nicknames for everyone. Roberta had been named Aunt Bert because of the way she doted on everyone's children. She stayed to help clean up after the party and had confided in Daddy that she'd never known her own father and would love it if she could call him Papa Eddie. We had all found the request a little strange after a first meeting, but, of course, Daddy agreed. From that moment on she was a self-proclaimed Naylor girl.

"Okay, okay. Tell you what. Come stay at my place, Bert. We have enough stress without fighting over you." Renee waved a white hankie as if surrendering.

"Where're you staying?"

"Give it a rest, Roberta. Please!" Estelle's authoritative maternal tone caused us all to pause.

Like an abused puppy, Roberta slinked her way into the kitchen.

"Estelle, when is Jimmy, I mean Jamaica, getting in?" Dawn asked, draining the last drop of doctored-up coffee from her cup.

"He will be in tonight around midnight. He's been able to get a flight from Paris and will be on a red-eye into Dulles."

"That boy's dancing sure has taken him around the world. I ain't mad at him. And he sho' 'nuff looks better in a dress than I do!" I said, laughing as I thought back to the days when we were all in junior high school. Jimmy had been in every musical the Harlem Park Junior High School ever produced. Daddy would drag us to his plays. "Estelle, did you ever know why we were at all of Jamaica's plays?"

"Because Eddie knew James wasn't going to show up. He said Jimmy needed the love of a good strong black man. We knew from the time that Jimmy was just a little thang that he was different. By the time he was in junior high, we knew he was funny. That's what we called it back in those days. Gay, homosexual, lesbian—

those are all new terms. It was funny, sissy, or bull dagger back then. But your daddy never made any difference with Jimmy. Jimmy will tell you when he gets here that he considers himself Eddie Naylor's son. He was so happy we were getting married because he said that now it could be official." Tears began to fall afresh.

"For as long as I can remember, Daddy was proud of his blackness. He would start to preach about what good strong black men did and didn't do. You know, Anthony is right. I always turned him down because he wasn't my daddy."

"Gurl, you betta hold on to that brotha if he's willing to stay with you after you have turned down his marriage proposal . . . what is it, six times now?" Dawn was adding her own twist to "You Betta Hold On to the Brotha If. . . ." "I didn't tell you all that Reginald proposed to me a couple months ago."

"Gurl, at least he's finally willing to marry you," Renee said, placing a pound cake and knife in the center of the dining room table.

"Hell, Reginald's been married five times. A marriage proposal from him ain't all that special," Collette interjected with her normal sarcasm.

"Oh, now that is chilly, but oh so true. That's why I told him thanks, but no thanks. He had the nerve to act like he was hurt."

"Y'all some funny modern-day women. Dat's fo' sho'! Way back when, a woman almost nevah said no when a man axed heh to marry him. Den she stayed wit' him 'til death did dem part."

"And I bet death departed the women first from putting up with all that mess. I'm not staying with a man who doesn't treat me like a queen."

Collette always made it so easy for me to bag on her.

"And you couldn't figure out they didn't treat you like royalty before you married them."

"To hell with you, Glynda. Just because you're scared of commitment, don't hate me because I'm willing to take a chance."

"Risky marriages are like flying on Take-a-Chance Airlines," Renee said, slicing pound cake and passing it around to each of us as though we had asked for it.

Collette took her plate and said, "Like the Dave Koz song says, 'I'm glad I didn't know the way it all would end . . . I would have missed the dance.' Life is too short, as Daddy has proven, to put happiness on hold. Even if the happiness is temporary. I don't regret my decisions, though I can guarantee you both the former Mr. Collettes are regretting their transgressions. This sistah got it going on!"

"Now I really don't want this to get out," I said, "but I agree with you, Collette. This has taught me that nothing is guaranteed. I love Anthony, and if I hadn't been so stubborn, he would be here to comfort me right now."

"Gurl, but then his foine brotha wouldn't be coming!"

Everyone in the room laughed at Dawn, and she looked around as though she didn't understand what she'd said that was so humorous.

"What did I miss this morning?" Roberta entered, carrying a freshly made pot of coffee in one hand and a bottle of Remy Martin in the other.

"Well, we met with the funeral director, and your friend over there handled Mr. Brown like he was a criminal, but she saved us a ton of money." I poured more Remy Martin than coffee into my gray coffee mug.

"Oh, she's a tough purchasing agent. I like watching her work. I wish I could negotiate like that," Roberta said proudly.

"We finally settled on what Daddy is wearing," I said.

"Actually, Uncle Thomas decided for us. We were arguing over what we are going to wear when you came in and we decided that picking on you was more fun."

Roberta didn't find my comment at all funny.

"I guess we should get back to it. I think either burgundy or gray suits with the opposite accessories would work. Does everyone have those color suits or dresses?" Estelle said, mindlessly stirring the black coffee in her burgundy mug.

"I think we should wear more traditional colors like black or white." Roberta acted as though someone had asked her opinion.

"We've been through all of this. It was decided we'd wear Daddy's favorite colors, Bert." Renee had a little edge in her voice.

"My burgundy suit is a winter one, and I don't know if I can find something lightweight enough that would match y'all."

Collette pretended to smoke an unlit cigarette. "Like we give a rat's ass what you wear."

"I can have Rico bring my gray suit and shoes. We tried to pack for the funeral, but we picked black and off-white. I haven't talked to her since I got here. I should call her." I tried to defuse the imminent storm rolling in from the direction of Roberta and Collette.

"Well, I just think I should be dressed like the rest of Papa Eddie's daughters," Roberta whispered to herself, loud enough for all to hear.

"That works for me, too. Derrick and Derrick junior have gray suits. Lette and Dawn?" Renee pretended she hadn't heard Roberta's comment. Her patience with her friend was growing quite thin.

"Fine with me," Collette said without emotion.

"Me, too." Dawn made it unanimous.

Roberta slithered into the kitchen, defeated.

I can't explain why it had been such a huge issue previously. The expensive cognac with a little coffee added had taken the edge off.

We continued to make small talk. Everyone around the table seemed to have aged ten years during the twenty-four hours that had passed since my arrival. Renee prepared to pick up her three youngest from school and make dinner. She promised to return before six with the entire crew. Dawn took my laptop into Daddy's office to search the Net for the casket he had requested. Pulling a cigarette from an almost empty pack, Collette hid her puffy, bloodshot eyes behind Ray-Bans as she picked up her purse to leave without a word. Uncle Thomas went home to gather more clothes and to wash his already immaculate car. Estelle followed Renee out the door, promising to return around six, as well. That left Roberta and me alone. What had they been thinking?

Silence descended on the house much like the fog rolls in off the Pacific Ocean to blanket San Francisco. We stared at each other, searching for something, anything, to say.

"I guess I should gather my things and go home to make sure my guest room is ready for Papa Eddie's friends."

"That sounds like a good idea."

"You know, Glynda, I don't mean any harm. But your family is the only people where I feel any real love. You all are as thick as welfare peanut butter. I envy that more than I could even explain. I don't talk to my real family except on holidays, and that is merely out of obligation, not desire. I know I bother you being around so much. I don't mean to, but I can't help it. Your family is my lifeline to happiness."

I was stunned by Roberta's candor. What was the

proper response? What would Eddie Naylor do? Without hesitation I walked over to embrace her with genuine feeling for the first time ever. Every pore in her body exuded anguish. Her trembling body gave off a scent of bitterness. Her stifled moans caused a silent wailing in my own soul. I realized, at that moment in time, Roberta had truly felt the loss of a father. We stood in the room where laughter had been shared around a table at which love was the only thing that overshadowed the food. We rocked back and forth crying for what seemed like hours.

11

A Cat's Curiosity

"I found the casket and ordered it. It cost twenty-five hundred dollars. I can't believe Mr. Brown was giving us a bargain at five thousand dollars. We saved half." Dawn rubbed the back of her neck, trying to relieve some of the muscle tension.

"But, of course, the merchants on the Net are charlatans!" We slapped high five. "Damn, it sure is good to hear the quiet. I turned off the TV since Devin is sound asleep."

"Gurl, my son has the right idea. We only slept a couple hours last night. We should take a few minutes to nap ourselves. Where'd Roberta go?"

"She went home to clean up her guest room. You know, a strange thing happened between us. I was ready to give her what-for again, but she started to tell me how being with us made her feel loved. The only real love in her life. My heart went out to her and I embraced her. I felt her pain. She is genuinely grieving."

"So now you like her?"

"I didn't say all that. But I do understand. We don't know what it's like not to be loved. I just know that Daddy would be mighty disappointed with us the way we've shown our natural behinds the past few hours."

"I guess you're right about Daddy. But Roberta must be real love-starved if this is the only love she gets. The only one who even tolerates her is Renee. Don't let her snow you. She's as fake as Tammy Bakker's eyelashes."

"You could be right, but what she felt just now was real."

"Whatever."

"I'm glad we're alone for a while. Let's go lie on Daddy's bed and rest," I said, and we headed to his room. "I talked to Uncle Thomas last night about the pills we found."

"Stop! What did he say?" Dawn asked as she folded back the comforter.

"He knew. He said Estelle tried to talk him out of taking them. But it was a man thang, and I just wouldn't understand. He also said he didn't think Daddy had even taken one of them because he had just gotten the prescription."

"Well, we can sure as hell find out!"

"How?"

"Count the pills, gurl! The number of pills is right on the bottle."

"Damn, why didn't I think of that?"

"Good thing you're not going to be a prosecutor." We laughed as she went to the bathroom counter, opened the bottle, and counted each pill.

My heart raced in my chest. Please let there be pills missing. I wanted a reason for Daddy being dead. "Well?"

"There's one missing." All of the vitality had drained from Dawn's voice and body.

"I see." I fell on the bed, at a loss for words.

"We have to tell Renee and Collette what we found."

"You know the fur is gonna fly! Renee has finally come around to at least being decent to Estelle. This'll surely cause an irreversible divide between us."

"But, Glynda, if she is responsible for Daddy taking these, are Renee and Lette so wrong?"

"She tried to stop him, remember? Uncle Thomas tried to make me understand how a man feels about sex at any age, but especially when he's older."

"Well, Reginald told me he would rather be dead than impotent. Is that deep or what?"

"Uncle Thomas told me the same thing." We slipped into bed fully clothed and pulled the cover under our chins the way we did when we were kids.

Sleep enveloped me instantly. I drifted into a peaceful dream. I was in a meadow and Daddy was pushing me on a swing. Beautiful flowers surrounded us. Clouds so white and fluffy, one would think a painter's brush had created them. In the distance a young woman in a beautiful yellow sundress ran in our direction in slow motion. Daddy stopped swinging me and began to glide without steps in her direction. As she came closer, I realized the beautiful woman with the angelic look was my mother. She stretched her arms in Daddy's direction. All of a sudden an air-raid siren sounded, and we all looked panicked. I wanted Daddy to make it stop, but he floated higher and higher as he and Mama met in midair. The siren took on the sound of a ringing telephone. It took several rings before I realized it was actually the phone. I groggily reached for the receiver.

"Hello, this is Glynda Naylor."

"Ms. Naylor, this is Chuck Morgan with Brown's Funeral Home. We just wanted to let you know that we got the call from the coroner's office releasing Mr. Naylor's remains. Mr. Brown had told us that you wanted to know when that happened so that you could contact Mr. Naylor's doctor."

"Thank you, Mr. Morgan, I'll let my sisters know. We'll have his clothes brought down to you tomorrow morning."

The phone conversation awoke Dawn. She raised

herself up on her right elbow and stared at me intently before speaking. "Well, mystery number one has been solved?"

"Yeah, the coroner released the body. We have to call his doctor to get the results, though."

"That's standard. You want me to call?"

"I guess. Should we wait for Renee and Collette to get back?"

"Well, only one of us can talk to the doctor, and I know all the right questions to ask. I'd rather do it without Collette in the background being Collette."

"I'll get the number. I'm sure it's in his phone book. I saw it yesterday in the den."

"Gurl, why didn't we think of this last night?"

"Think of what?"

"Nina Blackford's number is probably in that phone book. You know that raggedy old thing was his bible. We would buy him new ones and he just put them in the drawer. Where is it? I'll get it."

"On the end table next to the phone." The information that was held by the good doctor would have to wait. Mystery number two might be solved with just a minimal amount of snooping. I was on her heels so close that, when she stopped short in the doorway, I ran into her.

"What're we going to do if we find her number in the book?"

I hadn't considered the options once we had, in fact, found her number. "Should we call her?"

"Well, running the risk of sounding like Collette . . . hell, yes, we should call her." Dawn's hands trembled as she reached for the phone book held together with a rubber band.

"Let's take it to the table and go through it."

Sitting side by side at the table, we looked at each other

before removing the rubber band. There was a small explosion of paper that fell onto the table and floor. Gathering the small pieces of paper and business cards from the floor made me think this had to be the only area of Edward Naylor's life that was disorganized, though he had always called it organized chaos.

"I wonder if we should call all of these people to let them know Daddy died." Dawn seemed to be speaking more to herself than to me.

"Gurl, it seems everyone already knows. It was like there was an emergency broadcast message announcing his death."

"Sister Greene," we said in unison, laughing.

We began separating the pieces of paper from the business cards. The pages in the book were worn and browning. Many of them had freed themselves from the stitched binding. We silently started with the pages in the book. Every page was full, including writing in the margins. When Dawn sat up straight and stared at me, I knew my daddy's secret was about to be revealed.

"Did you find something?"

"Nina Blackford, 104 Elm Drive, Jefferson City, Missouri, 314-555-1611." Dawn had hit pay dirt.

As if I didn't believe her, I had to look at the information myself. I stared at the personal information of the stranger who meant enough to my father to receive an equal share of his estate. My palms began to sweat, my throat constricted, my vision blurred.

"Should we call the number?" Dawn spoke first.

"Maybe we should wait for the others to get back."

"I think we should do it before the real drama queen gets back. Collette will make a scene with the woman on the phone, demanding to know who she is and how she's eligible to be one of Daddy's heirs." Dawn's statement was logical but not practical.

"But then if we call without her, she'll turn that wrath on us."

"You act like you're afraid of Collette."

"And you're not?"

Nervous laughter filled the room.

"Who's going to call?" I asked, hoping she'd volunteer.

"You're older, you do it."

"Since when has my age been anything other than a source of ridicule?" I searched for reasons not to dial the number.

"Gurl, just make the call!"

With much effort I raised myself from the chair; the heaviness from the previous day had returned again. I slowly moved toward the phone by the back door. Did I subconsciously choose this phone because rotary dialing took longer? I let my hand rest on the receiver to calm the trembling. Slowly, I raised the receiver and dialed, hesitating between each number. After what seemed like time without end, the phone began to ring.

On the second ring a young woman with major attitude answered. "Yeah?"

"May I speak with Ms. Blackford, please?"

"She ain't here. Who's this?"

"When do you expect her?"

"Who wants to know?"

"My name is Glynda Naylor, and I need to speak with Ms. Blackford as soon as possible. May I leave a number for her?"

"Do whatever you want."

"Will you be so kind as to write it down?"

With a long, extremely winded sigh, the young woman finally managed a barely audible "Hold on."

"She's real pleasant. But at least we got the right number," I said while waiting on the line. I heard her moving items about, apparently searching for a pen.

"So, what is it?"

I repeated Daddy's number to her before I asked, "And with whom am I leaving this message?"

"You sure do ask a lot of questions. My name is Edwina." The next sound I heard was a click.

"Glynda, all of the color has drained from your face. What is going on?" Dawn asked.

"It may be a coincidence, but her name is Edwina." I was numb and feeling even heavier.

"No shit? Are you thinking what I'm thinking?"

"That she's our sister?"

"Yep, yep!"

"Gurl, I can't imagine Daddy having a child and not telling us. Plus she is way too arrogant to be a Naylor girl. Daddy would have broken a foot off in her rude ass."

"How old did she sound?"

"Definitely a teenager. She has that know-it-all attitude that comes at about age fourteen and sometimes lasts until half-past forever."

"That means I'm not the baby girl!"

"Oh, get over it! This is far more reaching than your level on the food chain. If Daddy had a baby and didn't tell us, what else could he have been hiding?"

"When did she say she would give Nina Blackford the message?"

"She didn't. I would assume around six or so. After work."

"So are we going to tell the others? If she calls and we haven't told the others, all hell's gonna break loose. I just don't want Lette to get the number and start calling every fifteen minutes."

"I'm so confused. Why are we the keeper of all the secrets?"

" 'Cause we real nosy?"

Laughing, I continued, "It would've almost been better if we hadn't found the number. That way the mystery would've stayed just that. The lawyer could have gotten in touch with her for us. Why did you insist we find the phone book?"

"Me? This was all your idea!" she yelled.

"What was all Glynda's idea?" Collette startled both of us.

"You need to wear a bell or something. We didn't hear you come in." I was sure she could hear my heart pounding.

"Oh, so now I'm a cow?"

"Oh, save the drama! I was thinking a cat, but why degrade cats!" Collette really seemed to be able to bring out the worst in me at will.

"Whatever, so what were you two talking about?"

Stalling for time to make up a believable lie, I asked, "Were you able to get all of your business handled this quickly?"

"I have a great assistant, and she just handled everything for me and sent me on my way. She asked me to convey her condolences to everyone. You still didn't answer my question. What was all your idea?"

"We were discussing flowers. I wanted white roses and Dawn said it was too feminine. What do you think?"

Collette eyed me suspiciously and slowly answered, "I actually think white roses would look great on top of the burgundy coffin. Why do you think that would be too feminine, Dawn?"

"Speaking of caskets, I found the model he wanted at half the price the funeral home was going to charge."

"Oh, really now? See, that's what I'm talkin' 'bout. So what about the roses?"

"I'm not really certain Daddy would like roses. He never had them in the house. He loved gardenias, though. They're white and smell soooo good," Dawn added casually.

"Gardenias? Do you know how—" Collette stopped abruptly.

"We'll take a vote when Estelle and Renee get back," I said, relieved that Lette's slip into fiscal scrutiny had diverted her attention away from Dawn's and my conversation.

"This voting shit is really working my nerves!" Collette pulled a cigarette from a fresh pack in her jacket pocket.

"Well, maybe *you're* working everybody else's nerves!" I screamed.

The multiple telephones ringing in stereo caused the three of us to freeze as though we were in a silly childhood dance contest.

"Saved by the bell," Collette said as she moved to answer the phone.

"I'll get it!" Dawn shoved Collette out of the way.

Collette stared at Dawn in disbelief. Now how did we plan to explain this one?

12

Cause of Death

"What are you two trying to hide?" Collette's narrowed eyes stared into mine.

Trying hard not to break her gaze, I answered, as any good lawyer would, "Whatever do you mean?"

"Shhhh, it's Dr. Sloane's office." Dawn waved us off.

Suddenly nothing else seemed to matter. The person on the other end of the line held the answer to the question that burned deepest in our hearts. Why?

Dawn's beautiful honey brown complexion became jaundiced, and the blood drained from her face. Tears filled her eyes as she shook her head in a denying motion. Her mouth moved, but no words formed. The imaginary concrete boots I wore precluded my movement toward her to take the phone. Collette looked from Dawn to me, and back again. She, too, seemed fixed to the floor. My palms became wet; my mouth tasted of onions; my pounding heart caused my ears to ring.

"Thank you, Dr. Sloane. I'll tell my sisters."

Dawn pushed the OFF button and stared at us through tear-filled eyes. She opened her mouth to speak, but only sobs escaped. We moved simultaneously to comfort her. But I wanted someone to comfort me. As we stood in a tight circle holding one another, crying, I yearned for Anthony's touch.

Collette spoke first. "What did Dr. Sloane say?"

"Daddy had an aneurysm. It ruptured and he died instantly. He never knew what happened. One minute he was talking to me and within a split second he was . . . gone. They're waiting for the toxicology report to determine if there were any drugs in his system. Dr. Sloane doesn't know what may have caused his blood pressure to rise quickly enough and with such force to cause the vein to rupture. But it is a good possibility if Daddy had taken that one Viagra in the past few days, the added pressure further weakened the wall of the vein and then suddenly it just blew."

"Drugs? Viagra? What in the hell are y'all talking about?" Collette pulled from our embrace.

Through the pinhole of light caused by Dawn's grief, the truth had escaped. Dawn's agony was now replaced by dismay. Collette's wrath was imminent.

"Don't make me repeat myself. What the fuck are you talking about Viagra, and why am I just now hearing about it? Y'all running around thinking you know every damn thing and keeping secrets from me. You trying to protect that Estelle bitch or something?" Like the roaring Mississippi at its greatest point during flood season, Collette's words rushed forth.

"Collette, there is no need to call Estelle names. This has nothing to do with her. We were going to tell you as soon as we heard from the doctor. There was no need to upset you if the pills weren't the cause of death." The calmness in Dawn's voice amazed me.

"Upset me? Upset me? Oh, in case you haven't heard, my daddy died yesterday. I'm already up-fucking-set! You and Glynda are always siding against me. It shouldn't surprise me that you two would conspire against me. I bet you told Estelle, didn't you? Oh, and I know Renee doesn't know. Give me the damn phone. I'm about to show your selfish, self-righteous asses the way you are supposed to handle information about the death of one's father." Collette screamed so loudly she woke up Devin.

"Wait, Collette. Let us explain!" Why did I feel so guilty? In the depths of my soul I knew we were wrong. But we had been trying to prevent a scene just like this one.

"Explain what? There ain't shit to explain. You knew Daddy was taking Viagra, and you chose not to tell Renee and me. You want to protect little Miss Estelle. Well, now that I see where the lines are drawn and what side of the scratch line you stand on, you can consider the war on!" The fury in Collette's eyes unnerved me.

"Estelle knows about the Viagra because Daddy told her, not us. Uncle Thomas knows, too. And you can't blame Estelle because she tried to talk him out of it." My shame had defeated me.

"So I get it now, it's just half of his children who have been left in the dark. I bet you and Dawn have been laughing about your little secret, haven't you?"

"Look, Lette, maybe we were wrong for not telling you and Renee as soon as we discovered the pills, but we made a bad judgment call. We didn't do this to hurt you, and we surely have not been laughing behind your back. I wanted to make sure that this was the cause of death before we said anything. Don't blame Glynda. It was my idea."

"I can't let her take all of the blame. You can be so irrational at times, and we knew you'd blame Estelle and treat her even worse than you are already. Uncle Thomas tried to make me understand how it is with a man when he can't perform the way he used to. He said despite Estelle's insistence that all was well in the romance department, Daddy refused to listen. Uncle Thomas said he didn't think that Daddy had actually taken the pills, but when we counted them this afternoon there was one missing." As I touched Collette, she snatched her arm away so quickly she knocked the cordless phone from Dawn's hand.

"Don't you dare touch me! You're no longer my sister. I don't want to sit next to you at the funeral. I don't want to ride in the same car with you!"

"Collette, just stop it. Listen to yourself. How did you get so mean-spirited and unforgiving? We messed up, and we're sorry. But to become divided now is crazy. What would it have accomplished telling you before?"

"I would've known. That's what it would've accomplished. I wouldn't be ready to kick your ass is what it would've accomplished. I can't wait to tell Renee what low and sneaky skanks you two are." Collette bent down to pick the phone up from the floor.

"Tell her whatever you want. I'm sure she will at least understand our motives and know that it was not to hurt either of you." I was hoping my even tone would calm her.

"I wouldn't count on it." Collette began dialing the phone.

For as long as I could remember Collette had been angry. She always seemed to need to prove something to someone. She had taken Mama's death the hardest of the four of us. Long after the police officer bearing the bad news had driven off, Collette had remained quiet. She had never asked any questions. She had never cried. For months, maybe even a year, Collette had said hardly a word. Gradually, she began to emerge from what we believed was a young child's grief, but with a mean-spiritedness none of us quite understood. Several years later, while cleaning under Collette's bed, Daddy found her diary. A father's natural curiosity into his daughter's mind got the best of him, and he sat on the floor between the twin canopy beds Collette and Dawn

shared and began thumbing through the pages expecting
to find the ramblings of a preteen girl's many puppy-love
crushes. Much to his chagrin he discovered pages upon
pages of guilt-ridden entries, including a letter to our
mother.

Dear Mama,
    I am so sorry that I got mad at you all those years
ago because you told me I couldn't spend the weekend
at Charlotte's house. Everyone was going to be there,
and we were going to tell scary stories and have a lot
of fun. I know it was family night and you said we always had to be together on family night. When you
told me that I couldn't go, I wished I didn't have a
mother and that way I could do whatever I wanted to
do. Daddy would never have said no to me. I wished
you were dead. So you see, I am the reason that car hit
you and you died. I have been feeling guilty all this
time. Please, please, please forgive me and ask God to
forgive me, too. I would do anything to take it back.
Anything. I would rather be dead myself. If Renee,
Dawn, and Glynda find out, they will always hate me
for killing you. I love you, Mommy.
                                                            Collette

That night, before we began clearing the dinner dishes,
Daddy confronted Collette with his discovery. Though
visibly upset, guilt clearly overshadowed her anger. Daddy
explained to Collette that a drunk driver killed Mama,
not the wishes of a six-year-old. Collette seemed angry at
the world that night as Daddy, Dawn, and I sat around
the table trying to comfort her. She was still angry today.
    Looking at Dawn, I knew she worried that our actions
might cause an irreversible rift between the four of us.
She'd been the peacekeeper. When she had been just a

toddler, she would stand in the middle of us sucking a pacifier while we argued, trying to keep us from coming to blows. In her teen years she would take the blame for our actions to prevent us from being mad at one another. Since she was the baby, we never seemed to get angry with her. She used this power for good and was the self-appointed head of family relations.

"Call me. You'll never believe this shit!" Collette said, leaving a message on Renee's voice mail.

"Please, Collette! Let's talk about this. We have enough to contend with. Being angry at one another will serve no purpose. I'm sorry. Truly sorry." I began to cry.

"Don't think those tears are going to move me a bit. So what other secrets are you two hiding?"

Dawn and I made eye contact. For sure we needed to share our latest discovery in Daddy's phone book. If Nina Blackford called us back before we told Renee and Collette, our relationship would never recover.

"Well, there *is* one thing," Dawn began slowly.

"See, I knew it!"

"Try to stay calm, please. This is why nobody ever wants your ass to know anything." My fleeting moment of remorse was over.

"You need to check yourself, Miss-High-and-Mighty-Just-Passed-the-Bar! You're the one here who's wrong. So don't be coming at me like I borrowed your favorite J. Renee pumps and walked through the mud." Though clearly still angry, Collette's fury was waning.

"Oh dayum. Walking through mud in her J. Renee's. Now that is foul!" Dawn managed to draw a slight smile from Collette.

"So what is it that I'm supposed to stay calm about?" If Collette was nothing else, she was consistently cynical.

Taking a really deep breath, I began. "We were talking

earlier about Nina Blackford, and I realized that we hadn't looked in Daddy's phone book for the number. We checked, and sure enough, there it was. We called the number, and a teenager with a bad attitude answered, told me she wasn't in, and took down the number."

"Damn, why didn't I think to look in his phone book? So we just need to wait for the return call—or have you tried again?"

"We had just called when you came in, and that's what you overheard us discussing. But there is one more thing," Dawn proceeded with caution.

"Well, what is it?"

"This could be nothing, but it caused us to wonder." I was relieved to be revealing everything we knew.

"I'm about a minute off you. Stop stalling."

"This teenager with the bad attitude's name is Edwina."

This time all of the color drained from Collette's beautiful caramel brown face. Her eyes glazed over, and tears formed instantly. She opened her mouth twice, but no words came forth.

13

A Friend Indeed

Suddenly the house was filled with activity. Sister Greene buzzed around the kitchen warming food and making iced tea. Three of Daddy's coworkers had stopped by with cards, food, and soft-spoken words. Church members were arriving by the carload. Most came, said a prayer, and left. David and Lillian Morgan had stayed to offer assistance to Sister Greene. Uncle Thomas entered with Mister Willie on his heels. We waited for Renee and her clan to arrive so that we could reveal our secrets to her. Thankfully, she hadn't returned Collette's call.

"Y'all wash up so you can eat. You need to put some food in your system." Sister Greene loved bossing us around.

"Call me Willie. Call me Silly. Just call me to the table." Mister Willie made a pathetic attempt at poetry.

"You need to go sit yo' old wannabe-playa ass down somewhere, Willie. There ain't nobody here for you to impress," Uncle Thomas jokingly chastised Mister Willie.

"I don't know what you talkin' 'bout, 'cause Sister Greene is lookin' good!" Mister Willie winked at Sister Greene, making her blush.

"Willie Johnson, you need to quit. I'm too old for that kinda talk. You need to be somewhere leading a prayer meeting." Despite her words, we all saw a twinkle in Sister Greene's eyes.

Laughing, I teased, "Sister Greene, now you know you're never too old for a little romance. Mister Willie here just recognizes a good woman when he sees one."

"Well, if he sees a good man he should send him my way!" Sister Greene snapped her neck so hard that her snow white shoulder-length ponytail danced a jig all its own.

"Oh, Willie, she done calt chu out!" Uncle Thomas teased.

"Yeah, she wants me!"

"The same way I want death and taxes. Everybody gather around the table so we can bless this food. We need to pray for Willie here, too. This man needs Jesus! David lead us, if you will, to the Throne of Grace."

"Gracious and Heavenly Father, we come before you asking that you give us peace in our minds, strength in our bodies, and joy in our souls. Bless the hands and homes of all those who have prepared this wonderful food. Amen." Deacon David Morgan, a long-time family friend, eloquently blessed the food.

"Where're Renee and Estelle?" Deacon Morgan asked as he scooped mashed potatoes.

"Well, you know how slow Renee is all by herself. So I figure she'll be here around seven," I said.

"Well, she needs to get here, because we need to talk." Collette was pulling a cigarette from her pocket.

"Put that cancer stick down and come here and fix your plate," Sister Greene scolded. "Y'all gonna start passing out around here, and then what we gonna do? We don't need any more drama!"

Collette, despite her respect for the wannabe matriarch of the Naylor household, retorted, "I'm grown, Sister Greene. I eat when and if I so please. But thank you for your concerns."

Sister Greene's face flushed red. "I'm just trying to help."

"Well, you don't have to tell me twice. I'll eat her share and then some of that fine Sister Greene's fine greens!" Mister Willie struck a pimp-daddy pose.

"Oh hush up, Willie!" Sister Greene blushed like a schoolgirl.

"Willie, you da man!" Dawn laughed. "You da man!"

Everyone gathered around the table filled with all our favorites: greens, yams, macaroni and cheese, fried chicken, baked chicken, chicken and dumplings, chicken, chicken, and more chicken. The food seemed endless. It appeared everyone in the state had dropped off a dish.

Using more decorum than Collette, I began to speak, "Sister Greene, everything looks wonderful. I have a bit of a headache. Would you mind making a plate for me and putting it away for later? I'm sure I'll feel more up to food then."

"See, that's why your head is hurting, not enough food and rest. All I see you young folks doing is walking around with bottled water. Since when is Baltimore water not good enough to drink straight out of the faucet? I'm willing to bet my pension that is exactly where that came from." She pointed at the bottle of Evian in my hand. "Just a license to print money in my opinion . . . a license to print money. But you know I'll put a plate up for you, baby." Sister Greene went into the kitchen muttering and shaking her head.

Recognizing the perfect opportunity to slip away, I made my way into the den. I needed solitude before Renee arrived. Although Collette was not visibly hostile, I knew she was angry and was lying in wait to pounce again. I hoped we could spare our visitors the airing of our family's funky laundry.

As I looked around the room where we'd spent so

much time, I felt a sense of peace. The last Christmas before Mama died came to mind as I sat on the window seat. Collette, Renee, and I had sneaked into the den on Christmas Eve for the annual package shake, thinking that Mama and Daddy had already turned in for the night. Much to our surprise, Mama's head lay on Daddy's lap sleeping as he stroked her hair. He smiled at us and put his fingers to his lips indicating we should be quiet.

He beckoned us to him and kissed us each good night, sending us off to bed. For the first time in my young life I understood what it meant for a man to love a woman. I knew then that a man had to love me enough to stroke my hair as I slept. The thought of that night gripped my soul. My soul yearned for its mate. I'd found the man who loved me enough—Anthony Sanders.

My momentary solace was interrupted by Renee and company's arrival. Three of the four children ran to me for hugs and kisses. Derrick junior was so tall and handsome. For sure breaking hearts was his pastime. Stephen was my daddy's spitting image. He was going to be tall, too. Shanelle was stunningly beautiful, with the best features from both Derrick and Renee. She was definitely no longer a little girl, but Krystal was the poster child for Daddy's little girl. She clung to his hand as Derrick walked into the den to hug me.

"How you holding up, Glynda? I see you're in here all alone, as usual. Renee is trying to be tough, but we're late because she was crying so hard she couldn't get dressed. This is a real tough pill to swallow. He was so alive, so happy, so healthy. I guess we just never know what tomorrow will bring. For that matter, we don't know what today will bring." Derrick held me close as he talked.

"That's for sure, Derrick. Thanks for taking care of

Renee. She always thinks she has to be so strong for the rest of us." I reluctantly broke our embrace.

We walked hand in hand to the dining room. Everyone seemed so happy, which just pissed me off. Didn't these people know that my daddy had just died and that *no one* should be happy?

As though Derrick could read my thoughts, he spoke, "It's okay, Glyn. This is how people show their respect. You and your sisters need to mingle with the people who have come here. I know y'all want to be alone, but it is best if you mingle. Best for everyone."

Though I wanted to be mad at Derrick for suggesting this was the cocktail hour at Martin's West, I couldn't. He was absolutely correct. I understood why Renee has loved this man for so many years. "I know you're right, brother-in-law. They all mean well, I'm sure."

"People just want to feel like they are making you feel better, even if they have no clue whether they are or not. Come on, let's get something to eat."

"Glynda, phone. It's Rico," Collette yelled from the kitchen.

"I'll get it in the bedroom." I was glad to take leave from Derrick's well-meaning optimism.

"Hey, gurl, I was wondering when I was going to hear from you." Relief washed over my tired body as I heard my friend's voice and fell onto the bed.

"Hey there, yourself. Are y'all holding it all together?"

I liked that Rico wasn't speaking to me in that whispered I-feel-sorry-for-you tone. "Other than being at each other's throats constantly and crying for absolutely no reason, we seem to be doing okay."

"I'm really glad. I've been worried about you all day. I have had one surgery after another, and then I had to get someone to cover the ER for me while I'm gone. Jonathan and I are on the red-eye tonight, getting in at five in the morning. We'll be staying at the Sheraton at BWI and will be over to Papa Eddie's place after we take a nap. Do you need me to bring you anything?"

"Why are you staying at a hotel? There's plenty of room here!"

"We don't want to be intrusive. We want any available space to be for family."

"You *are* family!"

"I understand you feel that way, but I know the rest of your sisters don't. You never answered my question. Do you need me to bring you anything? I just finished up at the hospital, and I'm heading home. We'll finish packing, have a little dinner, and then go by your place before we go to the airport. That way we'll miss the traffic."

"We're all wearing either gray or burgundy, so if you could get my charcoal suit and pumps I'd appreciate it. I guess you're right about my sisters. We've had more than a few heated discussions about Roberta imposing herself on the family, and now I'm being a hypocrite because I feel like you're family. Have I told you lately how much I love you?"

"No, gurl, and you're slacking on the job! Speaking of loving, Jonathan spoke to Anthony this morning. He's a mess! He wants to be with you so badly. He broke down, told Jonathan how much he loves you."

Like a switch had been flipped, tears filled my eyes. "He told me today when he called. I've been such a fool. I'm not going to find a more loving and devoted brotha, and I've just been too stupid to see that."

"Gurl, you got enough going on without concerning yourself with your stubbornness. I'll go by and pick up the clothes. Anything else you need while I'm there?"

"No, just get here. I need you."

"When's the funeral?"

"Friday evening, with a Saturday morning burial."

"Now when I get there, please put me to work, whatever you need, whenever you need it. Is that clear?"

"Yes, ma'am. There's something I need to tell you."

"Gurl, you know you can tell me anything."

"I think my daddy had a secret life," I whispered as though someone else was in the room.

"What are you talking about?"

"There's a woman in his will who no one knows. We don't know who she is or what she meant to him. But she gets an equal share of his estate. And that is a pretty sizable piece. Then Dawn and I being nosy found her number in his phone book, called it, and a teenager named Edwina answered the phone!"

"Oh my Gawwwwwd! Do you think he's had this woman on the side all the time? What's Estelle saying about all of this?"

"She just casts her eyes down and cries. This is so unbelievable about my daddy. And, are you ready for this? She's only three years older than Renee!"

"Damn, Glyn. I don't know what to say!"

"Gurl, there's nothing to say. We just have to wait it out and see what she says when she calls back. We contacted Daddy's lawyer about her, too. We just need someone to clear this up. My imagination is running wild! Can you imagine what this must be doing to Estelle?"

"There has to be a logical explanation. The Papa Eddie I know wouldn't have any major skeletons in his closet. He was such a good man. I hate to ask this, but did you get the coroner's report yet?"

After a long pause I answered. "Yes, an aneurysm. Never knew what hit him. As if I haven't laid enough heavy news on you, there's more. He was taking Viagra."

"Stop!" Rico gasped with laughter. "I'm sorry, I know that's not funny. But it is so hard for me to think of Papa

Eddie that way." It was hard for Rico to talk, she was laughing so hard.

Despite myself, I started laughing, too. Amazingly enough, it felt so good to have a belly-roll kind of laugh. It became contagious, and we could no longer maintain our conversation. I was finally able to speak. "See, you're so far to the left, you can't even see right! I shouldn't be laughing, and my daddy is lying in a funeral home."

"Gurl, you know I mean no disrespect, but Papa Eddie knocking pictures off the walls and lamps off the nightstand. I ain't mad at him."

"Yeah, that is pretty funny when you put it like that!"

"He embraced life with all he had, and you can't begrudge him that. They wouldn't have the toxicology back yet to know if the Viagra actually caused the rupture. Did they say when they would know?" Rico was serious again.

"In a few days. Rico?"

"Yes?"

"Thank you for being my friend. I feel so much better just talking to you. Just hurry up and get here."

"Hold on. I'm coming!"

We talked for a few more minutes and then said our good-byes. I tried to convince her to stay at Daddy's, but she was adamant. I couldn't wait to share this information with Roberta.

14

Facing the Music

The activity level in the dining room, den, and kitchen had increased threefold while I was in the bedroom on the phone. People seemed to occupy every square foot of the house. So many faces were familiar, yet I couldn't associate names with many of them. My fatigue weighed heavily, and I felt I was walking the thin line between grief and depression. I sought out Uncle Thomas. Being with him gave me an inexplicable comfort.

"See, I understand what my man was going through. Now you know ole Willie here got a few fillies in his stable. But I'm as much a man as I was twenty years ago. But with so many women, I need a little help from time to time."

"So what chu tryin' to say, Willie?" Uncle Thomas chuckled. "You wasn't much of a man twenty years ago, either?"

"You know how a man tries to get a woman to say his name? Ole Willie be havin' 'em spell his! W-I-L-L-I-E!"

"God gon' strike you dead lyin' like dat."

"Long as He don't strike mah johnson dead, we be just fine!"

"So what kinda hep you been gittin' wit' all yo' women? You taking them Viagra pills, too?" Uncle Thomas inquired. Both men were still unaware of my presence.

"I got me some herbs that do the same thang. Ole Sweet Daddy Willie here can go all . . . night . . . long!"

"See Ima move out of da way of da lightnin', 'cuz you just lyin'. Only thing that goes all night long on you is your pacemaker. Them young gals want one thang and one thang only from you. And it's dead!"

"Ain't a damn thang dead on me, Thomas. Nothing 'tall."

"I'm talking 'bout dead presidents, ya ole fool. Dem gals only want yo' money. Yo' ole ass can barely git out of bed in da morning."

"Maybe I gots me a reason for wanting to stay in bed, you old fart."

"Yeah 'n' dat reason's name is arthritis!"

"Thomas, my man, in case you didn't know, there are three thangs a man never wants to get out of."

"So tell me what dem three thangs is."

"Let me enlighten you, my brotha. A hot shower, a warm bed, and some good p—"

"Mister Willie!" I startled them both.

"Glynda, chile, how long ya been standin' dere?"

"Long enough, Uncle Thomas! Shame on you, Mister Willie!" I laughed.

"Glynda, baby, I just was speaking the truth." Willie grinned.

"Renee and Collette was looking for you, baby. They both looked kinda mad. But I guess that has been par for da course these past couple of days."

"I'll find them. You two better behave," I teased. I knew what lay in store for me when I came face-to-face with the terrible two.

I worked my way through the maze of friends and family, stopping occasionally to shake hands with some and hug others. The common thread connecting us all was disbelief that Eddie Naylor was gone. I found Renee,

Collette, and Dawn in the laundry room, with Collette hanging outside the door smoking.

"So, what were we supposed to do?" Dawn asked defensively.

"Oh, let's see . . . when all else fails, tell the truth!" Renee had that anger/sarcasm thing in full effect.

"We didn't lie to you." I came to my baby sister's defense.

"You're right. You didn't tell us anything. If Lette hadn't walked in when she did, God knows when we would have found out the truth," Renee spat.

"Y'all always overreact to everything. I'm sick of you two getting a little bit of information and then dwelling on it. You've always been that way. I admit, we were probably wrong, but all of this wasted energy and drama is what we're trying to avoid."

"Probably! See, that's what I'm talking about. You still don't see anything wrong with what you've done by keeping us in the dark. We know about two things. God only knows how many others there are."

"We've told you everything we know about everything. We swear." Dawn sounded like a ten-year-old pleading with her parents for forgiveness.

"She's right. But I've apologized all I plan to. You can either accept it or hug and kiss my narrow ass. Like I said, if you weren't such drama queens, we wouldn't even have to think about keeping stuff from you."

"All right, this is enough. We aren't going to start this ridiculous arguing again. It accomplishes nothing. Who were you talking to on the phone, Glynda?" Dawn tried changing the subject.

"Rico." I didn't feel like making peace.

"Oh, so when does the good doctor get here?" Collette closed the screen door as she crushed her half-smoked cigarette.

"My friend will be here tomorrow morning, along with her husband. I fully expect that you're going to be nice to her."

"As nice to her as you've been to Roberta?" Renee gladly interjected.

"Interesting you should ask. I begged her to stay here with me, and she said she wouldn't intrude. I find that quite interesting. Don't you?"

Rolling her eyes and working her neck sistahgurl style, Renee simply said, "Whatevah."

"So she thinks she's too good to stay at the house?" Collette pounced at the opportunity to start more mess.

"You know what? This conversation is over!" I turned abruptly to rejoin our guests.

If possible, it seemed as if even more people had arrived. Some spoke in low whispers while others laughed and made jokes about the good ole days with Daddy. Sister Greene was in command of the kitchen, and she barked orders to others wearing white uniforms with a patch on the sleeve that read WILLING WORKERS BOARD MEMBER. Everyone had either a plate or a cup in hand. There was another group of Willing Workers that was cleaning. Had I not known better, I would have thought this was a party. I stood in the midst of all these people, yet I felt so alone.

"You look lost." As I turned, I was face-to-face with my first love, Michael Brockington.

"Oh, Michael!" Instinctively I hugged him. Michael and I had been sweethearts from the fourth grade until I left for college. We'd promised to stay together no matter what as we went off to colleges on opposite ends of the continent. We had remained close the first semester of our freshman year, writing and calling constantly.

When we returned home for Christmas vacation, something was different about him. Though his mouth professed all was still the same, the guilt behind his eyes betrayed him. On New Year's Eve at five minutes to midnight, he finally told me he had met someone who attended Spelman. He said his nights at Morehouse had been lonely and that she was there. I'd thrown my drink in his face and ran to find a phone, crying.

Of course, the phone call I made was to Daddy to pick me up. Michael was pleading with me to forgive him on the steps of Delores Butler's lavish home when Daddy arrived. I fully expected him to pick me up and take me straight home, but instead he first wanted to have a tête-à-tête with Michael. Daddy leapt from the car and seemed to be on the porch with us in two steps. Towering over Michael, he explained to him he would never have a second chance to make me cry.

Despite his calling every fifteen minutes, Daddy wouldn't let him speak with me. After three days Michael simply gave up. When I returned to school in mid-January, a four-page letter waited for me from Michael, explaining that he would always love me but he needed to have a woman who was in the same city. It had taken us more than five years before we spoke again.

"I know this is a stupid question, but how are you, Glynda? You look wonderful!" Michael was as handsome as he was the first day I saw him in grade school.

"Sometimes I'm okay and other times I feel like I'm so out of control. And you ain't looking too shabby yourself." I slipped from his embrace.

"Well, just don't expect too much from yourself. This is really hard stuff to deal with. I heard you passed the bar. Congrats!"

"How did you know that?"

"There isn't much I don't know about you. I've always kept tabs."

"You're kidding me, right?"

"Why are you so surprised? I've loved you since I was in the fourth grade. When I got to college, all those fine sistahs across the quad sent my wrong head into a spin, but my heart always belonged to you. Mr. Naylor scared me so bad with his threats to castrate me that I just left you alone. I haven't been in one meaningful relationship in all these years."

"Wow! How did you find out about Daddy?"

"I work at the plant. I head up their engineering department."

"So you and Daddy worked together and he never told me?"

"Believe it or not, he was still mad at me for hurting you. He pretended like he didn't know who I was, but he did. Hell, he still scared me. When they posted the notice on our Intranet, I knew I had to come."

"Oh, Michael, I'm so glad you did! It's so wonderful to see you again. Have you eaten?"

"The good sisters here have fed a brotha well." He laughed, rubbing his stomach.

"Have you seen my sisters?"

"Yeah, but I didn't say anything to them yet. Dawn sure did grow up nice!"

"That she did. She grew out of her tomboy ways with style, didn't she?" It felt good to laugh with an old friend.

We continued to talk for several minutes, catching up on old friends and long-forgotten times. We made promises to stay in touch, and I told him I wanted him to meet Anthony. He declined.

The crowd began to thin. Each group left quietly, promising to return with more food and comfort in the days to come. Struggling for the right words played tricks with people's hearts and minds. Some barely said anything, while others rambled on endlessly.

"I'm heading out to pick up Jimmy from the airport,"

Estelle said. "We'll be back in the morning around ten or so. Miss Hollywood will be in on Friday morning at five." Estelle hugged me as she gathered her things to leave.

"She must be on the same flight as Rico and Jonathan, just a day later. Estelle, thank you for everything. We'll make it through these next few days somehow."

"Did you hear from the lawyer?" Estelle looked troubled.

"No, I'm sorry, we didn't." I wondered if I should tell her what we'd discovered so far.

"I just know my Eddie was faithful to me, Glynda. I just know he was."

I hugged her but said nothing.

"Tell Jamaica to call me when he gets to your house. I love him so much. He's like the brother I never had."

"Chile, now you know my Jimmy is more like the sister you wished you didn't have!" We both laughed and hugged each other again. The release felt good.

Shortly thereafter, Estelle and I said good night. The others followed close behind, leaving just immediate family. "Renee, are you and the kids spending the night?" I really wanted us all to stay together.

"No, we're going home, but I'll be back first thing in the morning. Derrick junior wants to spend the night with Devin, though. I wonder why the lawyer didn't call us back today?"

"I wondered the same thing. It couldn't take this long to pull the file. This seems a little odd to me," I said, holding Renee's hand.

"This whole thing is odd to me. Daddy taking Viagra. Naming strange folks in the will, us fighting like we live in the projects. Quite strange indeed." Renee spoke the words with no particular recipient in mind. I felt her anguish.

"Dawn, are you and Devin spending the night?" I yelled to the kitchen, where Dawn and Collette were drinking laced coffee and eating chocolate cake.

"Considering how much Irish cream and coffee I've had, I don't think I have a choice," Dawn answered as I entered the room.

"Good. Derrick junior is staying, too. What about you, Collette?" I asked, though I knew the answer.

"No, I need to be home in my own bed. Maybe tomorrow night. I guess we'd better get going so we can get some sleep tonight. This may be the last opportunity we have for a good night's rest until after this is all over."

I found it quite interesting that Renee and Collette didn't want to spend the night together, but Dawn and I did. "What time will you be over in the morning? I want to call the lawyer first thing, since he didn't call us back today."

"I'll be here at eight thirty." Collette responded quickly.

"I guess I'll be here at the same time. I saw you and Estelle talking before she left. Did you tell her what you found out today?"

"No, I thought about it and then changed my mind. We may as well wait until we have some definite answers before we start sharing information."

"My God, we actually agree on something!" Renee started to laugh.

"Yeah, I guess we do." I, too, laughed as I hugged her.

15

Mending Fences

I woke to the harmonious breathing of my baby sister. She lay next to me snoring lightly. We'd talked for what seemed like hours before I drifted into a dreamless sleep. Our conversation ranged from our teen years to her somewhat troubled relationship with Reginald.

Reginald and Dawn had been dating for more than five years. She loved that brotha's athletic supporter after a basketball tournament. Reginald White was twelve years Dawn's senior and was almost divorced from his fifth wife. In my opinion Mr. White had some serious issues. I thought back to a conversation we'd had at my college graduation party when I explained how difficult it was to understand his finger pointing to his five previous wives when he was the one who'd made the choices.

According to him, everything that had failed in his marriages was no fault of his. He'd been the model husband. Yeah, okay. I felt sad for Dawn because her self-esteem had plummeted her into a quagmire of self-doubt and she felt Reginald was all she deserved.

On one elbow I watched her sleep and said a silent prayer that she would soon realize that no one could neglect or use her without her consent. I leaned over and kissed her, then got up to head into the bathroom before the rest of the crew awakened. I was so grateful for my first dreamless sleep since all of this had happened. I really wanted to go for a run to clear my head, but I still felt so heavy. As I stepped on the scale in Daddy's bathroom, it revealed that I'd lost three pounds. I thought of Dr. Barnett from my flight and dismissed the inclination to call him.

I showered quickly and dressed in my running clothes in case I changed my mind. The smell of fresh-brewing coffee signaled Uncle Thomas's arrival in the kitchen. I went to join him.

"Good morning. How's my favorite uncle?"

"Yo' only uncle is jus' fine. How 'bout chu, baby?"

"I actually slept really good last night. Dawn's snoring didn't even keep me awake. Uncle Thomas, please don't tell the others, but I'll be so glad when this is over. I feel so guilty for even thinking that."

"Why ya feelin' guilty? Chile, lookie here. If I could git away wit' not bein' a part of all of dis mess, I'd be somewhere fishin' and remembrin' da good, good times."

"Oh, Uncle Thomas, I'm so glad to hear you say that. I didn't want anyone else to know I just want this to be over. It's too hard. And the hard part hasn't even started yet."

"Baby, don't I know it. I sho' 'nuff don't know how Ima be able to look down at my brother in a coffin. I just don't know." Uncle Thomas hid his face in his hands to muffle his sobs.

"It's okay, Uncle Thomas. Somewhere in the Scriptures it promises that God won't put more on us than we can bear. He's really putting that one to the test. You makin' any grits to go with that coffee?"

"Grits? Chile, I could undastan' biscuits or even toast. But grits?"

"Just a country girl caught up in a big-city world." I hugged him tight and kissed him on the cheek. "You remember when we were kids, shortly after Mama died, you'd come over every Saturday morning to make breakfast for us. Daddy was a wonderful father, but it was no secret he was gourmetically challenged."

"If dat means he couldn't cook, den say ya right!"

We both laughed.

"That was the only area in which he lacked, though. From the very first day as a single parent, Daddy was so dedicated. He never missed a beat. Sister Greene always came by, but she hardly had anything at all to do. Daddy cleaned, washed clothes, helped with our homework. I can't remember one time he failed to meet the challenge. He never complained, either. I know he'd be so tired after working all night, making sure we got off to school on time. I hadn't ever really thought about it, but I can't remember ever seeing him sleep. He was always up when we got home from school. Ready to help with whatever we needed. Made dinner, such as it was, then would watch TV with us until we went to bed. Then he would be here when we got up in the morning."

"He was some kinda man, dat's fo' sho'."

"Who do you think Nina Blackford is?"

"Honest ta God, I don't know. Yo' daddy was a proud man. According to dem papers, she is three years olda dan Renee. I sho' don't believe it's 'notha woman. He'd a told me fo' sho'."

"We found her phone number yesterday and called her." I braced myself for his reaction.

Turning slowly, he stared through me before speaking. "And?"

I was in emotional turmoil. I wanted to believe him, but how could I? "She wasn't there. Edwina answered the phone." I searched his face for a reaction.

There was none. I didn't know what to make of his lack of reaction. "Uncle Thomas, you know the truth will come out. You should tell me what you know. Don't make this harder than it already is!" My voice had raised a few octaves.

"I don't rightly know what chu talkin' 'bout. I was waitin' on ya to tell *me* who she is." He didn't make eye contact.

Cross-examining my uncle was the last thing I wanted to do. "She's a smart-mouth teenager who said she would give Nina the message to call us back. Since she didn't call last night, I plan to call back today after I speak to the lawyer. As soon as the others get here, we're going to get to the bottom of this mystery."

"Jus' be careful where you dig, 'cause you may jus' hit a gas line and cause an explosion."

"What are you trying to say?"

"Don't go lookin' fo' answers ta questions betta left unaxed."

"I'm a lawyer, Uncle Thomas. There's no such thing."

"I hope you don't make yo'self sorry, is all I'm tryin' ta say." Uncle Thomas busied himself with breakfast preparations. I watched his aging body move about the kitchen. He was hiding something. I could feel it.

"Call yo' sisters to see what time dey's comin' ovah. I don't want to make breakfast and have it get cold."

"They said by eight thirty. But I say we concern ourselves with those who are here and let those not here fend for themselves."

The phone interrupted Uncle Thomas's response. "Good morning. This is Glynda Naylor. . . . Good morning, Mr. Shapiro." My heart started pounding at the sound of the lawyer's voice. "I'm anxious to know the answer to our question."

"Well, Ms. Naylor, I don't know how much help I'm going to be. There's no indication in the file as to Ms. Blackford's relationship to your father. We do have an address and phone number for her, however. Do you want the information or should we make the contact? Are you aware you have been named as executor?"

"No." More eloquent conversation escaped me.

"Is that the answer to both questions?"

"I'm sorry. No, I don't want you to make contact, and no, I didn't know I was named executor."

"Again, we'd like to express our condolences to you and your family. Mr. Naylor had been our client for only a short time, but he left quite an impression with the staff."

"That's how Daddy was, Mr. Shapiro. I'll be sure to convey your message to my sisters."

"We'll need to set a meeting for the official reading of the will, whenever it's convenient for you."

"I'll get back to you in a day or so. I'd like to get that done before I return to California, if possible."

"Not a problem, just speak with my secretary, and she'll schedule it. Again, I'm sorry for your loss."

"Thank you." I hung up the phone.

Uncle Thomas was transfixed. Standing in the middle of the kitchen floor with the cooking spoon in hand, he asked, "Well?"

"We're no closer to solving the Nina mystery. He has the same information we found in Daddy's phone book. Who's this mystery woman?"

"Baby, I dunno." Uncle Thomas turned to the stove.

"You know the truth will come out eventually. So if you're holding out on me, there's no point. He's dead. What can we do to him?"

"I done tol' chu I don't know, now quit axin' me. Actin' like ya don't believe me!" An exposed nerve had been hit.

"Uncle Thomas, I don't know what to believe. Please don't get upset with me. We just need answers."

"Well, I ain't got 'em."

There was a long silence before I left the kitchen. I returned to Daddy's bedroom, where Dawn had finally stirred. She was sitting up in bed staring into space.

"Good morning," I said in a defeated tone.

"Morning. I reserve the good for later. I heard your conversation with the lawyer and then words with Uncle Thomas. I just don't understand this." Dawn climbed out of bed.

"Yeah, me either. But I know I couldn't stand to have Uncle Thomas mad at me. So I'm just going to leave it alone. The truth will come out sooner or later. I find it interesting that Nina Blackford didn't call back last night. I wonder if Edwina gave her the message."

"It's still early in Missouri. Why don't you call her now?" Dawn called from the bathroom.

I stared at her for a long moment. For the first time I realized I wasn't sure if I really wanted to speak to this woman who obviously held the answers to many questions. "I'll get the number."

Derrick and Devin had slept on the sofa bed with the television on low volume. The morning news told of overnight violence that had claimed the lives of two teenage boys. My heart immediately wept for the families of the victims. I could remember hearing news reports of deaths for nearly my whole life, but it had never affected me quite this way before. I could now comprehend the horrible pain that those left behind had to survive.

Thumbing through Daddy's phone book, I saw the names of many women whom I didn't know. Did they, too, have secrets about my daddy?

My hands trembled as I dialed the number. Ring one, heart pounding. Ring two, palms beginning to sweat. Ring three, mouth going dry. Ring four, voice mail. Breathing a sigh of relief, I began, "Ms. Blackford. My name is Glynda Naylor, and it's imperative that you call me as soon as possible. I left a message for you yesterday with Edwina. This concerns Edward Naylor." I left the number and hurriedly hung up the phone.

"I guess she's an early riser. This will all work out, Glyn." Dawn stood next to me, smelling of Listerine.

"Promise?"

"It has to. Did everyone get in okay last night and this morning?"

"I'm assuming they did. I didn't call Rico and Jonathan yet. They're probably still sleeping. I know Jamaica is still sleeping. I'll call around ten if we haven't heard from them. Should I call Lette and Renee to tell them what the lawyer said or wait until they get here?"

"Gurl, now you know you'd better call them. We're already in deep ca-ca!"

I laughed despite my heavy heart, and reached for the phone to dial. "You've got a point."

Renee picked up on the first ring.

"Good morning." I added about a teaspoon of cheer to my voice.

"Morning, gurl. How's everybody over there?" Renee sounded tired.

"The boys still aren't up, but the rest of us seem to be okay so far. What time are you coming over?"

"I'm getting everyone ready now. Derrick has them marching like little soldiers, of course. So I'd say around nine thirty or ten. Why?"

"A couple of things. Uncle Thomas, of course, is making breakfast, including stewed apples. And the lawyer called this morning."

"Already? Dang! So what did he have to say? Please tell me he told us who this Nina person is."

"Sorry, he was no help at all. He said Daddy didn't indicate his relationship to this person. He did have her phone number and address. Asked if I wanted to contact her or should he do it. I told him I'd handle it. I left another message for her, but this time it was on her voice mail. I guess she gets out kinda early."

"Have you told Collette yet?"

"No, I'll call her next. I guess we should've done a three-way."

"Hang on. Let's do it now. You know she is going to want to know why the lawyer doesn't know, why the woman didn't answer the phone. She'll just be ranting and raving. Maybe with both of us on the phone it won't be so bad."

"You're kidding, right?" We both laughed.

Collette was out of breath when she picked up the phone. "Hey, gurl, how're you this morning?" Renee's number had come up on Lette's caller ID box.

"As Sissy said, so far, so good. She's on the line, too."

"Good morning," she said.

I wasn't certain, but I think I heard a different tone in her voice as she spoke to me. "Good morning to you, too. Why're you out of breath?"

"Trying to work out some of this stress. This Tae Bo will kill your ass! Let me grab some water. Hang on."

"She sounds like she's in a good mood," Renee said, using Collette's time away from the phone to assess her mood meter—something we'd all learned to do when she was a teenager. When she was in the red zone, we all stayed out of her path. Misreading Collette's mood could prove fatal for one's psyche.

"But we know that can change in a microsecond," I added without hesitation.

"Okay, I'm back. So to what pleasure, or displeasure, do I owe this joint call, so early in the morning?"

"The lawyer called and said he doesn't know who Nina Blackford is either. Relationship isn't listed. He had her address and phone number, which of course we have already. I left her a message on her voice mail this time. Told her it was imperative she gets in touch with me. Hopefully that will do it."

"You shoulda told her she had some money coming. She would've called you by now. Well, let me shower and I'll be right over in case she calls. Where's Dawn?"

"She's right here. She says good morning, too."

"Tell her to pick up the extension," Collette barked in her normal, no-nonsense tone.

"I'll ask her to get the extension," I replied sarcastically.

"You know what I meant." Our civility was short-lived.

"Good morning, my sisters."

"Hey, baby sis," Renee responded.

Collette wasted no time with pleasantries. "So what do y'all think?"

"About what?" I asked.

"Like you aren't thinking the same thing. Do you think this Edwina person is our sister?" Collette couldn't help being the way she was all the time.

"I can't believe Daddy would have another daughter and not tell us. Didn't tell Uncle Thomas, Estelle, nobody?" Renee added.

"That's pretty hard to believe. Who the hell can Nina Blackford be? Why would he have an affair with someone, marry Estelle, and then leave her in his will? None of this makes sense," Dawn interjected.

"We should find out soon enough. I'm hoping she calls when she gets the message I left this morning. I'm not convinced that child, Edwina, gave her the message."

"You guys just get over here. We need to be together when she calls. I love you," Dawn continued. The feeling of love and closeness that Daddy had instilled in us returned to me.

And with a warmth and kindness I hadn't heard from Collette in a lot of years, she replied, "Give me forty-five minutes."

"Well, Derrick is getting the kids ready so I should be able to just get me ready in an hour. I'll see you all soon. Tell Uncle Thomas to save me some food." With Renee we all knew that meant two hours.

We said our good-byes and broke the connection. Dawn slowly entered the kitchen with tears streaming. "What if Daddy has a secret life and we find out he was a horrible person. That would be worse than him dying to me."

"First of all, there's no way Daddy was a horrible person. At worst he has a teenage daughter who's out of control. Why he chose not to tell us, we'll just have to wait and see. Second, with each other we can weather any storm. Remember God promised not to take us where His grace can't keep us." I hugged her.

"Y'all go wake dem boys up. I declare young people need da most rest I evah seen. Breakfas'll be ready in a few minutes. I want y'all ta have mah biscuits right out da oven." Uncle Thomas waved the spatula as he spoke.

We woke Devin and Derrick, telling them that Uncle Thomas was going to get the switch after them if they didn't get a move on and to clean up the mess they had made in the den.

Before we got through the first course of breakfast, Collette arrived. Though the dark circles under her eyes were prominent, she looked rested and color had returned to her cheeks. Even in biker shorts and a tank, my sister looked gorgeous.

"Good morning, all. Uncle Thomas, I worked out for

an hour and a half this morning, and I'm going to blow it all in a matter of seconds at this table."

"Oh, Auntie Collette, you're foine! My homies asked me just the other day how old you are. They wanted da hookup." Derrick beamed with pride.

"Boy, I would be put under the jail. But some of them brothas on the football team need to call a sistah when they get out of college." Collette laughed as she spoke.

"Lawdhamurcy, we gonna pray for your yellow school bus–chasing butt. Mothers hide your sons, my sister Collette is in town." Dawn looked to me for backup.

"Gurl, I can't help it I like 'em young. You only gotta date one old geezer to appreciate a black man in his youth. Whoa, Glory!" Collette pretended to feel the moving of the Spirit.

"See you ain't right," I said. "You betta get a plate. You can worry about that tiny waist if you want to and leave these grits here for me to finish off. This is why I wear stretch pants." Dawn and I high-fived each other.

It felt so good to laugh like old times. I didn't know how long it would be before grief would seep back into the very pores of my existence, but I was going to enjoy this moment.

16

And on the Third Day...

The phone started ringing nonstop before we were able to finish breakfast. Many were calls from friends expressing their condolences and offering to do whatever they could to help. Soon Renee arrived in her usual chaotic fashion.

We'd failed to decide on the floral arrangements. That became the first order of business after we'd stored the leftovers, made a fresh pot of coffee for lacing, and moved to the den.

"We'd talked about gardenias yesterday. I think that would make a lovely casket spray," Dawn commented, starting the discussion.

"What about white orchids? That's what I remember most about Ron Brown's funeral," Renee said, pouring Baileys in her cup.

"Oh, you mean the secretary of commerce who was killed in the plane crash?" I said, thinking back. "Those flowers were beautiful. All of his flowers were white. Very nice touch. Very, very nice." I really liked the idea of all white flowers.

"What do you think, Collette?" Renee asked.

"I'm sure it doesn't matter what I think. Sounds like you three have made up your minds."

"Please, Lette, let's not argue about this, too. It's such

a simple thing. Tell us what you want." Trying to appease Collette was making me sick to my stomach.

"White flowers are fine. But why do we have to pick the most expensive ones?" Collette looked at each of us in turn. "We could do a combination of white flowers that would be more cost-effective: gladiolus, carnations, a few roses. What you're proposing will cost at least five hundred dollars. This is a funeral, not a wedding."

Somebody needed to lay hands on this woman and have a word of prayer. She actually thought we would entertain her suggestion without incident. "May I remind you," I said, "that Daddy paid for not only a wedding but a divorce for you? And how much were the flowers for the marriage that didn't last as long as the car payments on a Hyundai?" I did nothing to hide my annoyance.

"What does that have to do with anything, Glynda? Why're you bringing up my marriages?"

"Not your marriages. Your wedding, a social event to be rivaled by the Kennedys. Daddy never hesitated to give you what you wanted. I know you had five thousand dollars in flowers. So if your only concern about our choices in flowers is the cost, don't worry your parsimonious ass one little minute about it because you have no say-so in the amount we spend. I told you two days ago not to mention money again, and nothing has changed."

"I see how this is. When Renee said we were spending too much for a casket, she was a hero. But every time I mention money, I'm some kind of heavy."

"It's not that." Dawn touched her arm trying to calm her.

"Then what the hell is it?" Collette pulled away. "I always knew you and Glynda took sides against me, but Renee, I'm really shocked at you!"

"No one's taking sides against you. You need to stop being so sensitive. The difference here is I knew we could get the desired casket for less money. You always want to compromise to save money. There's a big difference." Renee got up from the couch and moved to the window seat overlooking the backyard.

"How's that different? We both want to save money. We'll spend five hundred dollars for flowers that will last for two days, then be thrown away."

"Do you even realize why people send flowers for funerals?" Now I was starting to feel sorry for her because she was either so self-absorbed that she couldn't comprehend our stance or she was just plain stupid. Either way it was a very sad state of affairs.

"I'm about sick and tired of your attitude toward me, Glynda. You've done nothing but accuse me of being cheap since you got here."

"Hit dog will holler!" I was mad, again.

"This is getting us nowhere. We've done so well so far this morning. We should buy whatever flowers the majority agrees upon. Let's just put this to a vote and stop arguing." Renee was aggravated.

"Like I said in the beginning, you didn't care what I wanted anyway. So y'all pick your five-hundred-dollar arrangements and five-thousand-dollar caskets. Acting like we the Trumps. That is just too much money to put into the ground."

"Collette, let it go. This is not our money. Daddy left it here for us to spend on his funeral, and as I said before, anyone who has put as much money into their body as you have needs to just sit back, shut up, and agree with whatever we decide." All gloves were off.

"Yes, but whatever we don't spend comes to us. I just think it is irresponsible to spend money needlessly."

"All in favor of white casket spray with orchids and

gardenias, raise your hand." Two of my three sisters voted with me.

"Next floral arrangement is from the grandchildren," Renee volunteered.

"I hope that you're taking it out of their share of the estate money since y'all get more than the rest of us," Collette said.

The rest of us acted as though Collette were invisible.

"Are we going with the white theme throughout all of the family arrangements?" Dawn asked.

"I think Collette's suggestion of carnations, gladiolus, and roses would be a nice arrangement from the grandchildren. What do you all think?" Renee was trying to make peace.

"I like that idea and it won't cost that much, though we should make it really big." I didn't give a damn about Collette's feelings.

"That works for me," Dawn was quick to agree.

"Good, two down. We just need to speak with Estelle and Uncle Thomas," Renee added.

"Has Uncle Thomas heard from Thomas junior and Michael?" Dawn asked.

"Oh wow. I haven't asked him since Monday night. He said he'd left a message with Michael's wife. I forgot to ask him if he'd called back. He doesn't even know how to get in touch with June Bug." I was embarrassed by my selfishness.

"Gurl, it makes no sense for them boys to act like that toward their daddy. They're gonna be so sorry when he's gone. Their mother let her bad feelings toward Uncle Thomas ruin any chance of a father-son relationship for them. That's why Uncle Thomas was always so close to us." Renee stared mindlessly out of the bay window into the yard.

"Well, when a man cheats on a woman, he has to accept whatever fate comes his way." Collette spoke for the first time since we'd shut her down about the flowers.

"But he didn't do anything to June Bug and Michael," I said. "He wanted so bad to be near them. But she refused to give up any information on where they were. Then, when they got old enough to do it on their own, they looked at him as the one who never reached out to them. What a mess. Now their uncle is dead and they may not even come to his funeral because of some dumb shit from the past." I couldn't help pleading Uncle Thomas's case.

"How long has it been since we saw them?" Renee asked.

"At least twenty years. So I don't hold out much hope of them coming to the funeral of a man they hardly knew." I wondered where Uncle Thomas had disappeared to.

"Well, I just understand about a cheating man. Uncle or no uncle, if you're wrong, you're wrong." Collette pulled a cigarette from her pocket and headed toward the back door.

"Collette, you know, unless you let go of some of your hatred, you'll always be unhappy," Dawn said.

I don't know why Dawn always walked into the lion's den wearing a pork-chop jacket.

"Well, thank you, Dr. Grace Cornish! I'll take your advice into consideration. All of us can't be happy in bad relationships with losers the way you can. But when you have a bastard child, I guess you have to accept whatever you can get."

"That's quite enough, Collette!" Renee said, raising her voice. "You have gone too got-damn far this time, calling Devin a bastard. And with your choices in men, I don't think you have any room to talk. Why are you always so mean-spirited? You never have a kind or supportive thing to say about anyone. Dawn was just trying to help. You're never happy about anything but your investment portfolio. I have a news flash for you, and you can ask Daddy about his if you don't believe me. You can't take it with you! I don't care how much money and things you acquire in this life, it's all going to stay right here." Renee was pacing.

"She started it, indicating there's something wrong with me because I don't love and kiss everybody's ass the way she does. I could care less what people think of me, including y'all."

"I didn't mean to hurt your feelings, Lette. I just hate to see you so unhappy all the time."

"Who said I'm unhappy?"

"That's evident by how you always find reasons to argue and dislike others," Dawn said. "You're always doing something to alter the way you look naturally. And don't think we don't know you've had liposuction. Do you know how many women have died as a result of that procedure?" Dawn had opened a very sensitive wound.

"I haven't had . . ." Collette knew it was futile to deny her surgery. She dropped her head, then looked from one to the other of us to see if we were shocked by this revelation. "You all know?"

"We've known from the beginning, Lette," I said softly. "But we don't care. We love you with all of your strengths and weaknesses. You're grown. Do what you want to do, but you need to lighten up on other folks. You need to stop saying mean and hateful things to and about people. You betta apologize to Dawn and Devin, and if I *evah* hear you say something like that again, I'll personally slap you so hard your taste buds will be doing salsa on the floor."

"Y'all are always the ones picking on me. I'm just defending myself. If you think I'm so mean-spirited, why haven't you said something before now? Why did you have to wait until we're all going through the worst period of our lives to psychoanalyze me?"

"You're such a drama queen." Renee started laughing as she continued. "We tell your ass *all the time*. You just never listen. Now go on outside, get your smoke on, and don't bring your ass back up in here until you're ready to apologize for saying such a mean thing to Dawn."

"She doesn't have to apologize to me. But she sure as hell needs to apologize to my baby. You are a heartless, selfish bitch who'll die lonely and shriveled up. Hatred destroys the hater," Dawn spoke through clenched teeth, her bloodshot eyes firing daggers at Collette.

I agreed with Dawn and added, "I just know you need to check yourself before you wreck yourself. We love you, but your ugly ways are another story."

"Let it go, Glynda! We've made our point." Renee thought she was my mama again. "When Estelle gets here, we're going to have to sit down to do the obituary. Promise me we're not going to start World War Three over this."

"Ask me no questions, and I'll tell you no lies. I just know we're not putting seventy-five percent of the free world down as relatives and friends," yelled Collette from the back door.

Before I could respond, the phone rang. I picked up. "Hello, Glynda Naylor speaking."

"Just the diva I wanted to speak to." Rico always had perfect timing.

"Oh Rico, I'm so happy to hear from you. You guys get any rest since you got in?"

"Jonathan is still sleeping. But I'm having a hard time resting worrying about you. How's everything going?"

"Well, aside from the constant pain in our chests, we seem to be doing okay. What time will you be over?"

"That's why I'm calling, to see if you need me to do anything. I got your suit and shoes. Do you or your sisters need to go shopping for anything? We want to order flowers, too. Have you ordered yours yet?"

"We just decided what kind of flowers we're ordering a few minutes ago. We are using the florist the funeral home recommended. We've decided that all of the flowers from family and close friends will be white."

"When in the hell did we decide friends' flowers would be white?" Collette said, returning to the den.

"We have an arrangement we always send. It's all yellow. I hope that will be okay." Rico had overheard Collette's comment, which, of course, had been her intent.

"Yes, an all-yellow arrangement will be fine." I rolled my eyes at Collette. "Maybe I'll tell Roberta you're doing that and she can do the same. So all of the close family friends can do all-yellow arrangements."

"How's Roberta handling all of this?"

"It's been interesting, to say the least."

"I bet. Well, I'm going to crawl back in bed with my very sexy and handsome husband, and we'll see you around three. We're stopping at the grocery store to get food. Is there anything in particular you all would like to eat? Jonathan wants to barbecue. Would that be okay with everyone? He feels like he needs to do something."

"Oh, that sounds wonderful. You know that man can cook some meat on a grill! We have lots of food, but I guess if you want to bring something in particular, staples like bread, milk, and juice. The children are here, and people don't seem to think of the things they need and like."

"Consider it done. I'll pick up fun food for them, too. How are they handling the loss of their grandpa?"

"Devin seems the most affected. He just seems to be sleeping most of the time. Derrick spent the night with him last night, so he seems a little better this morning. Rico, just get yourself on over here, gurl, I need you!"

"I'll see you at three. Love you."

"Back at cha."

As I hung up the phone, I caught Renee's and Collette's gazes. "Why are y'all staring at me?"

"I just wanted to get a clear view of what a hypocrite looks like." There was no levity in Renee's tone.

"Now what are you referring to?"

"How you have a double standard for close family friends. While Roberta isn't as polished as Rico, she loves this family and me with all of her heart, and you have treated her with the same disrespect you have accused Collette of."

"I have issues with Roberta and how she imposes herself on this family. She always has. Rico knows her place, and that's as my friend. She only wants to do what she can, to lift our burden in any way she can. Roberta *is* a burden. But in all fairness, I had a talk with Roberta and I saw her pain, and I'm willing to back off a bit. I just need you and her to understand that she is not Eddie Naylor's daughter."

"Why y'all always at each otha's throats?" Uncle Thomas had returned.

"Where you been, Uncle?" I was thrilled he interrupted the potentially volatile situation.

"I had to git away fo' a few minutes. I went down ta da boys' and girls' club ta talk ta da director. Dey right heartbroken. I wanted ta see if some of dem boys wanted ta say somethin' at da funeral. Eddie'd really like dat."

"What an awesome idea. You're right, Daddy would've loved that. We should give time to anyone who wants to speak at the funeral. Limiting their comments to two to three minutes, though." Renee spoke the words I was thinking.

"We settled on white flowers from all of us and yellow from close friends of the family. Did you want to get a basket arrangement for the foot of the casket?" Dawn asked, walking over to hug him.

"Dat'd be right nice. Den maybe Estelle can git one dat matches it fo' da other end ta balance it out. Willie wants ta get flowers in the shape of some dominoes. Dat man is a mess fo' sho'. I tol' him I needed to check with y'all first."

"We can't tell him how to spend his money. But as Daddy's best friend, you may want to tell him about the yellow-flowers idea. Maybe the dominoes club could do the arrangement shaped like dominoes. Someone called from there last night asking for the details to send flowers," Dawn said.

"You think that is appropriate for a church funeral?" Collette asked.

"What's wrong with flowers shaped like dominoes? Daddy played all the time, and I surely don't think they would've kept him out of heaven!" Renee responded quickly.

"I just asked. Forget I brought it up. Whatever y'all want, since I'm outvoted on every issue anyway!"

"I went by Estelle's house on mah way back from da boys' and girls' club. She'll be ovah in a few minutes. I jus' wanted ta make sho' she was doin' aiight. This thang is weighin' on heh real heavy. Dis here mystery woman ain't helpin' none eitha."

"Did you see Jamaica?" I really wanted to see my buddy.

"Chile, that boy look mo' like a woman than any of y'all! He took one look at me 'n' started bawlin'. Dat chile loved yo' daddy!"

"Yes, he did," I stated. "He and I are in touch all the time by e-mail, and he always talked about how Daddy was so special. Daddy sent him e-mail, too, from time to time, and you would've thought he got a check in the mail he was so happy. I hope he agrees to sing at the funeral. He's so very talented."

"That would be good if he sings," Dawn agreed.

"Domino flowers and gay singers. First United will never be the same." Collette rolled her eyes and sucked her teeth.

"Chile, dat boy's heart is pure as gol', and while I know what the Bible says, I wish I knowed a dozen mo' good people like him."

Collette only stared at all of us.

17

Coming Home

Dawn placed the floral order and we decided we were hungry again. It was phenomenal how no matter what we ate, we were still hungry, and no matter what or how much we drank, we remained sober.

Collette was surprisingly quiet and withdrawn. As much as she worked my nerves, I didn't like to see her this way. "Hey, you. You okay?"

"What do you care?"

"You know it's not like that. We have very different opinions about so many things. But I do love you. I sure hope you know that. When you're not giving one of us a hard time, I get worried."

"Whatever."

Before I could respond, a clatter from the foyer caught our attention. Estelle arrived carrying several bags. On her heels came Jamaica, dressed in burgundy pants, silk shirt, and matching patent-leather shoes. His silky shoulder-length hair bounced with every step, and his nails were flawlessly French-manicured. Only a true diva looked so good this early in the day. Jamaica!

"Oh Sissy, I'm so sorry!" Jamaica ran into my arms and began crying.

"Jimmy, I'm so glad to see you. You're so kind to fly in from Paris."

"Kind? Your daddy was the man. He was enough man

in himself that me being me didn't bother him. I could tell you stories of so many times I came to him crying because I couldn't go to my own father. So please don't insult me by thanking me for doing what has to be done."

"Nonetheless, I'm so glad to see you. Let me look at you. You look stunning. I wish I rolled out of bed looking like this."

"I know that's right," Renee added.

"Renee, sis, how are you?" Jamaica hugged Renee long and tight.

"I'm better now that you're here. I agree with Glynda, you look marvelous, darling!"

"Oh brother," Collette whispered with a deep, over-exaggerated sigh.

"Collette," Jamaica said, nodding politely. "It's good to see you, too."

Collette refused to acknowledge Jamaica's greeting. Pulling another cigarette from her pocket, she again headed for the back door.

"What's a sistah gotta do to get some love up in here?" Dawn asked, extending her arms.

"Oh Dawn, I'm sorry, boo. You know I love you. You look so good! You snagged one of them fine doctors yet?" Jamaica kissed her on the cheek as he hugged her.

Though Jamaica and Dawn were only six months apart in age, he and I were by far the closest. Dawn was a close second, however. Dawn and I were the least judgmental and loved Jamaica even when he wasn't sure who or what he wanted to be.

"I'm sooooo sorry about Papa Eddie. I've been crying since the moment I heard. I couldn't even perform that night. My understudy is thrilled. I haven't missed a performance in two years."

"I'd love to see you dance. If you dance anything like you sing, then, man!" Dawn held his hand.

"I'm thinking of moving to Paris. They're so much more accepting of me there. I'm a real star in the city of lights, honey," Jamaica said, snapping his fingers in a Z formation.

"Well, baby, you've always been my star." Estelle held his face in both hands as she kissed him.

"Spoken like a true mama." Jamaica hugged her back.

"Guilty as accused," Estelle said, beaming with pride.

"Where've you fellas been?" Dawn asked, as Devin and Derrick junior entered the dining room.

"We went running. Mom, you should try it. It will make you feel better," Devin jokingly said to Dawn.

"Boy, you shouldn't even joke like that," Dawn said, laughing.

"We need to settle this obituary mess," Collette said from the doorway, a cynical look on her face.

"Collette, why does it have to be a mess?" Dawn said, annoyed that Collette had interrupted the playful banter between mother and son.

"You know it is. All kinds of folks who aren't related to him will want to be listed. And my vote counts about as much as those Florida folks' votes did back in two thousand. So let's just get on with it! Anybody want coffee or tea? I may as well have some purpose for being here." We heard the clatter as Collette filled the teakettle in the kitchen.

"I think I'll have some chamomile to calm my nerves," Jamaica said. "I'm really trying not to take these Valiums, but you know a girl gotta do what a girl gotta do."

"Let's hope the tea does the trick," I replied, smiling at my friend. "We've been lacing everything with cognac. I'm not sure if it has done much to calm our nerves. We've been fighting since the first phone call."

"Ain't dat da truf!" Uncle Thomas piped in.

"Uncle Thomas, thank you for coming by to see me

this morning. Seeing you really made me feel better. I didn't realize how much you look like Papa Eddie until today. I could have sworn it was him sitting in that wing-back chair. I always remember him sitting in that chair when he came to visit after my father left. He'd watch television with me. Play chess. Or just talk." Tears fell, streaking his mascara.

"We need to get this obituary done and to the printer's today if we want it back in time." Collette set a steaming cup of hot water in front of Jamaica with a tea bag.

"She's right. We need to get it there by four o'clock. I'm sure it will take until three fifty-nine to get it done." Renee placed my laptop on the table.

"You going to type, Renee?" I asked, relieved it would be anyone but me.

"I don't mind. The first order of business: Are we printing in color or black and white?"

"Color," demanded five of us.

"Black and white," the other four chimed in.

"Why would we even entertain the option of black and white? We plan to make a small booklet. It would look so much better with a nice color photo on the front. I thought we could do a nice color photo layout on the inside." As though we'd spent hours rehearsing, Dawn spoke the words in my mind.

"Here goes Ms. Trump again." Collette shook her head.

"That all seems a little fancy for Eddie. He was an elegant but simple man," Estelle said softly.

"I ain't seen no obituary book." Uncle Thomas scratched his balding head.

"Okay, Derrick, and why did you say black and white?" Renee looked at her son curiously.

"PaPa and I had been working on a family crest for the family reunion this year. It was almost finished, and

I wanted to put it on the program. But it's line art and I just thought it would look better in black and white."

"What's a family chest?" Devin asked.

"It's a family *crest*. It's like a logo. Why didn't we know about this family crest?" Renee quizzed.

"He wanted to keep it a surprise. We'd been working on it for a few weeks, getting it just right. So can I still put it on the program even if it is in color?"

"Where is it? I want to see it. Uncle Thomas, did you know anything about this?"

"Yeah, but I couldn't tell y'all neitha."

"Let's not start jumping to conclusions. Daddy just wanted to surprise us with it. You know how much he loved surprises." My words betrayed my heart.

"It's in my room at home. I was filling in Missouri."

"Missouri?" Like a mass choir on first Sunday, the word rang out in unison.

"Yeah, the crest includes the states of North Carolina, Maryland, and Missouri."

"Did he say why Missouri? We don't have any family in Missouri!" Collette's eyes darted from one to the other of us around the table.

"Naw, I never asked. I was just really jazzed to be working on it with him. He told me what he wanted, and I drew it," Derrick said defensively.

"Oh, baby, I'm sorry, we didn't mean to accuse you of doing anything wrong. We're just really surprised. That's all. Derrick, when your daddy comes back, I want you to go home and get this crest." Renee struggled to remain calm.

"I swear, every time we bring up the simplest thing, a new secret is divulged." I was beginning to believe none of us truly knew Daddy.

"I never would've believed Eddie had so many secrets," Estelle said with disdain.

"Well, secrets or no, Papa Eddie was da man as far as I'm concerned," Jamaica interjected. "We need to just wait and see what happens. So, are we doing the color booklet or will it be black and white? And Miss Collette, if money is the issue, then I will pay for it my damn self. Sorry, Mama."

"Well, you just do that. Then y'all can trim it in gold if you choose. I'm sick of everyone telling me how they are spending my money."

"Your money!" I was on my feet before I realized what I was doing.

"Sit down, Sissy! Jus' leave it be. Let's git on wit' dis obituary bidness. Don't it have to be at the printer by four o'clock?"

"Uncle Thomas, I'm sick of her and this money issue."

"I said, sit yo' ass down and move on!"

The smugness on Collette's face infuriated me even more. I made mental plans to ambush her ass. But I knew Uncle Thomas was right. We needed to move on.

"Uncle Thomas, is there anything you want included about your childhoods in the obituary? We have all the basic information: parents, schooling, Mama, et cetera," Dawn began.

"I think the proper way to do it is all of his personal information in the first paragraph, then family ties in the second paragraph, and then other information follows." Jamaica always talked with his hands flashing his amazing jewelry.

"You're right, Jimmy. Now the question becomes who do we list in the second paragraph?" Collette pulled the pin from the grenade, threw it, and sat back waiting for the explosion.

"Let's get through paragraph one first," Dawn said, rolling her eyes at Collette.

"We know full well what'll be in the first paragraph.

These are the facts: Edward Zachary Naylor was born June third, nineteen hundred thirty-eight, to Luella and Edward Naylor, in Rocky Point, North Carolina. The family moved to Baltimore in nineteen forty-three to pursue a better life. Edward was educated in the Baltimore public school system, graduating from Edmondson High School in nineteen fifty-six. He received a bachelor of science degree in engineering while attending Morgan State College after serving four years in the United States Army. He had been employed by Bethlehem Steel for more than twenty years at the time of his death on August twenty-seventh, two thousand and one. Now can we move on to the listing of survivors?" Collette twirled a cigarette between her fingers.

"Let's back up to the cover, Miss Fast Ass! I like the idea of a sunrise/sunset cover," Dawn continued. "I've seen a few different ones. We can use his baby picture as the sunrise and the engagement picture he took with Estelle back in June for the sunset. Then overlap them slightly, with his date of birth and date of death. 'Home-going Celebration' at the top, with his name at the bottom. All in a really nice font." Dawn's suggestion set well with everyone, including Collette.

"I can do all the graphic work, if you want," Derrick volunteered.

"Derrick, that would be great. Are you sure you don't mind?" His unassuming spirit warmed my heart.

"I really want to do it. I just don't want y'all to fight about this anymore. Devin and I are really bummed about everybody being so mad all the time. We talked about it while we ran this morning."

And a child shall lead them . . . I was too embarrassed being so respectfully put in check by my nephew to look at the others. The thickness of the quiet was suffocating. No one wanted to be the first to speak. Who among us could say anything in rebuttal? Combining death, secrets, envy, and money was causing irreparable family division. A family Edward Naylor worked so hard to preserve.

"Derrick, we'll do our best to stop the bickering," I said quietly. "We're sure leading by real poor example. Thank you for volunteering to do the layout of the obituary. I think I speak for all of us when I say we'd be honored to have you do it." I was so ashamed of our behavior.

"I think I'm going to be ill," Collette said. "You act like butter wouldn't melt in your mouth. You're the main one always starting some mess, especially with me!" She worked her neck.

"See, I could go there with you, but I'm not. I just promised my nephews."

"Whatever. Now that the cover is taken care of, let's move on to survivorship."

Dawn looked from me to Collette and back again before she started. "First, we need to include his marriage, the date, where they lived, and us."

"Shouldn't we also include when he became a Christian and the church he belonged to all of these years?" Renee asked.

"Yes, that should be listed in the personal part of the obituary, for sure," I added.

"Okay, we've got all that. What about the part he leaves to cherish his memory?" Collette wanted desperately to start some more mess.

"Of course, we're listed first in birth order, including Derrick, next his grandchildren, then Uncle Thomas, his children, Aunt Ida Mae, Estelle, her children, and then close friends like Mister Willie, Roberta, and Rico." Dawn never looked in Collette's direction.

"Oh, we forgot the mailman," Collette said sarcastically. "Daddy knew him for like fifteen years."

We each ignored her.

With tears forming Estelle spoke first. "I don't want to cause any problems. If listing us in the obituary will cause any more conflict than we already have, don't even give it a second thought."

"Don't be ridiculous, Estelle. Everyone knows you two were getting married. Do you know how bad we'd look to everyone if we didn't put you in there?" Renee rolled her eyes at Collette.

"I think Renee's right," I said. "If we didn't include Estelle, we'd be disrespecting their relationship. What difference does it make anyway whom we list. Daddy loved everyone, and everybody loved Daddy. Let's move on."

The remainder of the conversation was strained, but we managed to get through it with minimal disagreements. I looked around the table and wondered if I was the only one who'd thought of Nina Blackford and Edwina in this process. Should their names be listed in Daddy's obituary? I thought back over the years, trying to remember if there was ever the slightest hint that Daddy had a secret life. There was none.

Friends stopped by throughout the early afternoon, and they were a welcome diversion because we seemed to argue less when visitors were present.

"I think that takes care of the program," Dawn said. "Jamaica, do you really think you will be able to get through the song? You misted up when we read you'd be singing it," she teased good-heartedly.

"Gurl, I'll do the best I can. I'll make Papa Eddie proud, I should do a dance routine. That would bring down the house."

"Boy, this is not a theater production. This is a funeral! Hush your mouth."

"But, Mama, Michelle and I could do the freedom dance routine I choreographed a long time ago. I bet she still remembers it. It is so beautiful. It would be tasteful, and I think it would be a wonderful tribute. People do all kinds of things at funerals now'days."

"Maybe them theater people, but not at my Eddie's funeral!" Estelle was visibly angry.

"Well, I personally think it would be a great idea." The look in Collette's eyes was all-telling.

"I don't think Bishop would like the idea at all." I couldn't believe how evil my sister could be.

"It was just a suggestion. I don't want to start no mess." Jamaica was truly hurt.

"So we can send this document over to the printer?" Dawn asked.

"As soon as Derrick does his thing, it's a wrap," Renee said.

"That just leaves the limos," I said. "I think we need three. That's room for twenty-one people." I wanted this to move along. We'd spent way too much time and energy disagreeing.

I so wanted to get back to a life that I had taken for granted. A life filled with love, peace, and measurable harmony. But in my heart of hearts, I knew that was a castle in the sky. My life would never be the same.

With the next influx of people came Rico and Jonathan. Seeing my best friend brought such comfort. She busied herself in the kitchen, and Jonathan naturally migrated to Derrick senior. They'd become friends when he and Rico had attended the first family reunion after they were married. The hours on the basketball court and at the local billiard parlor had fused a lifelong bond. It seemed in the sea of women I had neglected to notice

Derrick had no allies. It was amazing to watch how men handled emotional stress. Derrick loved Daddy like a father, yet he hadn't shed a tear, at least none I'd seen. He'd taken care of Renee's every need. He'd tolerated her outbursts and held her until her sobs subsided. He'd been a rock. Yet when he was in the company of Jonathan he seemed less strong, and pulled from Jonathan's strength. They talked, briefly catching up on work, sports, and the latest car craze. Then the two old friends headed for the backyard to fire up the grill.

I went to join Rico in the kitchen. She was chopping onions to make her world-famous (or at least Southern California–famous) turkey salad.

"So, how are you doing? And I want the truth. You look really tired. Have you been sleeping?"

"Dang, one question at a time. I'm as okay as someone can be who is going to bury her father in a couple days. I'm really tired. We've done nothing but argue since I got here. Collette is so unreasonable. She's unhappy and not content unless the rest of us are there with her."

"She didn't speak to me when I came in. She made a big point of speaking to everyone else. I'll be here for you, but I won't take any abuse from her. While I couldn't possibly know what you're feeling, I do know what I'm feeling, and I hurt all over. When we pulled into the driveway, I felt like a boulder fell onto my chest. I loved Papa Eddie so much. It was all very clinical to me until I got here." Mascara-stained tears began to draw vertical lines on Rico's stunning face.

"I'll talk to her. But just so you know she isn't discriminating, she isn't speaking to me either." We both laughed.

"Is there anything else you need me to do? Any errands you need me to run? Airport trips, flowers, toilet paper, it doesn't matter. I'm here to help in any way I can. I brought some Remy Martin XO for later. We can make some herbal tea. This is for medicinal purposes, of course. And you can't argue with your doctor." Rico smiled, making her eyes sparkle.

"You're a pediatric surgeon. How're you my doctor?" I laughed.

"You're a big kid at heart?"

"I'll grant you that!" Her strength reinforced me as I hugged her.

"Where's Aunt Ida Mae? Will she be here? I do so love her. She's quite the character."

"She's taking the bus. She'll be here tomorrow morning."

"The bus?"

"Don't even ask. We tried to get her to fly. But she's so stubborn."

"I'm surprised Roberta's not here. She thinks she's one of you guys."

"Gurl, don't talk her up. I'm sure she'll be here later. Some of Daddy's friends are staying with her. They're flying in late tonight."

"As soon as I finish mixing the turkey salad, we'd better join the others. They'll get an attitude with you for hanging out here with me," Rico halfheartedly kidded me.

"You're probably right. But there's something I need to talk to you about first."

Rico stopped mixing to stare at me. "What is it?"

"I think Daddy has another child."

"What?"

"I think he has this whole secret life. Another woman named Nina Blackford, who has a daughter named Edwina. They live in St. Louis."

"You told me all of this yesterday, and it was hard to believe then. It's even harder to believe now that I've had time to think about it. Papa Eddie couldn't have another child. When would he have had time? How old is this child?" Complete astonishment robbed Rico of her reasoning.

"Well, she's a teenager with a major attitude. I'm not sure of her age. As far as time, I haven't a clue. But maybe when he was on one of those business trips. Maybe this Nina person lived here at one time. I just don't know, Rico. I don't know."

"Has she called you back? You shouldn't jump to any conclusions until you talk to her. You're the lawyer. . . . You know, innocent until proven guilty?"

"That doesn't apply to daddies with secrets!" My face smiled, but my heart ached.

18

Telling Secrets

I woke from a troubled sleep to the sound of muffled voices. The green digital display on the alarm clock told me it was four thirty-seven. Who in the world was visiting at this hour? Curled in the fetal position, snoring lightly next to me, was Dawn. Renee and Collette decided, after much debate, that they'd spend the night in their own homes and prepare to stay together the night after the funeral.

The funeral. My God. There was going to be a funeral. We had an appointment this morning at nine to see Daddy's body. The funeral director would pick us up and take us to give final approval before others were allowed to see him. How could I give my approval that the man I loved since my conception looked okay to be on display for all to file past him? Some would be crying softly. Others would be shaking their heads in disbelief. And, of course, at least one person would try to climb into his coffin. There was always one somebody who was determined to be more grief-stricken than anyone else. Someone who couldn't go on in life without the dearly departed. My money was on Roberta.

No matter how well dressed he was, no matter how nice the coffin, no matter how many beautiful flowers arrived, I would never give my approval. If I refused to give my approval, did that mean none of this would be

true? It would be so much easier to spend the day in bed.
I'd simply refuse to go to the funeral home. The laughter coming from the kitchen interrupted my thoughts
and made me more than a little curious.

Swinging my feet onto the floor took major effort. As
I sat on the side of the bed I was reminded of the paint-
ing *Monday Morning Blues*. Fatigue and heaviness
enveloped me. But I was drawn to the sound of voices.
As I stood, my joints ached and my head felt light. I
couldn't understand these physical manifestations asso-
ciated with emotional strain. Dawn stirred but didn't
wake.

Pulling on my robe, I headed for the bathroom to
brush my teeth and wash my face. A shower would have
to wait until I found out who was holding court at this
hour. Trepidation took hold of my soul. I couldn't explain my apprehension, but it made the hair on the back
of my neck stand. I picked up my water glass and headed
to the kitchen.

The den, hallway, and kitchen lights burned brightly.
The voices were more distinctive now, and one belonged
to Uncle Thomas. Another male voice offered condo-
lences, explaining they had made really good time over
Interstate 70. They'd come as soon as they'd heard. Uncle
Thomas offered coffee and breakfast. I sighed a breath
of relief when I realized the man must be a friend of
Daddy's from out of town.

Stepping into the kitchen, I knew nothing could have
prepared me for what I saw. Sitting at my daddy's table
was the spitting image of my sister Collette. An older,
plumper version with short red hair, but without a doubt
she could have been Collette's twin.

Seeing this woman caused me to drop the glass, still
partly filled with water. The sound of shattering glass
startled the trio. My eyes locked onto the eyes of the fa-

miliar stranger. My mouth moved to speak, but my jaw
was locked. I felt as if I was moving in slow motion as
the tall male stranger began to speak. His lips formed
words, but the noise that emerged sounded like a record
being played at the wrong speed.

Uncle Thomas's shout broke the spell. "Sissy, chile, ya
gonna cut yo' feet on dat glass."

"Let me help you." The male stranger led me around
the broken glass.

I stared from the man to Uncle Thomas to the woman
I knew shared my bloodline.

"Sissy, baby, ya need to come sit ovah here. Dese people got somethin' to tell you." Uncle Thomas took my
other arm.

"Who are these people?" My eyes pleaded for information.

"My name is Nina Blackford." The woman touched
my arm.

I looked at Uncle Thomas for confirmation that this
woman spoke the truth. My mouth opened three times
before words escaped. "Who are you? You look exactly
like my sister Collette."

She looked at the man before speaking softly. "That's
because I'm your sister Nina."

The sound of blood rushing through my head and my
heart pounding in my chest deafened me. My knees betrayed me, and I fell into the waiting chair.

"Sissy, baby. Say somethin'." Uncle Thomas was patting my cheek.

"What in the hell do you mean you're my sister?
You're too old to be my sister. According to the insurance papers, you're older than Renee. And who are *you*?
My brother?" I pointed in the direction of the male
stranger.

"My name is Victor. Victor Blackford. I'm Nina's husband."

"Wait just a got-damn minute! How're you going to waltz in here claiming you're my sister? How do we know this is not some kind of scam?"

"Sissy, baby, baby, look at heh. She's yo' daddy's spittin' image. She looks more like Collette than any of da res' y'all. We need to jus' sit down 'n' hear what she gotta say."

"I don't want to hear shit she has to say. I have three sisters, and Renee is the oldest. My daddy didn't cheat on my mama. I won't believe that! I'm going to get Dawn!"

"Wait, Sissy!" Nina reached for me.

I snatched myself away and turned in the same movement. "Don't you dare call me Sissy! Only my immediate family calls me that!"

"I'm sorry to have to break this news to you now. Poppee had planned to introduce me this year at the family reunion."

"Daddy? Who are you calling Daddy? Don't you dare fix your mouth to call Edward Zachary Naylor your daddy!"

"But Glynda, he is, I mean was, my father." Tears formed in her eyes.

"I don't believe you!" I broke into uncontrollable sobs as the realization of the truth took possession of my soul.

Uncle Thomas opened his arms, and I gladly flew into them. He held me until my sobs turned into a steady stream from my eyes onto his worn plaid bathrobe. "We'd betta call da othas."

Victor sat stoically, holding Nina's hand. She wept quietly. How dare this woman show up here this morning, talking about she's my sister? On the morning I had

to give my approval that Daddy was ready for the world
to file past him to pay their last respects. What nerve!

"You wants me ta git Dawn while ya call Collette 'n'
Renee? Or do you wants me to call them?" Uncle Thomas
rubbed my arm.

"Did you know anything about any of this?"

"No, baby. I sho' 'nuff didn't. But when I opened dat
do' 'n' saw Nina standin' dere, I knowed. I knowed she
was Eddie's chile.

"We needs ta hear what she gots ta say. I'm gonna put
on coffee and start some breakfast while we wait for
Renee and Lette ta git here. And ya tell dat sista of
yours, Renee, to hurry it up."

"You call them. I don't want to answer their questions."

I refused to look at Nina as I made my way back to
Daddy's bedroom. My swift gait turned into a sprint as
I grew closer to the door. I rushed inside, slammed the
door, and fell against it. The slamming door woke Dawn.

Glancing at the clock, Dawn stretched. "What is wrong
with you? Why are you slamming the door at this time
of morning? You gonna wake up the whole house."

"Nina Blackford is in the kitchen!"

"What?" She bolted upright.

"You heard me. She's in the kitchen, and she says she's
our sister."

"Stop lyin'!" Dawn came across the bed toward me
on her knees. "Where did she come from? When did she
get here? How did she get here at this hour? Oh my God."
Dawn stood and started pacing. "Did you call Renee
and Collette?"

"Uncle Thomas is doing that now. Apparently they
drove from St. Louis. I don't know how she found out.
Dawn, I don't know shit. She's supposed to tell us everything when the others get here."

"You said 'they.' Who else is here?"

"Her husband, Victor."

"Oh my God!" Dawn sat heavily onto the bed.

"Brush your teeth and get your robe so we can go back out there."

"Why don't we wait until the others get here?"

"No. If you don't want to go, I'll go back without you."

"I'm scared to face her. Oh my God. My daddy had an affair."

"Well, there is one thing you need to brace yourself for."

"Damn, there can't be more."

"She looks *exactly* like Collette. I mean, she's older and bigger. But she and Collette could be twins."

"Oh snap! You're kidding me, right?"

"You know I'd never joke about something this serious. There's no doubt she's related to us."

"Oh my God."

"Could you please say something else?"

"Damn!"

We both managed a nervous laugh.

I sat on the bed as Dawn handled her business in the bathroom. Again I looked around the room at the pictures. Now everything seemed different. Were there others? I felt as if I was in the middle of a twister. My mind raced wondering what the others' reaction would be.

Collette was sure to throw a fit and spend most of her time on the porch smoking. Renee wouldn't be able to listen because she would be crying uncontrollably. Dawn would be consistently trying to make peace. I wanted to see their faces when they took their first gander at Miss Nina Blackford. Had her name been Naylor, too? I had a million questions.

Dawn emerged from the bathroom, grabbing her robe. "You ready?"

"The question is, are you ready?"

"I guess. Let's do this thang!" She took my hand and led me back toward the kitchen.

Even though I'd prepared her for Nina's striking resemblance to Collette, Dawn hit an invisible wall with the force of a locomotive. She began backing up until the doorjamb stopped her. With nowhere to escape, she began shrinking to the floor. She just whispered "Oh my God" repeatedly.

Victor and Uncle Thomas rushed to her side. Each took an arm and helped her to her feet. Victor led her to the chair that had been my only shield from the gray linoleum.

"You must be Dawn," Nina said, leaning forward.

"How do you know my name?"

"I know everything about all of you. My daddy has always told me about you all."

"Then why didn't he tell us about you?" I didn't know what to believe.

"Poppee was tormented with this secret for so many years. He was so stressed about telling you all at the family reunion, it may be what killed him."

It still unnerved me to hear this strange woman refer to Edward Naylor as Daddy.

Headlights filled the kitchen window, announcing the arrival of another of the Naylor girls. The room fell quiet. It was like watching a disaster unfold before our eyes. We knew something needed to be done, but we were helpless to stop the devastation.

Within seconds the front door flew open, and Collette and Renee seemed to reach the kitchen in two steps. They both stopped short in the doorway, first looking at each other and then at Dawn and me. Collette opened and closed her mouth repeatedly, gazing from one person to the next. Question marks seemed to dance in the air around her.

"Who the hell are you?" Renee barked.

There could be little doubt in anyone's mind that this woman was related to us. The four of us stared at this stranger, then at one another.

"Ain't no need ta be rude. Come on in here 'n' grab a seat. Looks like we gots some thangs ta discuss." Uncle Thomas was pulling chairs to the table.

"Who is this woman?" Collette finally managed.

"This is Nina Blackford and her husband, Victor," I said. "I think I'll let her tell you the rest." I sat down opposite Nina.

"Well, well, well," Collette said. "So you're the mystery woman. Where did you come from? Why are you here? And what are you to our father?" Collette was ignoring the obvious.

"I'm your sister. Or, I guess I should say, your half sister." Nina looked at each of us in turn.

"That's some bullshit!" Renee screamed.

"I know how you must be feeling, but trust me, I am your sister. Poppee's been with me my whole life."

"Who's Poppee?" Collette asked weakly.

"Our daddy." Nina motioned to all of us with her hands.

"We're trying to be really patient with all of this, Nina, but I think it's time you explained," I said nervously.

"I'm the oldest." Nina stared at Renee.

"The oldest what?" Renee was livid.

Dropping her head as she spoke, Nina replied, "I'm your oldest sister. Edward Naylor is my father, too."

"Oh hell, no!" Collette was on her feet. "There ain't

no way Daddy had another child and none of us knew. Uncle Thomas?"

"Dis here is news ta me, too. I think we need to jus' listen ta what she gotta say. Go on, baby."

"I don't want to hear shit she's got to say. Comin' up in here on the day of my daddy's wake, starting some stupid mess like this." Collette's arms flailed wildly.

"Collette, sit your ass down. Look at her. She's your twin! We at least need to hear her out." Dawn pulled Collette into the empty chair next to her.

Nina raised her head to speak. Her voice faltered. Despite myself, my heart went out to her. "My name is Nina Lynette Naylor Blackford."

"Oh my God. You have his name?" Dawn gasped.

"Yes."

"Holy shit!" I said. "I think you need to start at the beginning! Before you do that, how did you find out about Daddy's death? I left messages, but you never called back."

"When I got your first message from Edwina, I panicked. I called here pretending to be a telemarketer, and when I asked for Poppee, someone told me he'd died. I then called the lawyer to get all the details. He told me Poppee had died suddenly and that you all had called, asking for information concerning me."

"Poppee?" Renee asked sarcastically.

"That's what I called him when I was little. I called my stepfather Daddy. It was just easier that way."

"Who's your mother? Who's this woman whom he cheated with for all these years?" I asked, not trying to hide my disdain.

"He never cheated on your mother. At least, not with *my* mother. They met when he was in boot camp. My mother was a waitress at the coffee shop right outside the base, and she had a thing for the soldiers. They dated casually, and obviously they slept together. He told me that this happened before he even met your mother. He said he never loved my mother, but when she told him she was pregnant, he never questioned whether or not I was his baby. By then he'd been transferred to another post, but they kept in touch by mail."

"Well, if your mama was a military ho, how do we know you are Daddy's child?"

"Collette! That's enough! Apologize," Renee chastised.

"Fuck her!"

"Stop it!" Dawn had tears in her eyes. "It doesn't take a DNA test to see she is one of us."

"She may be Daddy's love child, but she's not one of us." Collette was being Collette.

"It's okay. Poppee knew it would be like this. He planned to introduce me at the next family reunion. He told me the last time we spoke, which I know now is the night he died, that Derrick junior had almost finished the family crest. He was so relieved to at last divulge his secret after all this time. He was so afraid that you all wouldn't love and respect him because he'd kept the secret for so long."

"Why ya thank he kept dis here secret all dese years, even from me?"

"He originally was so ashamed to have gotten Mama pregnant in the first place. He was afraid his mother would have been disappointed in him. He loved his mother so much. Even though Grandmother died before I was born, he felt she would somehow know. He, of course, didn't want Aunt Ida Mae to find out either. Then when he started dating your mother, he didn't want her to think less of him. It wasn't like it is today with illegitimate babies everywhere. Then, after she died, he didn't know how to tell y'all for the same reason. Me and my mother were the only ones who knew the truth."

"You make it sound like you and your mother were always in touch with him." I didn't know what I was feeling.

"We were. I saw him three times a year. He called me every week. He was at all of my graduations, paid for my college, gave me away at my wedding, came when Edwina was born." Victor rubbed his wife's back between her shoulder blades as she spoke. "I had the best of both worlds. My mother finally married her a soldier boy when I was three and half, and he, too, is a wonderful man and father. But Poppee always took his responsibility to me very seriously. He sent money every month, bought school clothes, Christmas gifts, everything."

"When's the last time you saw him?" I asked, spell-bound by the information I was trying to process.

"The weekend after Father's Day. He came to tell me he was going to marry Estelle and wanted my blessing."

We all stared from one to the other.

"I have pictures of all of you from the time we all were children. He'd spend hours telling me about each of you. He wanted me to feel like I was a part of this family. Please don't be mad at Poppee. He did the best he could with the mistake he made. He was so stressed by all of this lately. I'd tell him every time we talked that he didn't have to do this if he didn't want to, but he insisted that the truth would set him free."

"Dayummmmmmmmmm." As usual, Dawn so eloquently expressed my feelings.

"I sure hope y'all not falling for this line of bullshit. She just came here to get her share of Daddy's money, and I'd sure appreciate it if you'd stop calling my daddy 'Poppee.' "

"He knew you'd take it hardest, Collette. He always told me how much you looked like me. And I saw a resemblance in the pictures, but we're mirror images. We even hold our cigarettes the same."

Collette threw her cigarette onto the table. "I don't know who told you I look like you. That's a load of crap. Uncle Thomas, what do you have to say about all of this? If you and Daddy had been any closer, you would have been the same person. You trying to make us believe that he never even told you?"

"I knowed dere was somethin' deep inside he was holdin' on to. I knowed it was eating at him even mo' lately. But I had no idear it was dis here."

"I assure you, ladies, my wife has no ulterior motive," Victor said. "We don't know anything about her share of anything. Poppee told her there was a will and who drew it up, but we don't know if she inherits one or one million dollars. She told me she had to get here and get here fast. We never even thought twice about it. Your father was a wonderful man who loved all five of his daughters with all his heart. I know this is a lot to comprehend, especially now. But Nina only speaks the truth."

As he spoke, I noticed how much Victor reminded me of Daddy.

19

Film at Eleven

"We need to call Estelle," Dawn said in a monotone.

"We need to get the programs altered. I'll call the printer as soon as he opens. The funeral home is picking us up at nine to go give our final approval of everything. I think you should be there, too." I realized as I spoke that I'd accepted this woman as my sister.

"Slow your roll. Slow your got-damn roll!" We all turned to stare at Renee.

"I agree we need to call Estelle. But putting Nina in the obituary? I think that's a little hasty. What are people going to think? This is a secret of the worst kind!"

"Who's going to pay for these last-minute changes to the program?" said Collette, predictably. "We're paying triple what we should have to pay anyway, thanks to the Trump trio."

"First of all, finding out Daddy was a child molester is the worst possible secret we can uncover." Dawn pounded the table for emphasis. "Nina being our sister, while a little shocking, is not a travesty. Daddy, for whatever reasons, believed that we weren't forgiving or understanding enough to share her with us. We've all been cheated. I don't want to waste another precious second on some bullshit. People will ask questions. We'll tell the truth and let them believe what they will."

"Uncle Thomas, what do you think? You're unusually quiet." I searched his face for the truth.

"I thinks Dawn's right. I don't know why Eddie thought he had ta keep dis all to hisself. But Ray Charles could see Nina is y'all's sistah. Her name belongs in dat obituary. She belongs in da family car. She belongs in da front pew. This is Eddie Naylor's young'un. And I wants to be the first to welcome her to da Naylor family."

"Welcome her? You trippin'!" Collette shouted.

"Look, Collette. You've disrespected Uncle Thomas about as much as I'm going to stand for." I was pissed. "Now you apologize and don't be cussing and acting like you weren't raised."

"We've all been cussing. Why is it always me that is getting picked on!"

"It's because you make it so easy."

"Don't y'all start!" Dawn said. "I agree with Uncle Thomas. I want to welcome you, too. But please be patient with us. This is a lot for us to comprehend. But you do look exactly like us, especially Collette. I don't know either why Daddy didn't think we'd understand. This is such a horrible way for us to be introduced. So where's our niece?"

"Listen at yourselves!" said Collette. "Welcome to the family? Where's our niece? This woman walks in here, weaving tales about our father, and we just take her word for it. What would Daddy think of y'all? He always taught us not to be gullible, and she just shows up on our doorstep talking about she's our long-lost sister and your arms fly open faster than a hooker's legs on a sailor's payday. Sorry, Uncle Thomas."

"Collette," Renee said wearily, "if we hadn't found her name in his will or the insurance policy, then yes, maybe we'd have cause to be suspicious. But we know she meant a lot to Daddy just from him leaving her an

equal share of his estate. And, Collette, look at her."
Tears began to form in Renee's eyes.

"I don't want to hear one more time how much she
looks like me. They say we all have a twin."

"I'll call Estelle," I said. "Nina, I know you're telling
the truth. Y'all can stay here with us. We'll make room.
Is Edwina coming for the funeral, too?" I said, heading
toward the kitchen phone. Everyone shushed while I
quickly made the call.

"My mother, stepfather, and Edwina will be here at
two thirty this afternoon," Nina said when I hung up.
"We don't want to impose. We know you have a lot to
talk about. But I assure you that I want nothing from
you, except your love and acceptance. I agree that we've
been cheated out of so many years. But don't think
harshly of Poppee. He just did what he thought was
best. When we struggle with truth, it sometimes seems
so much worse to us than it will to anyone else. Most
people don't even care. I know I'll cause a raised eyebrow or two by being here. But folks will get over it."

"Why did you call him Poppee?" Dawn asked.

"My mother said that when I started calling him
Daddy, he told me to call him Papa, but I couldn't say it.
So I called him Poppee, and Mother said he threw his
head back and laughed so hard that he began to choke.
She said when he stopped coughing, he hugged and kissed
me and told me he would always be my poppee. And
you know what, Dawn? He always was."

"So I guess when he said da plant was sendin' him ta
St. Louis fo' trainin', he was comin' ta see you?" Uncle
Thomas was putting coffee mugs on the table.

"He never told us how he would get to St. Louis so
often. But it seemed I was always looking forward to his
visits."

"What about holidays? You never saw him for Christmas or Easter or Father's Day because he was always with us." Collette's words dripped with sarcasm.

"From before I can remember until my grandmother died when I was thirteen, she'd bring me here. We'd stay at the Holiday Inn for holidays. He'd take me out to lunch and spend a lot of time with me."

"See, I know you lying now! Daddy was always with us on holidays." Renee was angry.

"I don't know what to tell you. On Christmas morning at around ten he'd show up at the hotel with all kinds of gifts, and we'd spend an hour or so together. Then the day after Christmas we'd spend all day together. We'd go shopping, and he'd buy all kinds of wrapping paper and decorations at half price. That night he'd put us back on an airplane, and we'd go home. Grandma would stay at the hotel while we were out. He'd always attempt to take her along, but she'd tell him we needed time alone.

"Oh my God! After we had a postdawn breakfast on Christmas morning, Daddy would leave, saying he needed to visit his buddies without families, but he'd be back in time for dinner, which was more like lunch because it was so early in the afternoon. And Daddy *always* went shopping the day after Christmas. I remember him telling Mama one year that she couldn't go because he may find more gifts for her. He always came home with wrapping paper, cards, and decorations for the next year." Renee got up to hug Nina.

"How could Daddy keep this secret from Mama all those years?" I said. "I was nine when Mama died, which would have made you seventeen?" I mindlessly stirred my coffee.

"Yes, I was seventeen. That was the first year Poppee ever missed my birthday. He loved your mother so much. He was different after that for a long time. In retrospect, I guess he felt guilty for holding this secret."

"So, Nina, baby, you sayin' Eddie nevah saw yo' mama durin' dese trips?"

"He'd pick me up and take me for a couple of days. Then he'd take me back to her. She loved Poppee, but she knew he loved Lorraine. She didn't love him when I was conceived. She hardly knew him. But she came to love and respect him greatly, based on how he took care of me. He sent a check every month and always bought my school clothes, and Christmas was awesome."

"Do you have other siblings?" As she spoke, Dawn tore her napkin into little pieces, something she often did when she was nervous.

"I have two younger bothers, Donnel and Chuck. They're Daddy's sons. Once my mother found a soldier who really loved her, she settled down, and they've been happily married ever since. There was never any threat to their relationship by Poppee. He made it perfectly clear that he was only interested in being with me."

"You know, when you take out the shock value of what you're saying, this all sounds so familiar, so Eddie Naylor." I smiled at her.

All of us, except Collette, seemed to have started to relax. There was no longer any doubt in my mind; this woman was my sister. Her husband seemed to possess the qualities of a good man, and his physical resemblance to Daddy was uncanny. Victor busied himself assisting Uncle Thomas with breakfast preparations. Uncle Thomas thought food could soothe any ill. I did so love that about him. I had a million questions for Nina and wanted them all answered now.

Collette was on the porch smoking and talking to herself. Even she had to recognize the truth. Renee's body language had relaxed, which meant she, too, had accepted the reality. Dawn looked as though she was in a haze. Sadness filled her eyes. I could only surmise what I saw to be disappointment. Her dream of the perfect father had been shattered.

Collette came back into the kitchen. "So, if I understand this right, your mother, stepfather, and daughter are coming here to my, I mean our, father's funeral uninvited. Just stirring up some mess. Well, I say you're not welcome here. We have an image to uphold. My father was a pillar of the community. What will all of the board members think? Bishop will be devastated. This is an outrage. I won't stand for it." Every toxic puff on her cigarette must have given Collette new momentum in arrogance.

"We mean no disrespect to Poppee's image in the church or community or family for that matter. But the fact remains, I'm his daughter. His name is on my birth certificate, and I'm in his will. I'll be at the wake and the funeral. Now, I can't force you to let me sit with you, but I'll be in that church with my husband and daughter. My parents are coming because they considered themselves his friends. Daddy and Poppee had a wonderful relationship based on love and respect. Poppee told him often how much he appreciated him taking care of his daughter when he couldn't be around to do it himself. I can't begin to really understand how you all must feel, but you can't imagine how I've felt all these years. I won't let you even try to tarnish my memory of the wonderful man who gave me life." Tears began to flow around the room.

"Alls I know is, everythang ya say, chile, sho' 'nuff sounds like mah brotha. My mama preached ta us from the time we were eleven and twelve that we'd betta not make no babies. She couldn't support us, let alone somebody else. And she said we had ta take care of any babies we made. I can undastan' why Eddie was 'fraid to let Mama know."

"But Uncle Thomas, wasn't Grandma dead?" Dawn asked.

"Yeah she was by da time Nina here woulda been born, but it was jus' somethin' 'bout da respect we had for our elders dat extended beyond dis here life."

"Nina, would you and Victor like to freshen up or take a nap before they come to take us to the funeral home? I really think you should come with us."

"I'd love to take a shower, and thank you, Glynda, for accepting me for who I am. I truly don't want to seem forceful with my stand on this issue, but I love Poppee just like you all do."

I stood to hug my new sister. "You couldn't help but love the man. Let me show you all to the guest room, where you can put your things and freshen up."

As we began to move down the hall toward the guest room, Estelle and Jamaica arrived. As her gaze fell upon Nina, Estelle lost her balance and fell against the wall. Jamaica reached for his mother, but he missed and she fell where she stood. Sheer horror filled her eyes.

"Estelle, are you alright?" Dawn rushed to her side. She switched from grieving daughter to nurse in point two seconds.

"This has to be Eddie's child. Lord, please tell me there's not another woman. I can't take any more. I just can't take any more." She began to wail.

Nina leaned down beside her to comfort her and spoke softly. "Estelle, there's no need to worry. I'm Eddie Naylor's daughter. But he and my mother were over before they ever started. You need not worry. He loved you and talked about you all the time. My name is Nina." She and Dawn helped Estelle to her feet.

"Lord, Lord, Lord. You're Eddie's child?"

"Yes, ma'am."

Estelle steadied herself, stepped back, and swept her

eyes over the full length of Nina's body three times. "Come here, chile, and give me a hug."

Nina broke down again and fell into Estelle's waiting arms. They both cried and rocked back and forth in a synchronized rhythm. They immediately seemed to have a bond that none of us had ever had with Estelle. Was it that they both felt like outsiders to the Naylor girls' circle?

"I guess this is the urgent news Thomas referred to when he called. I couldn't imagine what else could have possibly happened. How're all of y'all taking this?"

"Obviously not as well as you." An ice sculpture could have been carved from Collette's words.

"Just give this all some time. I guess I'm relieved to finally know who the mysterious Nina Blackford is."

"Estelle, this is my husband, Victor. My daughter, mother, and stepfather will be here this afternoon."

"You guys come on so you can get showered and changed. Where's your luggage?" I was motioning toward the guest room.

"I'll get our things from the car. Honey, you going to be okay?" Victor kissed Nina on the cheek.

"What do you think we're going to do to her?" Renee said, half-jokingly.

"Nina pretends to have it all together for appearance's sake. But, truth be known, she isn't doing so great at all. My comment had nothing to do with you all, but everything to do with my wife." Victor had put Renee in check quite nicely.

There was minimal conversation while Victor retrieved their belongings, but something seemed to pass between us nonetheless. I wasn't sure what would happen next, but I expected the next few hours to prove quite interesting.

After getting them settled into the guest room, I returned to the kitchen. I was more than a little fearful of the conversation that awaited me. The thirty-second walk back to the kitchen left me no time for meaningful reflection.

"This is the worst mess." Renee shook her head as she spoke. "What are people going to think? We all grew up in the church together. Everyone knows us. This is so embarrassing."

"I agree, we'll have some explaining to do," I said, "but to say that this is the worst it could possibly be just isn't accurate. Listening to what Nina said made me love and respect Daddy even more. What an incredible burden he carried around with him all these years. He did what he considered to be the right thing—shouldered his responsibility and did whatever it took to protect us. So I don't want to hear any of us say we're ashamed of him. Ever!" Tired didn't even begin to explain how I felt.

"All of y'all are just so accepting and goody-goody." Collette paced as she spoke. "If that woman rides in the family car, I'm not going. If she sits in the front pew, I'll sit on the other side. She's his love child. She has no place with us. Daddy had every right to be ashamed of her."

"Why ya gonna be like dat? Dat woman ain't done a damn thang to you. Chile, you need to git on yo' knees and ax God ta forgive ya for all dat malice ya got in yo' heart. God can't bless you when yo' heart is so full of hate, ya don't have room fo' Him in dere!" Uncle Thomas pointed his finger at Collette's chest as he spoke.

"Collette, baby, your daddy didn't do any more than anyone else," Estelle said. "He was just such a proud man. This explains so much of what was going on with him lately. He would just be mad for no reason. He'd stop talking. When I asked him what was wrong, he'd tell me I was being paranoid. But like a mother knows

her child, a woman knows her man. I've known Eddie
for many a year, and I knew something was bothering
him. Your uncle is right, you need to let go of some of
this bitterness. It'll destroy you. Hate only hurts the hater.
You have a unique opportunity to embrace another sister. Someone who loves your father the same way you
do. That will help to sustain his memory."

"We need to shower and change to go to the funeral
home. You coming, Renee?" Collette turned to leave as
though Estelle had said nothing at all.

"We'll be back by eight thirty." Renee's eyes begged
me not to say any more to Collette.

"If that woman is going, I'm not!" Collette spat.

"Have it your way," I replied simply.

Without another word Collette left with Renee in tow.
As the front door slammed, I breathed a sigh of relief.
We'd at least have a short time without any tension.

Dawn finally broke the silence. "I don't think Collette
is serious, do you?"

"Who knows what your sister will do. But her actions
will bring far more shame to this family than Nina does.
Can you imagine what people will think and say if she
doesn't ride or sit with us?" I shook my head.

"*My* sister? Hell, she was *your* sister first. And people
will say there goes ole crazy-ass Collette Naylor. Everybody knows she has issues. I do know we need to make
Nina feel as welcome as we possibly can. She's been
through a whole lot over the years. Can you imagine
knowing you have sisters and not being able to contact
them?"

"I'm happy to see at least you two have five good
senses," Estelle said. "That woman has done nothing
but be born. And if that's a crime, then we all stand
guilty. And how many of us are the product of single
parents? Collette just needs to check herself. She's so

self-righteous. Your daddy worried about her all the time. He said she needed counseling. But she insisted there's nothing wrong with her."

"She ain't nevah got ovah Lorraine's death. Ain't no tellin' what dis here thang gonna do ta her. But you right 'bout one thang, though; it gonna look real bad if she doesn't sit with y'all and ride in the car."

"She's probably just blowing smoke. I bet she'll be back here with Renee at eight thirty. Just to make sure we don't spend too much of her money." Dawn laughed as she spoke.

"Now that is probably the one thing that will bring her around," I said. "One thing all of this has done is made me forget the task ahead of us. We'd better get showered and dressed. I'm too stressed for Uncle Thomas's grits this morning."

"Oh Lord, you know if we don't want grits, we need prayer, therapy, or both." Estelle leaned over to hug both of us.

Estelle and I cleared the table as Dawn went to shower. I was lost in my thoughts as we worked in silence. Had Daddy's perfect image really been shattered? His crime had been to deprive us of our sister for all these years. Years we could never retrieve.

My mother had been a woman of impeccable character. She lived her Christianity rather than talked it. She was kind, loving, and forgiving. There was nothing that Daddy could have told her about Nina that would have changed her perception of the only man she'd ever loved. In any case, by all accounts Nina had been conceived before they'd met.

Daddy had carried this secret to his grave, a secret that very well may have put him there before his time. But Estelle's demeanor had changed; though still grieving, a burden seemed to have lifted with the unveiling of Nina Blackford.

I needed to call Rico. According to our body clocks, it was still very early in the morning. As a pediatric trauma surgeon, she was no stranger to being awakened by frantic phone calls. My mind and body craved Anthony. Making love to him was the ultimate pleasure, but sleeping next to him was the ultimate peace. I'd hoped he'd have a chance to call me again soon. Again, I felt as if I'd cheated us both by being so stubborn and independent.

Nina startled Estelle and me both when she entered the kitchen. "Thank you," she said, smiling. "I feel so much better. I'm tired, but the shower worked wonders. Can I do anything to help?"

"No, we're finishing up. Uncle Thomas made breakfast. Would you like some? We just didn't have much of an appetite this morning."

"A little much to digest: new sister, bacon, and eggs?" Nina laughed. She had a witty sense of humor. I liked that. I could learn to love her with minimal effort.

"I want to know everything there is to know about you, and I want to know it all now. I have to warn you, Collette says she won't ride or sit with us if you come along. We told her then she'll have to make her own arrangements."

"I don't want to cause any problems among you. Victor and I will get there on our own, and I can sit in the back. I just know that I have to be there. I don't have to go with you this morning. I really don't want to see him like this anyway."

"Oh hell, naw. If I gotta go, you gotta go. You're a Naylor girl. All for one and one for all."

"Oh Glynda, Poppee was so perceptive. He told me exactly what to expect from each of you. He told me you'd question me until you were satisfied that I was telling the truth. Then it would be like I'd been a part of this family since day one.

"He said Dawn wouldn't even question me. She'd take one look at me and she'd immediately love me. Renee would be a harder nut to crack, but crackable. He said that by the end of the family—" Nina paused, caught in her own thoughts.

I rubbed her arm.

"He said by the end of the family reunion, Renee would've reluctantly relinquished her position as oldest sibling, but relinquished nonetheless. Then there's Collette. He said that she may never come around, that she would be angry and spiteful and would say anything she could to hurt me. He told me not to be surprised if she never accepted me as your sister.

"But, Glynda, he promised me he'd be here to protect me. Why did he leave just when we were about to be a whole family?" Nina began to sob.

"I don't know, Nina." Of course I couldn't let her cry alone.

"Oh, so you thought you could have a good cry without me?" Dawn entered the kitchen fresh and looking so beautiful.

"Oh we're sorry. We won't start without you next time." Nina wiped tears with the back of her hand.

"Glyn, you'd better get showered and changed. Then maybe you'll be up to some toast and coffee before we leave. I think we need to eat something. Because if you faint, you on your own." Dawn kissed me lightly on the cheek.

"See how they do you, Nina? I'll be out in about thirty minutes. You two get to know each other. Estelle went into the den with Uncle Thomas. Ask him if he wants you to make some more coffee."

I left the oldest and youngest of Eddie Naylor's daughters to get acquainted. If Daddy could see Dawn and me, I knew he would be smiling. I showered quickly and wrapped the towel around me, then called Rico. I wanted so badly to invite her along to the initial viewing, but I dared not. I did, however, want her here waiting when I returned. Roberta was bringing Daddy's friends over at noon. By three o'clock the house would be a bevy of activity. All of the family and friends would be gathered before the funeral. Close friends had agreed to congregate at the house and follow us to the church.

She picked up on the first ring a little out of breath.

"Did I interrupt something?" I asked mischievously.

"Hey, gurl! Your timing is impeccable. How are you this glorious morning?" Mornings were always glorious when she made love with Jonathan.

"Well, considering what today is, I guess I'm doing okay. I really want you to be here when we get back from the funeral home. I also need you to pick up Aunt Ida Mae from the bus terminal at nine forty-five. Do you remember what she looks like?"

"Of course, I remember her. I still can't believe she wouldn't fly. I hear something in your voice. What are you not telling me?"

"Nina Blackford showed up this morning."

I heard Rico shift in bed. "What?"

"You heard me. Nina Blackford was here when I woke up this morning. She's my sister."

"Oh my God. So she's the sister, not Edwina?"

"No. Edwina is my niece."

"I can't imagine Papa Eddie having an affair. I just can't."

"Well, you're not wrong. She was conceived before he and Mama met. He took care of her all this time. She calls him Poppee. He was as much a father to her as he was to us, he just didn't see her all the time. He never missed any major occasions with her, though, and she knows everything about us."

"Damn. How're you dealing with all of this?"

"It's beyond comprehension, but when you see her, there'll be no doubt in your mind she's my sister. She's Collette's twin."

"Oh Lord, I know Collette isn't feelin' any of this. How are Dawn and Renee doing with all of it?"

"Dawn never missed a beat. Oh, new sister? Come on up in here so I can give you some love. Renee is stand-offish, but she's dealing with it. Collette says she won't ride or sit with us if we acknowledge Nina as our sister. I'm calling the printer as soon as I get off the phone with you to tell him to add her and Edwina's names. She'll ride with us, and she'll be sittin' in the front pew. Number one position."

"Gurl, Jonathan and I will pray for you right away. Today is going to be so hard. And Collette is going to do everything she can to make sure it is even worse."

"I'd better get dressed. I'll see you when we get back. Roberta should be here around noon or so. Why don't the two of you team up to make sure everything runs like it should."

"Whoa, what is this I'm hearing? You and Roberta allies?"

"I've learned something in these past few days. Life is way too short to sweat the dumb stuff. Roberta is way too fast. *Waaaay* too fast, but the bottom line is, she loves Daddy and he loved her. Her intentions are good. And who in the hell do I think I am to say she can't do whatever it is she feels she can. She's Renee's best friend. Renee needs her best friend. And I fully understand that!"

"I love you, Glynda."

"I love you, too, Rico." A sense of comfort washed

over me like the warm water during a much-needed shower.

I quickly called the printer and made my request. Despite his protest, he found it in his best interest financially to grant my wishes. I dressed in black stretch pants and a black tank top. I started to put on makeup, then thought better of it. What was the point? I'd have it cried off by ten o'clock.

"Daddy, I'm on my way to see you," I said softly, looking at myself in the mirror before turning off the light.

20

All for One?

True to her word, Collette didn't return before the long black car with tinted windows arrived to transport us to the funeral home. We waited an additional fifteen minutes before deciding to leave without her. Pain encircled my chest at the thought of pettiness robbing us of one another's comfort.

Nina cried softly on Victor's shoulder. Though we explained she was not responsible for Collette's actions, we failed miserably at convincing her. Once we were settled in the car, we all fell silent. I presumed we were all lost in our thoughts. Fear gripped my very being as I anticipated my reaction to seeing Daddy in a casket.

The ride seemed to take forever, but at the same time it was over in an instant. The well-appointed three-story facility loomed over us. The driver opened our doors and assisted us to the sidewalk without uttering a sound. We assembled in a small circle, no one taking the lead to enter the building. Dawn gripped my hand.

"If you all don't mind, I'd like to say a little prayer before we go inside," Victor offered.

"Okay." I couldn't manage to say anything else.

"Most gracious and merciful Father, I come before you praising and thanking You for this opportunity to call on You. I ask in Your Son's holy name that You send Your guardian angels to watch over these sisters as they embark on this seemingly impossible task. But Father, we stand on Your promise that You shall not allow more trouble to fall upon us than we will be able to handle. Lord, I also ask that the building of relationships between Your daughters begin right now. In Christ's name we ask, amen."

We all murmured, "Amen."

"Victor, thank you. Are you a minister?" As Renee asked the question, I realized we knew nothing about my new sister and brother-in-law.

"No. But I'm a believer. And I know that prayer makes everything a little better."

"Amen to that," I added, feeling a little steadier than when I first took steps onto the pavement.

Nina took her husband's hand and started toward the building. The driver opened the door to allow us entry. Soft music filled the air, and the foyer was decorated in soft pastels. A massive marble table dominated the space. A young woman dressed in a beautiful charcoal gray designer suit stood to greet us.

"You're the Naylor family, I presume." She extended her hand while smiling genuinely. "We here at Brown Funeral Home would like to express our heartfelt sympathy and stand ready to make this process as stress free as possible. If you would please step this way, I'll take you to the office of the director assigned to your family. May I offer you tea, coffee, juice, or water?"

We each declined. She led us to an office that was lavishly furnished. The walls were filled with pictures and plaques that bore the name of the man who founded the establishment.

"Mr. Brown will be with you momentarily."

"Thank you," I managed. Everyone else sat stoically.

In a matter of a few seconds, Mr. Brown entered carrying a file. "Good morning. I'm sorry to have kept you waiting. I was reviewing your father's file and making our last-minute checks before we escort you to the private viewing room. I see everything is in order. I wanted to commend you for getting the casket delivered to us on time. We were able to have everything prepared on schedule. Your father is being laid to rest in style. I think you'll be pleased."

What in the hell was he talking about? Pleased? Pleased about seeing my daddy in a casket. No matter how nice the casket, how fine the clothes, how beautiful the flowers . . . nothing could please me about this.

"Mr. Brown," Renee said, "we're sure you have done a good job. Before we go any further, I'd like to introduce you to our sister, Nina Blackford." Renee was very matter-of-fact.

"Your sister? In all the years I've known your father, I never knew you had another sister." Mr. Brown raised his right eyebrow.

"Nor did we." Renee smiled.

"The program booklets should be delivered to you by three o'clock this afternoon. If they haven't arrived by then, please call me." I maintained a business-as-usual tone.

"I'll be sure to notify the receiving department right away." Curiosity was surely getting the best of him.

"Ms. Blackford, I'm very pleased to meet you. I wish it were under different circumstances, however." He extended his hand.

"Thank you, Mr. Brown. I, too, wish we were meeting for a social occasion."

"I think we're as ready as we'll ever be to see Daddy," Dawn interrupted.

"Certainly, Ms. Naylor. If you all will follow me this way." He stood and led us from the office and down the hall. We passed three private viewing rooms, each with an occupied coffin. I assumed each awaited the approval of the next of kin. Mr. Brown stopped on the far side of the door to the third room on the left. We each froze where we stood. Looking from one to the other, no one wanted to enter first.

After a long moment, Nina took Renee's hand and they made steps toward the doorway. Uncle Thomas and Estelle followed them. Dawn, Victor, Derrick, and I fell into step behind.

A deep moan escaped from Renee before she collapsed. Derrick rushed past Uncle Thomas and Estelle to his wife's aid. Nina's knees betrayed her as she began sobbing uncontrollably. Victor was at her side before she hit the floor. Uncle Thomas, Estelle, Dawn, and I were so consumed with our own grief we were unable to be of any assistance. Renee and Nina had blocked the entrance to the room. Mr. Brown managed to get on the other side of the incapacitated sisters. He helped their husbands get them to their feet and into waiting chairs.

Estelle entered the viewing room next. With each step toward the casket her moans became more pronounced. She began chanting Daddy's name. I walked slowly toward Daddy, holding on to Uncle Thomas's right arm. Dawn held his left.

We felt Uncle Thomas falter, and we both braced him. Words seemed so inconsequential. We each emitted a torturous sound of anguish. I realized for the first time that this viewing wasn't for our approval. It was to allow those closest to the deceased a time to display their grief privately.

We were a mess. Renee couldn't even sit in the chair. She was on her knees with her face buried in the cushion of the seat. Derrick rubbed her back while tears streamed silently down his flushed cheeks. Estelle had laid her head on Daddy's chest and was stroking his bearded face. She babbled something incomprehensible. Uncle Thomas was bent over with his hands on his knees rocking back and forth, saying, "Lord, Lord, Lord," in rapid succession. Nina had buried her face in Victor's chest, and her body quaked from her sobs. He stroked her hair. Tears filled his eyes but refused to fall. Dawn had turned her back to the coffin. She held herself tight and swayed back and forth. I stood in the middle of the chaos.

I stared from one to the other. I couldn't make my mind process the situation. I knew something horrible had happened. I was an unwilling observer, not a participant. I couldn't comprehend what was making these people act this way. The man in front of me in the casket looked a lot like my daddy, but that couldn't be him. My daddy was too happy and healthy to be dead. Everything went black.

For someone who had never fainted before in her life, I'd now hit the floor twice in three days. I could hear someone calling my name. The voice was familiar. As much as I struggled to open my eyes, they seemed glued shut. I could hear everything happening around me, but I didn't know where I was. My head ached as I willed myself to open my eyes. Slivers of light found their way to my optic nerves. Then glaring light. Nothing was in focus, but I knew people stood over me. I could feel their presence. Someone asked if he should dial 911. Someone else said I was coming around. I remember wondering, Who are these people? As my eyes began to focus, I recognized Victor. My new sister's husband knelt over me softly calling my name. As though electric currents passed through my body, I jerked. I remembered we were in a small viewing room in the funeral home that had possession of my father's remains.

"She's awake. You alright?" Victor asked.

"I think so. I can't believe I've fainted again. What is wrong with me?"

"Let me help you up. I want you to sit up first. Then we'll help you to your feet. You ready?" Victor took one arm, Derrick the other.

"Glynda, I think you need to see a doctor. This fainting can't be a good sign. Are you pregnant, baby?" Estelle asked in her best motherly tone.

"No, Estelle, but I think I'll see a doctor when I get home."

"Okay, we're going to help you to your feet. You ready?" Derrick asked compassionately.

"I think so."

Victor was very strong. He lifted me off the floor and stood me upright in one smooth movement. Though my head was spinning, I was steady.

"Gurl, you scared me half to death. Come sit here." Dawn led me to a chair directly in front of the casket.

"I'm sorry y'all. I guess I just can't deal with this." I gestured toward the casket.

"There's absolutely no need to apologize, baby. We were so busy taking care of you we had to stop thinking about ourselves for a minute." Estelle pressed my arm.

"Yeah, Estelle's right. I came to my senses real quick when you hit the floor." Renee laughed weakly.

"Mr. Brown, I guess we should take a look at everything to make sure it meets with our approval. After all, that's why we're here." Dawn managed a smile.

"Ms. Naylor, please take your time. We're here to serve. May I get anyone some water or juice?"

Again we declined. Everyone was gathered around me as we all put off the inevitable. We would have to approach the casket and look at Daddy. I made the first move. I stood, hoping my legs wouldn't betray me. I moved slowly toward the exquisitely crafted, oblong eternal dwelling for the remains of Edward Zachary Naylor.

My family followed. None of us spoke. I touched Daddy's face and snatched my hand away immediately. His skin's frigidity shocked me. I realized I'd never touched a dead person before. Renee stood very close to me, stroking my arm. She touched his perfectly manicured hands, which were crossed at his waist. Dawn ran her hand along the edge of his suit lapel. No one uttered a sound, but we spoke volumes.

"Everything seems to be exactly as we requested, Mr. Brown," Dawn said in a preoccupied voice. "You've done a wonderful job. He looks so peaceful."

"Yessah, y'all did a mighty fine job. He looks like he's sleepin'," Uncle Thomas said, wiping his eyes.

"My Eddie would be very pleased."

"We'll have him moved to the main chapel right away for public viewing. We've had a lot of calls asking when they could come by to pay their respects."

"Then we'll see you at the church this evening, Mr. Brown?" I asked, turning away from Daddy.

"Yes, I'll be handling this service personally."

"I guess we can head back to the house?" Renee asked of no one in particular.

"I'll have the car pulled around. I just need two signatures and we do have a final bit of business to handle."

"Oh yes, the payment. I almost forgot. I guess we should go back to your office?" Renee asked.

A sense of relief found its way to the funeral director's face. He was glad Renee had brought up the payment first. "Right this way."

We filed out of the room and back to the office in which we'd been seated before. Dawn had a faraway look that mirrored my feelings. I understood why the funeral home provided car service throughout the process. I don't think any of us was in any condition to drive.

Renee paid the full amount due and thanked Mr. Brown again. Unusually quiet, we slowly left the building and descended the stairs toward the waiting car. Nina startled me when she began to speak.

"You may think I'm overstepping my bounds, but why did *you* have to pay for Poppee's expenses? He told me he had lots of insurance."

"Oh, we'd had words with Mr. Brown when we were first making the arrangements. He was trying to charge according to what he perceived was our ability to pay. So when he asked for the policies, we told him he needn't concern himself with the insurance because we were paying cash."

"Very good business move. Poppee always talked about your business savvy."

"We know so little about you and what you do, Nina. We're so caught up in all of this we haven't even asked," I said, waiting my turn to get in the car.

"I know. There's not a lot to tell, I guess. I'm a clinical social worker with a master's degree in psychology. I manage a unit at a hospital for emotionally challenged teens. I've been in social work my entire adult life. I met Victor while I was working as a counselor in the justice system. He's a parole officer. We fell in love on our first date, and that was eighteen years ago. We were married seven months after our first date and have been more than happy ever since. You've spoken to Edwina; she's our only child."

"We have a million questions," Dawn said. "I'm sure you'll answer them in time. I know I speak for Renee and Glynda when I say we're happy to have you as a part of our family. It'll take some adjusting to on our part, but we'll all be just fine. Don't worry about Collette; she'll come around."

"The last thing I want to do is cause any more grief. I think my greatest disappointment is that Poppee isn't here to help us all get through this."

None of us responded. We spent the remainder of the ride home in silence. As we turned the corner, I was amazed at the number of cars parked in front of Daddy's house. The one car I wanted to see was conspicuously absent: Collette's.

Before we had all congregated on the sidewalk to thank the driver for the transportation, the front door flew open and Roberta rushed out to greet us. She carried a white linen handkerchief, which she brought to her mouth as she approached us. Tears were surely not far behind. I braced myself, determined to be kind.

"Oh, I should have been with you when you went to the funeral home. Are you doing alright?" Her question was directed at Renee.

"We're doing."

"Why don't you come on inside? Rico and I have prepared a light snack. I brought the Bowmans over, too. Everyone is inside. I thought you would have called me to go with you this morning."

"It was just for immediate family. We had a private viewing and some business to handle. But you'll be riding from the house with us tonight, right?"

"Well, if it was for immediate family, why are these people with you?" Miraculously, Roberta's tears vanished.

Renee looked from Nina to me, as if asking permission to divulge our family secret. I was expressionless. I knew we'd have to tell this story a thousand times over during the next two days. I wanted to print flyers and pass them out with the service programs. *This woman is*

*our sister. She is my daddy's illegitimate love child. We
know as much about her as you do, so please don't ask
us any questions.*

"Roberta, this is Nina Blackford. She is our sister."

"Your sister? So when I said I was your sister, it was
unacceptable, but this woman, whom I've never met,
can say *she's* your sister."

"Roberta, she can say she's our sister because she *is*
our sister. She is Daddy's oldest child." I was praying for
fortitude.

As the color drained from Roberta's face, she began to
speak. "What do you mean she's Papa Eddie's oldest
child?"

"What part of that are you not comprehending?"
Dawn said, uncommonly rude. "Daddy had a child with
a woman other than our mother and here she is!"

"She just shows up and says she's Papa Eddie's child
and you take her word for it? Well, I surely do not!"

"Roberta, we don't give a damn whether you accept
her word or not. This is none of your business. Please
don't make me remind you of your place and put you in
it." I felt my blood pressure rising.

"Well, you haven't heard the last from me on this."
Roberta turned to walk away.

"Wait just a got-damn, fly-fucking minute," Renee
burst out. "Who do you think you are? I have put up
with your butting into my family business longer than I
can remember. I always felt sorry for you because you
didn't have a close family of your own. I've been defending you, causing friction between my real sisters and me.
But you have gone too damn far this time. You better
take your ass back in the house and find your place and
stay the fuck in it. Or if you don't like what I'm saying,
you can take your ass home. Because you see, that was
not *your* daddy that I just saw, and you have the option

of leaving!" Renee was sweating and out of breath by the time she finished.

I couldn't understand where Roberta got her nerve. But I was more than a little glad Renee had finally told her off. Maybe now she'd get it. We stared after her as she walked away in tears, without responding to Renee.

"Poppee had talked about Roberta from time to time, but nothing prepared me for this. She's a bit possessive, isn't she?"

"That she is. We've had more than a few words in the past few days. But her heart is in the right place, I think. She loves Daddy, but she doesn't know when to be seen and not heard." I couldn't believe I was defending Roberta.

"We should go inside. Brace yourself for the questions and dirty looks. No one is going to want to believe you're Eddie Naylor's daughter, despite how much you look like Collette." Renee took one of Nina's arms, leading her toward the house.

"I'm ready. To be with you all is worth anything these people can throw at me. I've longed for this my entire life. I'm finally with my sisters. . . ." Nina smiled as her voice trailed off.

21

All God's Children

Like a Cling Free—softened blanket falls onto a freshly made bed, a hush fell over the house. One by one, the visitors stopped talking to stare at Collette's mirror image. As we moved through the room, the buzz of conversation behind us gained volume like the roar of an oncoming train.

The words on almost everyone's lips resounded throughout the house: "Who is that woman? Is she a cousin?"

The atmosphere in the rooms had shifted so drastically, I felt tension choking me. I wanted to scream for all of these people to mind their own damn business. This was for the Naylor family to handle, and we weren't interested in anything they had to say.

Renee's and Dawn's faces showed the same stress I felt. I thought we had prepared ourselves for the stares. Was I imagining they were pointing fingers? Uncle Thomas sensed our distress and rescued us.

"Y'all, can I have e'rybody's attention? I has me a announcement ta make. I know y'alls all wondering who dis here lovely young woman is. Well, she's mah niece. She be Eddie's oldest chile. I knows y'all are wonderin' where she come from, where she been, 'n' such. We don't have them answers just yet. But we loves her, 'n' dat's dat!"

"I guess that pretty much covers it," Dawn continued.

"Our sister's name is Nina, Nina Naylor Blackford. And this is her husband, Victor. They're from St. Louis, and we met them this morning. So we're as surprised as all of you. But we know just by looking at her she is one of us, and we've embraced her. This has been a very stressful day and we'd appreciate it if you'd hold any questions, which we probably don't have answers to at this point anyway, until later." Dawn's voice cracked several times during her monologue.

"Well, Miss Nina, let me be the first to introduce myself. I'm your uncle Willie. Me and your daddy was the best of friends for a many a year."

"I've heard so much about you, Mister Willie. Poppee spent hours talking about that candy apple red sports car you bought. Secretly, I think he wanted one, too." Nina shook his hand and kissed him on the cheek.

Willie, blushing, said, "Oh, ain't you the sweet one. I don't know why Eddie didn't tell me about you. I just know we got a lot of years to catch up on!"

"Watch it now, Mister Willie. You're gonna make me jealous. You know you're my godfather." Dawn hugged him.

Mister Willie broke the ice, and soon everyone began introducing themselves to Nina. They went out of their way to make her feel welcome. Looking at each of my sisters, I knew they felt the same relief I did. If anyone was shocked by this revelation, they kept it well disguised.

"Glynda, baby, where's Collette?" Sister Greene pulled me toward the kitchen as she whispered.

Her question immediately opened my floodgates. "I don't know, Sister Greene. She never even showed up at the funeral home. She told us if Nina went along, she wouldn't come. She said she wouldn't ride with us or sit with us at the funeral. Why is she doing this?"

"Ahhh, come here, baby, it's going to be alright. She'll come 'round. You know this is a bit of a shocker, I have to admit. But your daddy was human. Just like any other man. He loved your mother, of that you can be sure!"

I explained that Nina was conceived before Daddy and Mama even met. At that moment I wondered how many more times I'd have to explain this before it was all over.

The noise level had once again elevated to a low roar as various friends and family members followed Rico and Jonathan as they gathered around Nina. I was pleased she was being so well received, and I slipped away to Daddy's room for solitude and to call Collette. She picked up on the first ring. "Why didn't you come to the funeral home?"

"I told you if that woman went, I wasn't going. I don't understand how y'all can be so gullible."

"Lette, it's not a question of whether she's telling the truth or not. We all, including you, know that she's Daddy's daughter. But how could you not come with us? It was really hard. I fainted . . . again," I explained, hoping to solicit a warm, sympathetic response.

"I despise that woman for coming into our lives now. How dare she even begin to tarnish Daddy's memory! I won't have anything to do with her or the rest of you, if she's taken in as one of us."

"You're being so unreasonable! She has every right to be with us—right down front. We don't know why Daddy chose to cheat her, and us, out of a lifetime of love and sharing. He did nothing wrong. We all need to be able to grieve for him together. Please come over here now. We have a few hours before we have to leave for the funeral, and a lot of people are asking for you."

"I don't give a damn about people asking for me. Tell

them to ask Nina why I'm not there. I'm sure they're all making kissy-kissy with her by now."

"Are you jealous?"

"What the fuck do I have to be jealous for? Eddie Naylor didn't hide me from the rest of the world. If anything, I should pity her."

"You're exactly right. We should all feel sorry for her and treat her with love and respect."

"You know what?"

"What?"

"See you at the church, because this conversation is over."

"Does that mean—"

Colette broke the connection before I could ask her if that meant she wasn't riding to the church with us. Pain engulfed my heart at the thought of the devil's hand at work, destroying us little by little. I thought of the many years of happiness we'd shared in this house, the laughter and tears. Nothing was stronger than family. Yet family was tearing us apart. I yearned for Daddy to console me. There was never anything that Mr. Naylor couldn't fix—until now.

A soft knock at the door brought me from my torturous thoughts. "Come in."

"Hi. May I come in?" Nina stuck her head in the door.

"Sure, I was just sitting here feeling as sorry for myself as I possibly could."

"I think you're entitled. I needed to get away for a few minutes. Everyone means well, but it's just a little too much to handle at the moment. I feel like I need to explain my relationship with Poppee."

"Did he ever explain to you why he never told us about you?"

"When I was a little girl, he said that your mother would understand and love me like I was one of her own, but he couldn't bring himself to hurt her. He said Grandmother, his mother, had always told him never to bring any illegitimate babies home. And though she was dead, he felt he couldn't do it. He never made me feel like I didn't belong. He sent pictures almost every month and long, long letters. On his visits he showed me the pictures and explained each one in detail until I knew each of you personally.

"Then Lorraine died. Oh, Glynda, my poppee changed. He didn't call or write for months. He called my mother to tell her that Lorraine had been killed and said he'd speak to me when he could."

"Why do you think he stopped calling?"

"My mother said she thought it was guilt, because he hadn't ever told her the truth about me."

"I want to know everything about you, Edwina, and Victor. And I want to know it all right now!" I clapped my hands together for emphasis.

"I see we must have inherited our patience from the same place." We laughed and hugged each other.

"Gurl, Daddy was as patient as Job on one hand; then on the other, he could be as anxious as a welfare recipient on check day." I felt as if I was chatting with an old friend.

"Thank you, Glynda."

"For what?"

"Not making this any harder than it already is."

"I can't explain it, but I feel close to you already."

"That's called family."

"Yeah, I guess it is."

We sat in silence for what seemed like an endless time, and soon we were holding hands. I wondered where Nina's mind had taken her. Mine raced with a zillion questions. We'd have to make time to talk when the funeral was over. A knock at the door interrupted my thoughts.

"Sissy, baby, y'all alright in here?" Sister Greene carried a tray with two cups, which I presumed to be coffee.

"Thank you, Sister Greene, we're fine. Just getting to know my sister. I heard the roar getting louder. Are there many people here?"

"Baby, there's almost no place to walk out there. Mostly people are coming and going, though. I told them y'all were resting for a minute since you were at the funeral home earlier. They understand, though the newcomers are more than a little curious about Nina. Chile, it's like they put a billboard on the front lawn about her. People seem to know when they come through the door."

"In case I haven't told you, thank you so much for how you are holding everything together for us. You're runnin' thangs in that kitchen."

"It's the least I can do. I been knowing y'all before y'all knew yourselves. But speaking of the kitchen, Mildred Williams brought some dressing. Now I'm not one to talk about folks, but you know her house is half-past nasty. And roaches applied for Section Eight last week. I don't want to hurt her feelings, but I'm just scared to serve any food she brought. What should I do?"

Nina fell over on the bed laughing at Sister Greene. It took all within me to keep a straight face. "Well, Sister Greene, I trust your judgment. Maybe we can tell her when she comes back from the funeral that it's all gone?"

"I'll think of something. That woman needs to clean up that house. I knew her mama, and she was raised better than that! Y'all come on out when you feelin' up to it." Sister Greene patted both of us on the hand and left.

"What a sweet woman. Poppee told me about her,

too. He said she had a thing for him when Lorraine first died. She seems like she'd have been a great catch. But in matters of the heart, who knows."

"True, that. I guess we should get back to the people. Maybe we can relieve Renee and Dawn. I'm sure they could use a minute alone to regroup. You ready?"

"Let's do it!" Nina grabbed my hand, almost dragging me toward the door.

As we reentered the hub of the activity, all heads turned toward us, and a hush fell over the room once again. No one seemed to know what to say. Nina broke the silence.

"Good afternoon to everyone I haven't had the pleasure of meeting yet. I'm sure you've heard about me. I'm Nina Naylor Blackford, Eddie Naylor's oldest daughter. My sisters and I will answer any questions you may have to the best of our ability. I want to thank you for coming by this afternoon to check on our well-being and to lend your support."

The stunned group managed a greeting and some moved toward her to make introductions. Nina seemed perfectly at home with the people we'd known all of our lives. Perhaps because Daddy had made sure that she, too, knew them. They hadn't met face-to-face, but Daddy had made sure she knew everyone who was important in his life. I felt a sense of pride and love for both of them at this moment. As I stared at Victor, the song "When a Man Loves a Woman" came to mind. The love he'd felt for his wife for so many years dominated his face.

Within a very short time the level of activity had returned to normal throughout the house. Most people stopped by briefly to talk with each of us and express their sympathy and offer a piece of advice. The one comment that seemed to antagonize me most was: He's in a better place. Without exception, when someone uttered those words, the hair stood up on the back of my neck. How dare they tell me such a thing . . . even if it were true?

Sister Greene and the other Willing Workers made sure everyone had something to eat or drink, if not both. I thought back to how many times I'd been the visitor expressing my condolences. When Mama died, I was too young to comprehend all that went on around us. I can remember Sister Greene, even then, being in charge of the kitchen. It had been Sister Williams's job to make sure the children were always kept occupied.

This time was different. I was expected to act like an adult. I had to make decisions. I didn't like this job description one little bit.

Marvin and Martin, the identical twins from down the block, stood before me like two African kings. They exemplified the word *Alayé*. I hadn't seen them in more than ten years. They had sho' 'nuff filled in those six-foot-five-inch breath-and-britches bodies quite nicely. At nearly thirty years old they still spoke in stereo.

"Glynda, we're so sorry about Mister Eddie. We just saw him down at the boys' and girls' club last month. He'd talked us into coaching swimming and track. Then we started mentoring last year, and it's changed our lives. Your dad was da man! We're all going to really miss him." Martin had started, and Marvin had finished. Or was it the other way around?

"Thank you, guys. You're right about one thing, my daddy will be sorely missed. Have you eaten? There's plenty of food, and it seems another dish appears magically every few minutes."

"We're fine. We're actually guilty. Mom and Dad sent us over with the food. They'll see you at the services tonight. We'll be there, too, of course. We'll be speaking on behalf of the club." I was reasonably sure it was Marvin speaking to me.

As I looked around the room, I saw my sisters having what appeared to be similar conversations. Without any spoken plan we'd each taken up residence in a different area of the house, each with her own command post.

Marvin and Martin excused themselves and found Derrick. I'm sure the good strong brothas would do whatever it took not to show any emotion. I envied them.

"How you holding up?" Rico rubbed my shoulders as she spoke.

"Where've you been? I saw you when I first got here and then you disappeared."

"Jonathan and I had to take care of some business for the service tonight. We went by the funeral home. I wanted a more quiet time to see him before the service. There were so many people there it took a long time to just get in the viewing room. You guys did a phenomenal job. Everything is first class. As only Papa Eddie would have had it."

"Yeah, he looks pretty good for a dead man, huh?"

Rico only smiled at me.

"I'm sorry. I guess that was in really poor taste."

"You're entitled. I see Collette isn't here yet. Do you think she'll make good on her threat?"

"Rico, I'm so afraid she will. I tried talking to her earlier, and she's being so unreasonable. She said she's not riding or sitting with us. Can you imagine?"

"Because she's your sister, I'm not going to tell you what I really think. I'm just really sorry she's stressing you out even further. Roberta went with us. Gurl, I thought I was going to have to perform CPR on her. She turned blue. And say what you want, you can't fake that. Everyone there was crying; some were wailing. I'm just glad

Jonathan suggested I go before the service. Will the casket be open?"

"Yes, for the first hour, the wake portion. Then we'll close it for the service, and we won't open it again. I'll never see Daddy again, Rico." With that tears began to fall.

"Aunt Ida Mae is still sleeping. I don't know how she's sleeping through all of this. I guess the bus ride was a little more than she bargained for. How old is she anyway?" Rico had very smoothly changed the subject.

"Gurl, she was Grandma's older sister, so I'd say at least eighty-five."

"Damn, she looks good. She doesn't look or move like she's a day over sixty. She was dressed so fly, too."

"Did you warn her about Nina?"

"No. I know my place, and all up in y'all's business surely wasn't it."

I laughed at my friend's down-to-earth nature. She was my grounding rod. My gaze went to Renee, and I saw Roberta rubbing her shoulders as Rico had done mine. I couldn't help but wonder if she was only trying to emulate Rico.

My attention was drawn to the sound of gold bracelets and beads. Much to my surprise, Aunt Ida Mae stood in the middle of the floor demanding a Bloody Mary. Rico was correct—she was very fly.

"Aunt Ida Mae! You look fabulous." I ran over to hug her.

"Baby, now don't tell me. Who is you? You Glynda, ain't chu?"

"Yes, ma'am. I'm so happy to see you. How're you feeling?"

"I be feeling a whole heap a lot betta if I could get me a Bloody Mary. I need the tomato juice to settle mah stomach. Where's mah nephew?"

"He's out back, Aunt Ida Mae," Dawn said, hugging and kissing her.

"You Dawn, right?"

"Yes, ma'am. How do you remember us like that? I haven't seen you in a long time."

"Chile, ain't a thang wrong with my eyes and brain. Now mah back and hips is a diff'rent story.

"Collette, come on ovah here and give your auntie some sugah. You been sick, chile?"

We looked from one to the other before Renee approached Aunt Ida Mae. Hugging her first, she then spoke. "Auntie, this isn't Collette. This is Nina."

We waited for some sort of recognition. There was a long pause as Aunt Ida Mae rubbed her temple. Then with a perplexed look, she asked, "Who the hell is Nina? God knows she looks like Collette. Just older. I thought she'd had a spell of sickness or sumin'."

"I'm your great-niece, Aunt Ida Mae," Nina said softly.

"Well, Ray Charles could see you look just like yo' daddy. So why come I don't know you? And where is my Bloody Mary? I swear I needs it now."

"None of us knew about her until this morning. But we agree with you she looks too much like Daddy not to be our sister, and we have accepted it."

"Where da hell is Collette? I guess this is what your daddy had to tell ole Auntie. He was going to send for me for the family reunion. But said he was going to come down and have a heart-to-heart with me after his wedding. Lordy, lordy. This is sumin, I tell you. My sister wouldn't have liked this one bit. No sirree, Bob."

"Collette is a little upset about Nina being here. She said if Nina is accepted as our sister and participates in the services as our sister, then she isn't coming with us." I wasn't sure, but Dawn's voice seemed to have a tattle-taleish flavor to it.

"Nina, baby, come ovah here and help Auntie ovah to dat chair? Who your people and where is dey from?"

"I'm from Missouri. I live in a suburb outside of St. Louis. My family is from a small town called Bolivar. My mother moved to Fort Leonardwood when she was eighteen. That's where she met Poppee. But we all live somewhere in Missouri."

"You don't have no people in the South? Arkansas way?"

"Not that I'm aware of."

"Well, I guess I jest betta welcome you to the family. Eddie ain't done no mo' than a million otha men done. It ain't easy to let your *real* family know 'bout your secrets."

Nina winced at the words "real family," but she said nothing.

"Go git Thomas. I needs to talk to him. Is his boys here?"

"No, ma'am. They aren't coming as far as we know. They haven't even called," Renee volunteered.

"I don't know what be worst. Not knowing you got family or got family and they don't even call or come 'round. I do declare."

"Auntie! 'Bout time you woke up. I was going to come in dere and put a mirror unda yo' nose! Give me some sugah, gal!" Uncle Thomas ran over to where Aunt Ida Mae was seated.

As he leaned over to kiss her, she slapped him.

22

Kinfolks

"Ow! What was dat fo'?"

"Not telling me about this here chile."

"Auntie, I swear I didn't know eitha! Eddie didn't tell me nuthin'."

"Then it fo' your brotha not tellin' me."

It took everything in us not to laugh. How many times had we been on the receiving end of someone else's disciplinary reward? Aunt Ida Mae grabbed Thomas's hand and pulled him close so she could hug and kiss him. Again, how typical, whip your behind and then kiss it and make it better.

We spent a long time exchanging pleasantries, answering Aunt Ida Mae's questions about our careers and families. More people filtered through bearing food, paper goods, beverages, and words of comfort. The last influx of people brought Estelle, Jamaica, and Michelle.

Grief had drawn lines on Estelle's flawless skin. She had aged years in hours. Jamaica's normal flamboyancy had given way to a quiet, subdued state. Michelle, however, floated in on an imaginary cloud.

Jamaica gave kisses all around. He spent a long time with Aunt Ida Mae, fussing over her beautiful designer jogging suit. Auntie loved the attention. Estelle spread polite greetings to everyone, then settled quietly in Daddy's favorite chair. Michelle stood around waiting for someone to acknowledge her presence. I guess I had to be the one.

"It's good to see you again, Michelle. It's amazing we're never in contact living in the same county." Small talk was wasted on her.

"Well, I'm always available for family. You should call my assistant to schedule a meeting."

"I'll do that." What I didn't add was, when Don King gets a haircut.

"I can't believe I had to rent an American car. I haven't driven anything but European cars since I started working in Hollywood." Michelle waited for one of us to bite.

"I thought your mother picked you up from the airport?" I'd found an easy mark.

"Oh, ummm, well. She insisted."

"Michelle, what's it like to work in Hollywood? Who do you hang out with? Do you know Master P?" Derrick was rapid-firing questions.

"Oh no, I work with the upper echelon of Hollywood. I work with Denzel, Steven, George, people like that."

"What exactly do you do for these upper echelonees?" Dawn expertly served up sarcasm.

"I'm working with the behind-the-scenes crew."

"Oh, a friend from law school did that to put herself through school. It's called production assistant, right?"

"Well, I'm not just a production assistant. I work closely with the directors and technical crews."

"So just what are you then?" Renee asked.

"Stop frontin', Michelle. You're a Starbucks-runnin', Krispy-Kreme-gettin', dry-cleanin'-pick-uppin' flunky. We're your family. And you couldn't rent a Gremlin with your no-credit-havin' ass." Jamaica's hand flared as he spoke.

"Why are you talking to me like this? You have no idea the advances I've made since you took your faggoty ass to Paris."

"You betta watch your mouth, gurl. We have some elderly people here," Renee chastised.

"At least I know exactly who and what I am," Jamaica said. "You're still trying to find yourself. You need to climb down off that high horse before you get knocked off by a tree limb." He rolled his eyes and snapped his neck so hard I thought he'd get whiplash.

"I know full well what I'm doing, and I'm very proud of my accomplishments. Just because you're onstage performing doesn't make you any better than me behind the scenes. We're both in show business."

"Those of us who can perform, do; those who can't, hate!"

Michelle turned quickly and disappeared into the crowded living room. We each shook our head and smiled. Michelle hadn't changed. She'd always been a legend in her own mind.

I brought Renee and Dawn up to speed on Collette's absence and suggested we not expect her to do the right thing.

"Explain to me what's wrong with that woman?" Dawn started pacing.

"She's angry because you all have accepted me as your sister. I'm sorry that I've caused a division. I wanted more than anything to be accepted and to become one of you. I realize now that was a pipe dream. When I'd heard Poppee was dead, I never thought of anything except getting here. I knew this is where I belonged."

"Dis prolly ain't my place, but it ain't nevah stopped me befo'. You right, chile, dis here is 'xactly where you belong. I don't rightly know why Eddie didn't tell us 'bout you. But we yo' fam'ly. No ifs, ands, or buts—just love." Aunt Ida Mae took a long swig from her Bloody Mary.

With that we all said, "Amen."

All heads turned as we heard an unfamiliar voice call, "Nina!"

"Mom!" Nina ran to the newcomer, embracing her and starting to cry.

"Oh, sweetie. I'm so sorry, so, so sorry." The woman I presumed to be Nina's mother stroked her back as she hugged her.

"Where's Edwina?" Nina managed to say as she stood upright.

"She's right behind me."

"Everyone, this is my mother, Delores Cannon."

We did our best to make her feel welcome with our greetings. She seemed nice enough on the surface. I spoke up first. "We're so glad you could make it here. We've had a little time to get to know Nina, and we love her already."

"I couldn't let Nina go through this alone. She has loved her father since the first day he came to visit her, and he was wonderful to her and Edwina. Your father was a man of great integrity. He never let his lack of love for me influence his relationship with Nina. And I don't know what I can say to make you know that as far as . . . I know he was always faithful to your mother." Fragmented words conveyed what obviously lay deep in her heart.

We looked from one to the other before Renee moved toward Mrs. Cannon and embraced her. "Thank you for telling us this. You have brought a great sense of relief to me knowing that everything Nina has told is the absolute truth."

"What's up?" A teenager with much attitude entered.

"You be more respectful, young lady!" Nina chastised.

"Edwina, these are your aunts: Renee, Dawn, and Glynda. This is your grandfather's fiancée, Miss Estelle." Nina smiled with pride as she introduced her newfound family.

"Where's the one who looks just like you?" Edwina said, popping gum.

"She's not here at the moment."

"I bet she ain't!" Edwina laughed sarcastically.

"You have to forgive Edwina. She's a bit hostile about the family situation. She's wanted to meet you all for years and is a little bitter about not being a part of this family," Nina said, trying to make excuses for her daughter's rude behavior.

"We all have some pretty strong feelings on this situation, but you really need to put her in a more respectful frame of mind." Estelle didn't try to mask her irritation with Edwina.

"She's a typical teenager. Hormonal changes have made her a little difficult at times."

We said nothing. I did say to myself, however, *Eddie Naylor must not have spent a lot of time with Miss Thang!*

I stood looking in the mirror in Daddy's bathroom contemplating the practicality of applying makeup. I looked so pale and washed out that I needed at least a little color on my cheeks. Dawn and Renee sat on opposite sides of Daddy's bed. Dawn had her control-top panty hose around her ankles. Renee just sat staring into space.

Derrick and Victor had undertaken the major chore of making sure the children were ready when the funeral cars arrived. They'd bonded instantly and were conversing like old friends in very short order. It was good for Derrick to have another man who shared his feelings. Loving a Naylor girl could be taxing, to say the least.

As I stared at the bathroom clock, the reality of the day seeped deep into my pores. All of the crying, all of the arguments, all of the disagreements had come down to this moment in time. In an hour someone would say a prayer for our strength. Someone else would direct us to the waiting cars. We'd ride in silence. We'd then line up outside the church in order of birth and march in slowly to music Daddy had chosen specifically for the occasion.

"Do you think Collette is going to show up?" Renee asked in a defeated tone without looking up.

"I'm praying she does. But you know how she is. She's hell bent on hurting us even further than we already are because she thinks we've betrayed her. And do you know what's so ironic?"

"Nina looks most like her?" Dawn asked the rhetorical question.

"Exactly! Hell, they look identical."

"I can't believe she'd embarrass us like this. She's a piece of work, I swear." Renee finally stood.

"Well, there are going to be some questions, you can believe that shit. Collette's not with us, but Nina's there. Man oh man!"

"Maybe no one will notice it's not Collette."

"That would be hilarious. She'd be doing this to get back at us, and no one will notice."

"Do you think word of this has spread like a rumor on the Internet?"

"Sister Greene *does* know."

We all laughed. I slipped on my skirt, only to find it

was too big. I'd lost at least five pounds since Daddy had died. I realized I hadn't eaten all day. There had been only one endless cup of coffee.

My sisters dressed in silence. I wanted to be ready to greet our visitors who arrived to follow us to the church. As I slipped on my jacket, the feeling of heaviness returned to my body. Lord, please don't let me faint again.

"I'm going to go and greet our visitors," I managed weakly.

"Gurl, you look terrible. I'd ask if you're okay, but we can see you're not. You'd better sit." Dawn helped me to the bed.

"I'm okay, honest."

"Yeah, right. I think we need to pray." Renee held my trembling hands.

"Come on, Dawn. We have so much to deal with today. Not the least of which is your silly sister." We took one another's hands, forming a small circle.

"Father, our God in Heaven," Renee began, "first we want to thank You for Your continued blessings. Lord, You loved us when we were too stupid to love ourselves. You've protected and carried us when we didn't even know we'd fallen. We don't understand why You've taken Daddy home to be with You, but we have no choice but to accept this very difficult cup from which we are forced to drink. Lord, we ask that You strengthen our steps, and give us an inner peace today and in the weeks, months, and years to come. Whatever it is the enemy is putting on my sister Glynda, I rebuke it in Jesus' name. Strengthen her body. Please bring our sister Collette back to her senses. Help her to see this is the way it is, period. Help us to understand the Nina situation. Let us show her Naylor love and accept her the way You've accepted us. Lord, be with Estelle as she says good-bye to her true love. Strengthen Aunt Ida Mae and Uncle Thomas. Give us patience with one another. In Jesus' name, and we all say . . ."

"Amen," Dawn and I said together, and we hugged the woman we'd always known to be our oldest sister.

"Now, let's go do this thing." Renee grabbed her jacket from the hanger suspended from the bathroom door frame.

As if I'd been given a shot of B_{12}, I felt a renewed strength. "And what do you mean, our sister?"

"When she trippin', I disown her," Renee said as we all laughed.

"Damn, I wish I'd thought of that!" I laughed, knowing humor would be elusive for the next several hours, if not days.

Dawn opened the door. It was show time.

Uncle Thomas sat looking handsome and so much like Daddy, I wanted to just hold him. Auntie sipped another Bloody Mary. I wanted to remind her we were going to church shortly but then thought better of it. Mister Willie and Sister Greene were the first to arrive. They sat talking to Uncle Thomas and Aunt Ida Mae.

"Hey, girls. Don't y'all look beautiful. Nina was just out here, and she should be right back. Can I get you anything?" Sister Greene rose and walked toward us.

"Nothing for me. Thanks. Has anyone heard from Collette?"

"I called her to try to talk some sense into her. But she's your daddy's child. Stubborn as June twenty-first is long." Sister Greene was fussing about the room, unable to not be working on something or someone.

"I don't rightly know what's done got inta dat chile. I'm 'bout sho' 'nuff shame of da way she be actin'."

Uncle Thomas crossed and uncrossed his legs as he spoke.

"We just said a little prayer for her in the bedroom and actually for all of us that we just make it through the next few hours." Renee sat next to Uncle Thomas, laying her hand on his.

I checked my watch as the members of Daddy's domino club arrived. The funeral director would pick us up in thirty minutes. I needed to busy myself with some sort of activity, to do something with my hands and my mind. Nina and Victor entered the den wearing burgundy pants suits. They were so elegant. Nina looked even more like Collette dressed up. She hugged each of us.

"How much longer before the funeral director arrives?" Victor asked, never leaving Nina's side.

"About thirty minutes or so. Maybe most will meet us at the church."

Derrick arrived from the basement with five well-polished little soldiers, and said, "Well, looks like the gang's all here. Everyone looks really nice."

We smiled politely. Before we could respond, a clatter came from the front door that caused us all to turn. Estelle and crew arrived with Roberta on their heels. Roberta had a handkerchief at her face. I rolled my eyes and sighed deeply. *Let the drama begin.*

"Good evening, everyone. I see we're all ready to go. Lordy, I don't know if I can do this." Estelle emptied her lungs as she spoke.

"Mama, we'll be there for you. We got you!" Jamaica kissed Estelle on the cheek.

"You got me? Who got you? You've been crying all afternoon." Estelle managed a weak laugh.

"Shhh! Don't call me out like that, Ma!" Jamaica performed in his best dramatic fashion.

"Oh hush, boy. You just make sure none of us have to come and pick you up off the floor. Thinking you're so strong."

"We're much too intelligent for all of these antics. I've been to funerals where you didn't even hear the people crying." Michelle ran her index finger around the rim of a glass filled with orange juice.

"Were these black folks?" Nina asked, amused.

"No."

With a snap of her fingers, Nina said, "And there ya have it."

"I just know I'm not going to be able to handle this one little bit. I had my doctor prescribe Valium." Roberta held her head. "I took one just before I left home. Someone else is going to have to drive my car. I'm just not going to be able to."

This slick hussy was trying to jockey for a place in the family car. "I'm sure we can find someone to drive you in your own car, or you can ride with Rico and Jonathan."

Roberta's eyelashes fluttered, and she seemed to have a small seizure. "I was hoping to be able to ride with y'all."

"Hope floats, my sistah. We'll find someone to drive your car, or you can leave it here." I wasn't bending, despite the pleading look in Renee's eyes.

People again began to fill the house, each bearing a casserole dish, bag, plate, bowl, or some such container of food. Everyone spoke softly. Some stared at Nina, but asked no questions. I watched our family and friends mill about making polite conversation. Had it not been for the Sunday-go-to-meeting garments, I would have thought everyone had come over for one of Daddy's famous barbecues. No one spoke of death. No one said that Edward Naylor's resounding laughter would never fill this house again. I became angry. Like the swelling crest of the mighty Mississippi, anger finds it own means of escape.

Someone needed to be scared.

23

Until Death Brings Us Together

I could see Rico smiling at me as we made our way up the aisle toward the casket. I couldn't remember the ride to or the assembly outside of the church. Surely if I was inside the church those events had taken place. The large sanctuary was filled beyond capacity. Flowers covered the expansive altar and spilled into the pulpit. Every conceivable color was represented in very simple to extraordinary designs. The arrangement that dominated the front of this Pentecostal temple was a pair of dominoes. Big six and the six-three, with a huge sash that read SIZ-NIX, BIG ED, WE'LL MISS YOU. Several rows were reserved for family, but every other available seat was occupied. People lined the back of the church, and I assumed the overflow room was filled to capacity, as well. Though the majority in the sea of people were expressionless, many could be seen whispering and pointing. The focus of everyone's attention was Nina Blackford.

"Rough Side of the Mountain," Daddy's favorite song, played as we moved closer and closer to the front of the church. With every step I felt a constriction in my chest. My breath was labored and shallow. Though I tried to breathe deep, my lungs failed to respond. My ears began to ring. In front of me Derrick held Renee upright. Her feet dug into the rich blue carpet as her husband dragged her along. Nina's mannequin-like posture made me think

she would break at the slightest bend. Victor did his best
to move her forward.

My eyes searched the crowd for Anthony. I refused to
believe that some miracle hadn't made it possible for
him to be here for me. Dawn's eyes darted back and
forth. In my heart I knew she looked for Reginald, the
same Reginald who hadn't shown his face since I'd arrived. Feeling cheated by the fates yet again, I sank deeper
into the quagmire of despair.

We walked what seemed like an endless aisle until we
reached the front pew. As we neared the casket I averted
my eyes. Nina and Victor were seated first, followed by
Renee and Derrick. I sat next to Derrick, then Dawn.
Collette was conspicuously absent. Uncle Thomas sat
next to Dawn. The rows behind us filled quickly as the
choir sang softly. Bishop raised both hands and slowly
lowered them, indicating the congregation should be
seated.

After a long silence Bishop, with his most resounding
voice, began. " 'If I can affect one person, help one young
person reconsider the path they've chosen, I may be the
only Jesus anyone ever sees, and I need to be as much
like Him as I can be. Understand that has nothing to do
with sittin' in the front pew, but everything to do with
what I do for my brother.' Those were the words Edward Zachary Naylor said to me consistently. He was
tireless in his mission. Well, saints, I can surely say this
evening that this man affected the many, not the few.
He . . ."

A cross between confusion and dismay found its way
to Bishop's face. He opened his mouth, but words refused to come. Loud whispers could be heard throughout the congregation. Following Bishop's gaze, I turned
but refused to believe the picture my retina had cap-
tured.

Up the center aisle of the church, where her father lay in state, strolled Collette Bernice Naylor-Cunningham-Grisham-Naylor, wearing a tight, pumpkin orange miniskirted suit. If wind had found its way under the matching hat, she would have become airborne. She took careful steps so she wouldn't trip in the four-inch pumps with straps that crisscrossed her ankles. Her shoulder bag, which rounded out this atrocity called an outfit, was of the beachgoing variety. Huge 'round-the-way-girl gold hoop earrings, bangle bracelets that jangled with her every movement. To hide what must have been shame were matching orange-framed sunglasses.

She sashayed toward the front of the church as if she were on the red carpet at a Hollywood premiere. The sight of Collette caused something inside of me to snap. The Mississippi was overrunning its banks. Before Dawn and Derrick could stop me, I was out of my seat and headed toward her. Her disrespect for my daddy was not comprehensible. I wasn't going to stand for it. As though Scottie had beamed me up, I stood before Collette. The church fell silent.

"How dare you come in here looking like a Cal-Trans ho!"

"You better get outta my face. Why don't you go back over there with your new sister? There isn't even room on the front row for me. I'll find my own seat." Collette tried to move past me.

Like Bryant blocking Iverson, I obstructed her every move. "Why're you doing this? You acting like you were raised in the projects, or better yet, not raised at all."

"You have two choices. You can step aside or be stepped aside. I don't give a damn about being in a church, I will clock you like you are Big Ben." She pushed me.

I'm not sure what happened next, but I remember seeing orange sunglasses go in one direction and the orange hat fly into the air. Suddenly I found myself suspended in midair with my arms flailing. As I became cognizant, I realized Jonathan had me by my waist. I was screaming as tears streamed. A small group of family and friends had surrounded us, trying to calm us both. Collette was swearing and threatening to whip my ass as soon as Derrick let her go.

"Y'all stop it! How can you do this to Poppee?"

"Stop calling my daddy Poppee!" Collette screamed.

Renee grabbed me by the hand and pulled me back toward the front of the church. When we got to the pew she slammed me down into the seat as if I was one of her children. "If you move from this seat, I will hit you myself."

With that she returned to the crowd gathered in the middle of the church. The entire congregation was on their feet. The crowd surrounding Collette parted like the Red Sea, and Renee emerged dragging a struggling Collette. She tried to force her into the seat next to me, but Collette refused to bend. She snatched away and found a seat on the opposite pew with the pallbearers. An usher brought her her hat and sunglasses.

The congregation returned to their seats, and the choir began to sing. I felt shame beyond measure. I couldn't believe Collette had ignited such a flame of fury in me. Dawn and Nina cried uncontrollably. Victor held Nina. Uncle Thomas held Dawn. I had no one to hold me.

Bishop returned to the pulpit and began speaking softly. "Grief does strange things to us. Let us pray for peace and strength for this family."

Bishop prayed a powerful prayer that helped to calm my nerves. I'm not sure what he said. I just know it soothed my soul. I made a mental note to make a public apology for my shameful behavior.

During the wake portion of the service, people were

invited to visit with the family and view the body. Bishop was kind enough not to say we were on opposite sides of the church. An endless stream of friends and people I'd never had the pleasure of meeting previously stopped by to shake hands and express how sorry they were for our loss. I couldn't make eye contact with any of them. Lord, what had happened to me?

The church band performed one beautiful gospel song after another. As the last of the friends filed past the casket, Bishop returned to the pulpit and invited the family to pay their last respects, to take our last view.

The ushers started with the fifth row. Rico, Roberta, Jamaica, and Michelle were among those making their way toward the coffin. Rico and Jonathan spent a few moments talking to Daddy before Rico leaned over to kiss him on the cheek, placing an object inside the coffin. Jonathan helped a clearly shaken Rico back to her seat. Roberta began screaming as she fell onto Daddy's chest. A nurse rushed to assist her, which gave her license to collapse. Others came to assist. Michelle simply stepped over her to return to her seat. Jamaica spent a long time just staring down at Daddy. I felt his pain. He'd lost one of his best friends.

The nurses got Roberta to her feet and took her from the church. The remainder of the family members behind us had their parting view without incident. Jamaica returned with his mother. Estelle spent several minutes talking to her soul mate. It made me realize how fragile life and love were. I yearned once again for Anthony.

The funeral director approached Renee, asking if we wanted to walk to the coffin or have it brought to us. She chose the former. The director assisted Uncle Thomas first. For the first time in my life Uncle Thomas seemed feeble. His steps were slow and deliberate. Before he reached the coffin he stopped, stood erect, and saluted

Daddy. That simple gesture opened the floodgates of grief from what seemed to be the entire church.

Dawn rose slowly with the assistance of a nurse. Her body trembled and she began saying "Daddy" repeatedly. She laid her head on his chest and loudly proclaimed her love. As the nurse tried to help her up, she refused. She grabbed onto Daddy and began screaming a chorus of no's. Prying her fingers loose, the nurse was finally able to return Dawn to her seat.

Now came my turn. As I tried to stand, I knew I could never do this. I could never say good-bye to Daddy. The director asked if I wanted to remain seated. That was unacceptable, as well. I didn't know what I wanted to do. In my peripheral vision I saw a familiar figure. As the man dressed in combat fatigues approached, I leapt to my feet and flew into his arms. My Anthony had somehow come to me.

Right in the front of the filled church, I hugged and kissed him. He gently pulled from my embrace. He took me by the hand and we took steps toward Daddy. As I hesitated, he gently encouraged me. Finally, I stood before the man who had been my hero my entire life, the man who had always been my role model. The man who'd sacrificed everything for my sisters and me. Even the sister I didn't know.

My knees weren't strong enough to hold me. Anthony felt me falter and held me. "Go ahead, baby. Tell him you love him. Tell him how you feel."

I was fortified by Anthony's words and presence. I leaned over and kissed Daddy. His cold and rigid skin brought me to the startling reality. "I love you, Daddy. I'll see you on the other side. Hug and kiss Mama for me. I'll take care of everybody for you. I'm sorry for what happened here. Please forgive me." Emotion overtook me, and I couldn't continue. With my chin to my chest I cried softly. Anthony helped me back to my seat. I tried to ask him how he'd gotten there, but I wasn't able to form the words.

Renee and Derrick went to view Daddy next. I was so caught up in my own grief, I'm not sure what really happened. As I became coherent, I saw Derrick pick Renee up and carry her back to her seat. Like overcooked pasta, Renee's body seemed to have no form or functionality. A nurse fanned her as Derrick spoke lovingly to her. She turned to me and we embraced, crying.

As the funeral director focused his attention on Nina, she whispered something to him that caused him to look at Collette. He nodded and crossed the center aisle to where Collette sat. Though her body language was defensive, she wasn't hostile. He extended his arm, and she took it.

Collette stood and braced herself before taking her first step. As she moved closer, her body relaxed. Nothing else seemed to matter as she looked down into our father's face. She touched Daddy's lapel and leaned over to kiss him. I read her lips as she told him she loved him. She shot a glance to our pew. Ice cubes were warmer than her eyes. She returned to her seat.

Victor stood and took his wife's hand. With a regal style that so reminded me of Daddy, Nina stepped to the coffin. "Poppee, I love you. I promise you, I'll do my best to fulfill your dream." Nina turned and extended her hand to Renee. Derrick helped her up, and Renee moved to take Nina's hand. Renee then turned and extended her hand to me. Anthony helped me up, and I turned to take Dawn's hand. We walked to them together. Nina then turned the other way and extended her hand to Collette. Collette looked away, mascara-stained tears streaking her face. But Nina refused to accept the rejection. She removed her hand from Renee's and went to Collette. She fell to her knees in front of her and looked up into her face. "Please, Collette," she said.

After a long pause Collette took her hand. Victor walked over and helped his wife to stand. Collette and Nina walked hand in hand to rejoin us. As the five Naylor girls stood hand in hand in front of the casket, tears streaming, the congregation seemed to feel every ounce of our emotion.

Collette slipped her hand out of Nina's and began to walk away. I was devastated that she would break our newly formed bond. Instead of returning to her seat, she moved toward Estelle and extended her hand.

Someone in the distance could be heard saying, "Thank you, Jesus." Then another, and another, until praises rose as a crescendo and everyone was on their feet, clapping and praising the Lord. From that moment on, the service transformed into a homegoing celebration.

Estelle joined us at the casket, and we had a group hug for longer than I can calculate. I then stepped to Collette to apologize. Before I could say anything, she said, "I'm so sorry, Glyn, for *everything*. Can you ever forgive me for just acting a pure fool this entire week?"

"Only if you do one thing for me."

"Anything, just ask."

"Please come sit with us."

"Daddy would have had it no other way." We hugged and walked arm in arm back to our seats.

Epilogue:
The Business of Living

As I placed my bags in the back of Renee's minivan, I felt a sense of peace. The two weeks since the burial had flown by in a flash. Nina had finally left the night before, after the most amazing time I could have ever imagined. A smile found its way to my face as I remembered the times the Naylor girls had shared. All five of us.

One week after Daddy died, we sat around the dining room table, still numb, but coping with all that had happened in seven short days. Our lives were forever changed. Uncle Thomas had gone home to leave us alone. Derrick had taken Victor to shoot hoops. It was just the five of us.

"The funeral service was more like Sunday morning worship. That choir just showed out!" Dawn said, pouring coffee for each of us.

Renee spooned sugar into her cup. "Honey, them folks were moved by the Spirit, from the singing to the moving tributes to Daddy and the wonderful eulogy. Without question, the most stirring homegoing celebration I've ever attended."

"Jamaica's dance number brought people to their feet. Even Bishop was standing and applauding. Daddy would have been so pleased," I said.

"I don't believe I've ever seen that many cars at a burial. It must have been at least two hundred," Nina said, slicing cake.

"Gurl, don't I know! When I got out of the car and turned around, I almost had a non–King James Version moment." Collette laughed at herself.

"No, see you had that non–King James moment when you stepped your hoochie ass up in a Pentecostal church wearing that orange miniskirt." Renee brought up the most embarrassing moment in Naylor history, yet again.

"Oh do I have to hear about this again?" Collette lowered her head in shame.

"Maybe we should focus our attention on the welter-weight bout in the center aisle instead?" Dawn sipped laced coffee.

"Gurl, can you imagine if Daddy had been alive? He would have whipped our natural behinds. I still don't know how I got to Collette in the first place. I was just magically there."

"You took like two steps and you were there. Swangin'!" This time Nina was teasing me. "That miniskirt was up around Collette's waist when they were trying to hold her off of you. It was like watching Ali and Frazier—the daughters!" Dawn was shadowboxing as she laughed.

"The whole church was on their feet, but you could have heard a mouse pissing on cotton it was so quiet. All we could hear was your bracelets clanging." Renee added her two cents to the harassment.

"But there was also not a dry eye in that church when Nina went over to get you, Lette. That changed the whole service." I smiled as I thought back to the pivotal moment in our family history. Nina had made a real impact on Collette with her extension of the olive branch.

"Gurl, it was when Collette went to get Estelle. Man!" Tears began to form in Dawn's eyes.

"Gurl, do you know what Anthony risked for you? I ain't mad at cha. That man got six hours to come be with his woman. Came up in the church still with twigs stuck in his collar. Damn, that was romantic. You should have seen your face." Collette wanted to change the subject. No matter how we assured her it was over, she was still embarrassed.

"I sat there hatin' Renee and Nina," I said. "Of course, I was having a pity party for you, Dawn, and me. When I saw him out the corner of my eye, I thought it was an illusion."

"Anthony is some beautiful illusion. Poppee had told me what a wonderful man he is. In the few hours we were together I saw for myself."

"Gurl, I know you're not talkin' about a brotha being foine. Victor is raggedy-edge-Martin-Luther-King-church-fan foine!" We all fell over laughing.

"Gurl, I know one thing. Reginald is history. He left me a message talking about he just doesn't do funerals. I deserve better than this. I may not be sure what I want, but I sure as hell know what I don't want." Dawn tried to hide hurt and disappointment.

"Glynda, when are you going to marry Anthony? With all of that fainting, my money says there's another Naylor on the way," Renee teased.

"I'm going to ask him as soon as I get home. And I'm not pregnant!" I protested, though not so certain my dear sister wasn't having a psychic moment. "I'm still in shock at all he did to get here Friday night. Convinced someone to give him congressional escort duty to D.C., flew with the senator and his entourage, escorted them to their hotel, traded six hours of guard duty, rented a car, drove here, and was back in Washington to relieve the guard at midnight. That is my man!"

"Gurl, I got that Gerald Levert song rambling through

my head, 'Baby, Hold On to Me.' " Nina snapped her fingers in Z formation.

We all high-fived.

"Ooooo, y'all a mess! Yeah, he *is* a wonderful brother. You know if Edward Naylor was your daddy, you had a helluva benchmark."

"Say, you're right!"

The house of Naylor would never be the same, but it would once again know love and laughter.

Don't miss the unforgettable return of Catherine Hawkins (you met her in *The Shirt off His Back*) in *What Goes Around* by Parry "EbonySatin" Brown. Read the first chapter here!

.

"But, Dad, we're eighteen. Why can't we stay out all night?" Alisa pouted. "You act like you don't trust us or something!"

"It's prom night, Daddy!" Ariana piped in. "All our friends are going to the after party."

Exasperation drew lines on Terry Winston's face. "And I have to tell you how many times, I don't care what your friends are doing because they're no concern of mine?"

"You know we really don't need your permission," Alisa said, testing the waters of defiance. "We're legally adults!"

Ariana stared at her mirror image in disbelief. She had to think quickly to counteract her sister's temporary bout of insanity. "I think what Alisa means is that—"

"Girl, you are straight up trippin'." The veins bulged in Terry's forehead and neck as he got into Alisa's face. "As long as my name is Terrance Winston and it appears on your birth certificate, my blood runs through your veins *and* you're slipping your key in *my* front door every day *and* driving the car that I make the payments on *and*—"

"Girls," their mother, Jackie, interrupted, "let me talk to your father for a moment. And, Alisa, I recommend you take a few moments to adjust your attitude before this family meeting reconvenes."

Ariana pushed her sister through the arched opening that separated the family room from the kitchen. Alisa jerked away, turning slightly to roll her eyes at her sister. "You're just tryin' to be Miss Goody-goody," she hissed. "You know you want this as much as I do!"

"Just go," Ariana whispered. "If you keep this up, we won't even get to go to the prom."

The two bounced up the wide staircase, splitting at the landing and going in different directions, though their rooms adjoined. "You seem to forget we're grown," Alisa yelled after her sister just before stepping into her bedroom and slamming the door.

Terry sat with his head in his hands, trying to understand where his sweet, almost-perfect daughters had gone and when the imposter who'd taken over Alisa's body had made the switch. In the scheme of things he really needed to count his many blessings. Ariana and Alisa Winston were top honor roll students as they approached high school graduation. They had been accepted by their top three choices of colleges with offers of full scholarships. To everyone's surprise, the girls were contemplating going separate ways in pursuit of their very grand academic dreams, which included environmental design for Ariana and journalism for Alisa.

By anyone's standard, Terry Winston had been a wonderful father since the day he decided he couldn't let Catherine Hawkins, their birth mother, put them up for adoption. He'd brought his darling princesses home from the hospital, determined to be the best father he could be, while Catherine went off in pursuit of her career goals. In spite—or perhaps because—of it all, he knew today as he'd known then that there had been no other decision he could have made. He loved those girls so much that he would have given them the shirt off his back if they needed it. Moments like these, however, made him understand why his temples, mustache, and five o'clock shadow bore the distinction of time.

Thank goodness for his wife. Jacqueline Rogers-Winston was the anchor in the many stormy seas of his life. A sense of calm began to radiate through him as he felt the warmth of her touch in the center of his back. "Are you okay?"

"Not hardly!" Terry took her hand and pulled her around to sit on his lap. "When did she get so belligerent?"

"Honey, she's just feeling her womanhood. She *thinks* she's grown. Every girl goes through the very same thing," Jackie said as she slipped her arms around his neck. "Count yourself lucky it didn't happen any earlier."

"Then why is Ariana so different?" Terry pulled back to make eye contact with his wife of seven wonder-filled years. "They look like the same person, walk and talk the same, but when it comes to personality they are as different as sunshine and rain."

"You seem to forget that it's all still weather. But amazingly they really aren't that different. They both work you like a baker kneading dough, but Ariana just has more finesse." Jackie kissed him gently on the forehead. "And then, toss a little estrogen and oxygen into the mix and, voilà, there you have it—women!"

Staring deeply into Jackie's eyes, Terry wondered what he'd done to deserve such a woman. His soul had connected with hers the moment he'd seen her in the supermarket on the rainy afternoon nearly thirteen years before. "What am I going to do?"

Laughing, Jackie pulled back and stood. "Oh, you thought I had a solution?" She walked around the couch into the kitchen, retrieving coffee mugs from the dishwasher. The sound echoed through the large, airy space as she placed them on the counter. She placed her hand on the cool granite and thought a moment before she turned and continued. "This is such a difficult age for everyone. They *are* in fact adults, though you think of them as your little girls. Look at them. They're built like supermodels with beauty to match, yet they still want nothing more than to please their daddy. They have the pressure of friends and adversaries alike to do this or to act like that. You seem to think that you're the only one with a hard job in all of this." Jackie poured two cups of coffee, added a little Baileys Irish Cream in both and moved back toward the family room.

"So you're saying I should let them stay out all night?" Terry wanted to be angry, but confusion won out.

Terry removed two coasters from the cut-crystal holder and placed them on the cherrywood table. Jackie set the mugs down and turned to her husband in the same movement. "Not at all. What I am saying is there should be some kind of compromise."

"I'm their father. I don't have to conciliate with them!" Terry stood, looking down at Jackie. "Teresa Winston never negotiated with me. It was her way or the highway."

"Times are different." Jackie grabbed his hand and pulled him back to the sofa. "And you'd lose your natural mind if Ariana and Alisa decided they wanted to *take the highway.*"

"Alrighty then, Ms. I've-got-all-the-answers, what do I do? No daughter of mine is going to be out all night with my blessings. The only things open after two A.M. are legs!"

Laughing, Jackie found it difficult to be serious. Trying to compose her thoughts for a clever comeback, she gave birth to what she considered sheer genius. "Let's have the after party here."

Speechless and staring at her as though she were an alien, Terry finally said, "Are you nuts? Do you know what a house full of teenagers could do to this place? Look around you. We have beige carpeting and hardwood floors, antiques, fine crystal. We'd have to take out a rider to our homeowners' policy." Terry picked up the coffee mug and blew on the mocha liquid absentmindedly.

Touching his knee and forcing Terry to make eye contact with her, Jackie continued, "But look at the beauty of this. They get to party all night with their friends, doing whatever it is eighteen-year-olds do, with your watchful eye right upstairs the whole time. And even if the floors get scuffed and the carpet stained, isn't that a very small price to pay for their happiness and your peace of mind?"

This woman is as smart as she is sexy. Terry smiled. He had to admit her plan did seem without flaws. "Do you think they'll go for such an idea?"

"In the words of the great don, make them an offer they can't refuse."

"Such as?"

"First find out what the other after party is offering"— Jackie grinned with satisfaction—"then trump it!"

Smiling at her, Terry thought back to the many times she'd been the answer not only to his prayers but also the desires of his heart. "How do you come up with this stuff?"

"Just brilliance, my love, sheer brilliance." She winked. "I think you should call them back down, first making Alisa apologize for her behavior, which immediately puts her at a disadvantage."

Just as Terry was about to summon his firstborn, Michelle, Michael, and Terrance Junior rushed up the stairs from the basement playroom. "Mommy, can we have some popcorn?" Michael yelled as he approached his parents.

"Boy, you just had dinner not more than an hour ago. Where do you put it all?" Exasperated, Jackie smiled. "There's a new box in the pantry. I want to see your homework when you're done with the popcorn. Yours too, Michelle and T.J."

"Yes, ma'am," T.J. said with the enthusiasm of a six-year-old who hadn't completed his assigned task.

Michelle beamed with pride. "I'm done. You can check mine now, Mommy."

"Whatever," Michael mumbled in a baritone voice reserved for someone well beyond thirteen.

As the children headed for the walk-in pantry to retrieve an evening snack, Jackie's heart felt full, remembering how the two families had blended seamlessly seven years before. Only those who had known them for many years knew the story of how Terry's identical twin daughters and Jackie's fraternal twins became the loving Winston clan. And the cement that brought it all together was Terry's namesake, Terrance Winston Junior.

"So you think this will really work?" Terry interrupted her reverie. "I mean, how do we even begin to plan a party for teenagers who *think* they're grown?" A serious look crept across Terry's face. "I mean, what do we allow? Do we chaperone?"

Rising, Jackie looked back at Terry and smiled. "You convince them this is a great idea and I'll handle the rest."

Terry watched Jackie's full, round behind as she switched into the kitchen. Opening the door to the built-in refrigerator that blended with the oak cabinetry, she bent to retrieve a fruit drink, and Terry found himself moaning involuntarily. Jackie stirred him in ways he had never even imagined a woman could. He couldn't understand why Jackie had such issues with her size. The thought of her softness, silky smooth skin, round bottom, full breasts, thick thighs, the heat that radiated from her booty as they slept . . . lawdhamercy! The rumbling taking place above his head shifted his attention from the woman with whom he desperately wanted to sneak into the pantry for just a few stolen moments.

"What in the . . ." Terry leapt to his feet and took the stairs two at a time. "I swear, sometimes they act like they're the babies in this house," he mumbled as he reached the landing leading to the east wing of the house.

He stood outside Ariana's room and listened to the two argue before knocking. "I don't need you to talk for me. I can tell Daddy what I mean." Though Terry couldn't see who was speaking, he knew it was Alisa.

"You need someone to keep your stupid behind out of trouble. If you don't stop this, I'm scared we won't get to go anywhere at all!" Ariana's voice had a tone of pleading. "What's the big deal about going to the after party anyway?"

"Everyone will be there is the big deal. How can the most popular twins in the senior class *not* be?"

"Alisa, we're the *only* twins in the senior class!"

Terry knocked lightly.

"Go away."

"This is *my* room!" Ariana yelled just before she snatched the door opened. "Daddy?" Ariana said, taken aback.

With his hand positioned to knock again, Terry said, "Oh, so you were expecting whom?" He struggled to calm the anger he felt at Alisa at that moment. "May I come in?"

"Sure, Daddy. I thought maybe you were Michelle. She asked me to help her with something." Ariana didn't make eye contact with her father, which was a good sign she was fishing for a believable response.

"What's going on up here?" Terry stepped into the large space decorated in various shades of yellow and blue. The queen-size canopy bed with canary-yellow and cobalt-blue netting draped over the posts showed signs of a tussle. "It sounded like you were coming through the ceiling downstairs." Terry eyed the matching pillows that were tossed about the room.

Alisa turned away from her father, folding her arms. "We're having a private conversation."

"The minute you threatened the structure of this house, it became public." Terry moved to the blue-and-yellow patchwork-covered footstool and sat. "What are you two fighting about this time?"

"She's such a suck-up! I want to go to the after party and so does she, but she's saying whatever it is that you want to hear!" Anger filled Alisa's beautiful face. "You always taught us to be our own person and to stand up for whatever it is that we believe."

"And you believe what about this?" Terry asked calmly.

"I believe we're adults, and legally you can't tell us what we can and cannot do." Alisa eyed her sister, asking for collaboration, but Ariana's stony face yielded little support.

Terry was stoic.

Alisa continued, "I know we still live in your house and with that comes certain rules . . ."

Terry saw Alisa start to squirm and, enjoying the assumed shift of power, he said simply, "Go on."

"But I think you need to relax our curfew." Confidence fleeing rapidly, Alisa lowered her head and voice. "At least on prom night."

"I see." Tension began to permeate the air as Terry turned to Ariana, who stood with her back pressed against the door. "And what do you have to say, young lady?"

As she dropped her head, the only sound that could be heard in the room was the ticking of the clocks representing the four time zones of the United States, each slightly off cadence with the other. "I'd like to hang with our friends after the prom. Could we compromise and go out to eat and maybe come home by four?"

"I would have considered this counterproposal, but your sister's attitude has me more than just a little concerned. Since you're *grown,* then perhaps we need to make other living arrangements." Terry toyed with them. "Grown is as grown does. I think you need to have your own place."

"Daddy!" they sang in unison.

Terry suppressed a chuckle. "Daddy what?

"When you think you can apologize to me and your mother for that outburst downstairs, you let me know." Terry rose. "Then we can discuss your loss of good standing and what it will mean to this prom and graduation season."

Ariana shot a penetrating stare at Alisa and returned pleading eyes to her father. "Daddy, I didn't do anything!" Unshed tears caused her expressive brown eyes to sparkle.

Though his heart melted, he stood firm. "All for one and one for all! You'd better have a come-to-Jesus with your sister. I won't live in the same house with disrespect, ever!"

Without another word Terry walked to the door, and Ariana moved aside as he opened it and stepped into the hallway. He expelled more air than he contained. It was so difficult to be stern. Deep inside, he'd always felt the need to overcompensate for Catherine's abandonment of them. Even after Jackie had adopted the girls, deep in his heart those feelings never changed. In recent months Alisa had become more and more combative. Jackie assured him it was a long time coming and totally normal. What scared him even more was that Ariana must have just been lying in wait to spring her split personality on him when he least expected it. The thought always made his head ache.

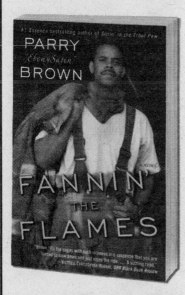